Under the House

ff

UNDER
THE HOUSE

Leslie
Hall Pinder

faber and faber

LONDON · BOSTON

First published in Great Britain in 1987
by Bloomsbury Publishing Ltd, London
First published in paperback in 1989
by Faber and Faber Limited
3 Queen Square London WCIN 3AU

Printed in Great Britain by
Richard Clay Ltd, Bungay, Suffolk

Acknowledgements to Christine Clark,
Penny Goldsmith, Clarine Ostrove, Mary Schendlinger,
Lael Whitehead and Lorita Whitehead.

All characters in this book are fictitious,
and any resemblance to actual persons
living or dead is coincidental.

British Library Cataloguing in Publication Data

Pinder, Leslie Hall
Under the House
I. Title
813'.54[F]

ISBN 0 571 15214 7

For Trish

1986

Maude Mason was losing her place.

Time was starting to melt and mix like a thick liquid. At the beginning of her sentence she was married and at the end she was widowed. Sometimes in the very midst of things she fell asleep: between her lifting the tea cup and it reaching her lips she drifted, waking with the cup at her mouth. It startled her, so that delicate drops of tea spilled.

This confusion had come early in her old age. She was seventy-one and her skin was smooth. Her cheeks were rosy. But if you looked closer the red colour was made of tiny root veins come to the surface.

Time in her life was liquid, moving between stone thoughts in underground places.

The new doctor asked her if she'd had any operations.

"No, no I haven't. Not really."

The doctor was surprised, then, to find only one breast. "Mrs. Mason, you've had a mastectomy."

"I have?"

"Yes, look."

"Oh, yes, so I have."

Her hands were gnarled. She weighed the same as she did at age eighteen. Her thin hair wouldn't hold a curl.

Most of her possessions were small. The big things she had moved to the lower floor where her husband used to smoke cigars in the evenings with his men friends. They would sit in the armchairs smoking and laughing, so that all of their large teeth showed.

Sometimes she made sandwiches and took them down the stairs on a tray. She always knocked before opening the door. A cloud of smoke hung in the air, sinking into the pine boarded walls and into the leaves on the plants. She could smell liquor. Laughter faded as she entered the room. Always it was the same. Geoffrey, her husband, would say, "Why, thank you Mrs. Mason, thank you."

7

As she closed the door it resumed, the harsh, big-fisted laughter. She paused, then, at the top of the stairs, the sounds curling after her, winding onto her feet and ankles. She was safe at the top of the stairs. The laughter was some good joke Geoffrey had told. It wasn't about her. Probably he had said something funny about the stock market or business, but not about her.

She never heard the men leave. Geoffrey let them out through the garden room. She only sensed his presence afterwards in bed, the pressure of his silent laughter.

He was dead now. Sometimes she remembered him. But she never went downstairs any more. All the plants had died, their curled leaves shrivelled around a thin layer of dust mixed with ancient smoke. As far as she was concerned there was nothing under the main floor of the house, where she lived. She kept her house perfectly clean and neat, just the way she wanted it. Always the same. No dust in her house. Even the birds that came to eat the bread crumbs she placed on the front balcony left no mess. Bits of feathers sometimes, that she brushed away. The birds flew out of the mountains and went back into the mountains.

Often the girl came to visit. Maude was glad to see her, but didn't always know how they were related. When the girl said "Aunt Maude, I'll help you," she remembered this was her niece, Evelyn. The girl stirred an old memory, standing outside the door, wanting to come in. Maude wanted her to come in too, because she was sure the girl loved her more than anyone did. She just couldn't quite remember how to do it; and then this nice girl would say the very helpful sentence, "Open the door, turn the handle. It's your niece."

Sometimes the girl would look at the fireplace and say, "Aunt Maude, you haven't been burning papers, have you?"

Had she? "No, no I haven't."

"You mustn't burn papers when I'm not here. You can have a fire when someone is with you. Otherwise it's too dangerous. Put the papers in the garbage."

"I always do."

"Yes, well, don't forget."

"No, dear, I won't."

Maude didn't like it when the housekeeper came to clean. Those chores were for her. She didn't have money to hire someone to do the work she had to do. And the housekeeper always went over the line. No one paid attention to the line, even the girl—what did she call herself, the niece—she didn't seem to see it. The line marked where she could vacuum. The next day she could do over that line, to the next line. Like

8

a farmer doing fields. The line was in the fabric of the rug.

But it was hard to cross over the line the next day, even when she wanted to. Maybe she was supposed to keep inside the line. S.D. claimed the part on the other side. Did he claim it? No, he was dead. And Stanley, he always tried to take everything. He couldn't make it stick, though, like in court. If that nice girl came today, Maude would ask, just to make sure S.D. was dead and couldn't take anything from her.

The niece liked to ask her questions, about long ago. That was nice. But Maude didn't always like to think about those things. Answering the questions was like touching something cold. It hurt her skin. Her jaw stiffened so that she had to speak between clenched teeth. It was better just to have tea and watch the birds fly out from the mountains.

"How are you feeling, Aunt Maude?"

"I'm fine. Just fine."

"Mr. Cox called me. He said he was in to see you."

"Oh, was he?" She didn't mean to say that. She meant to say yes, he was, but it was so difficult with all these people who needed to be remembered.

"He told me he used to be a friend of your sister's, a friend of Isabel, when she was alive."

"Oh, yes."

"He said he knew Isabel when she lived on Gerard Street?"

"Yes. That's right."

"What was it like then?"

"It was nice."

"Did you live near Isabel?"

"We had a two-storey house. It was a lovely house. Isabel used to visit. I was young then."

"You're not so old. You're only seventy-one."

"Yes. Seventy-one. Maybe that's not too old. Is there anyone left older than I am?"

"Your brother."

"Yes, my brother. Who's that now?"

"Clarence. He's older."

"He's still alive." She tried to say it as a statement, not a question. "But S.D. is dead."

"Yes. A long time ago."

"Isabel has trouble with the stairs."

"You mean where you used to live?"

"Yes. She can't make it up the stairs any more. She's getting old."

"You mean here, in this house?"

9

"She had trouble the other day making it up to her room."

"Aunt Maude, there isn't an upstairs in this house."

"Yes there is, dear. But the stairs are too steep for Isabel."

The girl didn't understand about stairs, or the line. If S.D. made the line, Maude couldn't cross it, or—maybe he'd kill her. He always meant what he said. And he hated birds. He'd shoot them and laugh. Or was that Stanley? No, it must have been S.D.

"S.D. is a mean bugger."

"But he's dead now."

"Is he?" Yes, that's right. She was confused. "He's still mean."

"Why was he mean?"

"He can't help it. He's drawn the line."

"What line?"

"The borderline. I can't step over it."

"Where? Where is it?"

"There, beside you. Right here in my living-room."

"I can't see it."

"Can't you? Is Stanley alive?"

"No."

"Who killed him?"

"No one. He just died."

"Somebody should've killed him."

1915

Maude Mason was raised on a farm in Saskatchewan. Gradually her father acquired the property around the farmhouse for seven miles in every direction. Everyone called him S.D. Kathryn, his wife, wasn't involved in her husband's acquisitions. She had her children and S.D. put the sons to work with the hired hands. One girl, the first born, had died.

The winters were too long and the baby's death had broken Kathryn. She had become withdrawn; some even thought she was slightly stupid. Then Maude, the last child, was born. Kathryn loved this one who stayed alone with her. She would rock her back and forth, shielded from the loud voices of the men, singing:

> Sweet Maude, sweet Maude
> You're sent from God

10

Come to me
From far away
Maude, sweet Maude, my own.

It was cold that night. Everyone in the house was in bed. All the big-boned men were heavy in their sleep. Maude stopped crying as Kathryn sang. The house was dark except for the embers of the fire Kathryn could see through the grate on the stove. Lawrence, the hired hand, had brought in enough wood for the day and evening, but it was now late into the night. There was no more wood. Kathryn went to the back door and picked up a stack of newspapers and magazines, as many as she could carry with the baby in her arms. She opened the stove with the cast iron lever, removed the metal plate, and placed the papers on the fire. They flared, making a harsh light on Maude's face. Then Kathryn heard the loud voice of her husband. "Kathryn. Come to bed."

The baby started to cry. She clanged the metal plate back on to the stove. Her tent of calm had been shredded by his voice and the sound of the child.

"Kathryn."

"Yes, I'm coming."

She felt her way up the stairs. S.D. would not allow the baby in their bedroom. She put her in the spare room that had been set up for the child. She rocked Maude again, but didn't sing. She could hear S.D.'s heavy breathing in the silent house, but dared not return downstairs for fear he would call again and wake the child. She got into bed, taking up a small space. His breathing did not alter.

In the middle of the night Kathryn awoke, coughing. Smoke filled the room. Then she heard the word she dreaded. "Fire." She couldn't see anything. "Fire. Fire." She crawled along the floor, reaching for the door handle. When she opened it, the smoke banged into her lungs. "Stanley, Clarence." She called for her sons. A hand came forward and grasped hers, leading her down the stairs and out through the thick smoke into the cold air. Everyone streamed from the house and out beneath the cackling yellow moon. One side of the farmhouse was in flames.

Kathryn suddenly remembered she had a baby. "Maude. Where's Maude?" She ran towards the house but was pulled back by Stanley, the older son. "Let go. Maude's inside. She's inside, Stanley. Let go of me." Kathryn screamed and clawed his arm.

Stanley heard her, but he could not let go. He was drawn into the panic of his mother's face. Maude was in the house. Time stretched and stilled.

It stopped in the grip he had on his mother's arm.

"Stanley, for God's sake," she yelled. "Maude's inside."

Maude was inside. His mother was weak and pitiful. Wanting to save Maude.

"Please, Stanley." She was begging him. His mother begged him to let her go.

"Please."

With enormous effort he released her arm. "I'll go in."

Kathryn watched and cursed her husband and her son.

The men yelled, their voices like bats darting through the shadows.

"Get the pumps."

"Pa's gone for them."

"The baby's inside."

"Canvas. We need canvas."

"Stanley's gone back in."

"Get the tarp."

The men ran to the window and stretched out the canvas.

"Throw her down, Stanley."

"Stanley, out here."

The baby was thrown from the window. She landed on the canvas with a sound like soft butter dropped into a pan.

"Jump, Stanley."

"Jump, Stanley. Jump." The voices tossed up to the window.

"I can't. I'll make it down the stairs."

Kathryn hugged the child. "Maude, my Maudie." She encircled the baby and took her to the corner of the yard, to the edge of the mown grass, where the endless fields of wheat began. Kathryn could barely hear the baby's screams above the voices of the men. The fire from the house webbed Maude's face in streams of shadow.

Kathryn started to sing again the song of Maude, sweet Maude, come from God, and saved from a fire.

1924

"Maudie, Maudie, she's an oddie. Maudie, Maudie, she's an oddie." The other children were chanting her name outside in the playground. "Maudie, Maudie, she's an oddie."

Maudie listened to their voices coming through the door of the school-room. She never went out for recess after that, but kept to her books or helped the teacher clean the blackboards. Whenever her name was spoken she would sit up straight, expecting the insult.

Maude took her name from the first-born child who had died. Her shield against the schoolyard taunt was the first Maude. They were like twins. It was her twin who was odd. The cruel jokes of the ugly children were meant for the other one. The real Maude wasn't odd, she was only different because she had a dead sister who bore her name. People were confused. Even her parents were confused; they treated her as though she were a baby, filmy and insubstantial. She wasn't allowed to go too far from home. She shouldn't visit neighbours. She couldn't ride the horses. Her parents guarded her from everything. They had a secret she shouldn't know about. It had to do with her twin. It had to do with the apples.

The apples were kept in the dark root cellar where it was cool and close, full of rot and decay. Going down into that cellar was clouded with terror. There was a sticky clamour of earth smells as Maude pushed the heavy wooden door and entered the darkness. She was always afraid that the door would close behind her and she wouldn't have the strength to lift the latch and get out. The scented darkness would catch her, keep her, and forget her. That was the first terror.

The apples were in a rough burlap bag at the farthest corner, next to the potatoes. She would feel inside the bag and pull out the apples, one by one, putting them into her bowl. They were the eggs from the earth that she took to her mother.

This time when she reached inside the bag, she touched a withered thing, soft on one side. She screamed—a short, choked sound that pushed her back, stumbling against the sack of potatoes. She lay on the ground, looking at the monster apple bag.

Now she was caught between two terrors: going back upstairs without any apples and touching again that wrinkled shape. The shrunken head of the first Maude, her other sister, there in the bag, withered and rotten.

She crouched on the ground, her eyes darting from the bag to the door and back again. She rubbed her hand back and forth in the dirt of the floor, trying to get it clean. If she didn't get the apples, she couldn't return to her mother. She would have to stay under the earth with the other Maude. Forever. Her mother would find them there, shrunken and vegetable.

She stood up. With one hand on the bowl and the other on the outside of the bag, she forced the apples out, whispering, "Baby Maude, stay back. Please stay away."

She ran out into the cold winter light, unable to look at the things in her bowl. She lifted the bowl up to her mother. Kathryn's face didn't change; she took the bowl. Maude waited. Still nothing happened. The other Maude had stayed under the ground.

And every time her mother asked Maude to get apples, her fear was mixed with victory, her death with survival. She had to go down where her dead sister was waiting. If she could keep her there, she would be safe above the earth. She had to make her stay back.

Maude had this secret. It was so cavernous and rooted that she could never be like the rest of them. When she lifted the bowl of apples, she offered up the possibility of exposure: not only of herself but also of the other Maude and the dark place under the house. She held tight to her secret.

1946

Maude woke at six o'clock in the morning. Although the train didn't leave until noon she wanted to be there early. Geoffrey would take her to the station. Isabel, her sister, was supposed to go with her, but she'd changed her mind yesterday. Maude had to arrive at the station early to make up for Isabel, who would have been late.

Maude and Geoffrey sat in the railway cafeteria drinking coffee. People came and went. The station was noisy. Another cup of coffee. Maude didn't have anything more to say. She was calm. She was thirty-one years old; she was married to Geoffrey Mason; she had a nice home, a nice husband. Since waking, her anxiety had slowly diminished until she was now superficial and pleasant. She worked hard to achieve this emptiness.

Her train was being called. Geoffrey paid the waitress and they went into the crowded hollow of the station.

"Mrs. Mason, you look slightly glum."

"Do I?"

"You do."

"Sorry."

"No need to be sorry. I could have gone with you."

"That's kind of you, thank you." Maude looked at him. She felt almost nothing for this man, compared to how she felt about Isabel, who was absent. That was wrong; he was her husband; he cared for her. But he didn't even know her. Of course he didn't know her, and she didn't really know him either. That was fine. They were married. Husband and wife. That was knowing. That was being related.

14

"So, have a safe journey," said Geoffrey.

Maude felt deeply ominous. Everything that was said had an unnatural measure to it, as though the words would later be remembered as the last words spoken. They wouldn't be of course, that was just stupid. But they stayed with her, like an insistence: once when spoken and once when she repeated them again in her mind, word for word, with the ominous tone.

She tried to deflect the danger by glancing Geoffrey's words off the hard surface she had created of herself.

She moved towards her husband and tilted her head back, trying to unpurse her lips as much as possible. The kiss was tight and thin.

"Maaaude." She was being called across the cavernous dome of the station. "Maaaaaude." She cowered at the public sounding of her name.

But it was Isabel. She was weaving her way towards them, wearing a purple coat with large padded shoulders. On her head was a brimmed hat, also deep purple, with a huge plume riding above it. She looked trim and elegant, and every bit of her carried the assumption that others would think the same.

"My God, she's changed her mind." Maude felt colour come back into her face and then drain. Whenever Isabel was around Maude's neat arrangements were thrown into the air. Nothing ever fell to the ground again until afterwards, and then not in the same order.

"I'm glad I caught you." Isabel was panting and her feather bobbed furiously as she tried to catch her breath. "The cab driver was so slow I could have shot him."

"You're coming?" asked Maude and knew immediately the question was a mistake. It showed too much.

"No, no. Wanted to say good-bye. Has your train been called?"

"Just now." Maude sensed that her mouth was hanging open. She clenched her teeth.

"I'll walk with you to the platform."

"Will they let you?"

"Of course. Geoffrey, wait for me." Isabel started through the crowd and then called back, "Which gate is it?" She wheeled around and returned to Maude who was still standing in the same place. Maude lost most of her initiative in Isabel's presence. She stood listless and confused, even though she had prepared, for days, to be calm.

"Get a red top for the bags, Geoffrey. Is this all you're taking? Never mind, we'll carry them ourselves. Which gate is it?" Isabel scoured Maude's face and paused. "You do look pretty." Then she picked up the leather suitcases and set off again through the crowd.

"Let me help," said Geoffrey.

"No, no. We're fine."

"Isabel, I'm sure I've forgotten something." Maude lingered and rustled aimlessly through her purse.

"Come on," Isabel called.

She was disappearing. Maude could only follow by tracking the feather which bobbed above the heads of the other travellers. Maude hadn't said good-bye to Geoffrey, and she looked back as she moved through the crowd, but he had disappeared too. She had only the wild plumage ahead of her.

Isabel led her onto the dark and steamy platform. It was a cave which picked up voices and echoed them back and forth like searchlights. The grey figures on the platform, distinct and yet illusive, like a dream. And Isabel, with her large and vibrant feather, was an exotic bird: wild, strange and unattainable.

Although Isabel was fifteen years her senior, Maude had this attraction, this viscosity for her. She preferred being with her more than anyone in the world. Her brother Clarence was nearest in age. But Maude loved Isabel.

They walked down the wooden slat between two trains. Maude didn't think to carry any of the bags that Isabel shouldered.

"Have you got enough money?" Isabel asked.

"Yes."

"Here, I want you to have this." Isabel put down one of the bags, handed Maude a small package, and proceeded with her pace. "Spend it for me."

"Really, I have enough."

"I know. Take care. Don't let them push you around. They can be such bullies."

"I wish you were coming," Maude said. She made the same mistake, telling Isabel that, but now she didn't care.

"Especially Stanley. Watch out for him. Say your piece."

"My piece?"

"You'll be just fine. Which coach is yours?" She took the ticket from Maude's hand. "B-l2. Here. Good-bye, Maudie dear. My thoughts will be with you."

"Do you want me to tell them anything for you?"

"Do come back—I mean, don't let them swallow you up. We're the only ones who have really left home. Remember that. To give you comfort. They might try to hold it against you."

"Will they?"

16

"It's just the family pride. Remember me..." The conductor yelling "all aboard" drowned the rest of what Isabel was saying.

Maude leaned out through the half-door, as Isabel was enveloped in a cloud of steam. The train emerged from the cave. The light hurt Maude's eyes.

"Remember me" double echoed in the ominous way.

Maude would have to make Isabel a memory, anything instead of this palpable absence as the last words lingered. She tried to fix Isabel as part of a past which she could recall or not. The train picked its way uncertainly through the city and reached the open spaces. Then Maude shifted from the edge of the seat in her bedroom cabin and leaned back. The wheels against the tracks clicked out the distance from her sister who was becoming memory and forgetfulness.

She played a childhood game of saying her own name just as each telephone pole passed. If she didn't do it right, she would be annihilated. "Maude." "Maude." "Maude." She closed her eyes against the game. Her own name, repeated, conned her into sleep.

There was a knock on the door. The porter called her to dinner.

She was most pleased, sitting at a table by herself with the freshly ironed white tablecloth and flowers in a small vase. Someone else would cook for her now. Out of her window an array of mountains passed.

It was too cramped for Isabel; if she'd come they'd be irritable and out of sorts with one another, Maude becoming more and more compliant as Isabel became more demanding. It was best as it was. To Maude, Isabel was like a walking stick. Somehow the stick had become quite broken so that it was short and useless for support. Still, if it was dark, she could use the stick to drag along the ground and the sound would tell her if she was still on the path. Or she could swing it the way a blind woman might, hunting out trees and objects in her way. As the spokes of the telephone poles spun miles between them, the stick became even shorter. Isabel was not here. Not even to warn of danger.

She tried to think of her family. Isabel never wanted to go back home, not ever. She always made excuses. The letter from her mother said that all the children were to come home because something had to be done about a family cairn.

> S.D. wishes that all of the children be here for this decision.
> It is of deep significance to him to make a record of the
> family's history. I have stressed with your father the
> difficulty and inconvenience of the trip, especially for
> you and Isabel, but he insists. You will have to do

17

everything you can to fit in with his wishes.

Isabel said they would go together. But then something urgent had come up. Maude didn't believe it. Isabel was a coward sometimes, pushing Maude out in front to take on the family. And S.D. would be angry.

On the second day, she opened the package Isabel had given her. She didn't count the money. There was a note in the package, and a scarf. It was light blue. At one end was a white shape marked in the silk. Abstract. A cloud; or perhaps a bird. Maude put the scarf around her neck, and noticed that the corners of the scarf were frayed.

> July 18/46
> Dear Maude—
> I do hope you understand why I didn't want to return with you, even if no one else does. If questions come up just stick to what you know. The scarf is for your protection. And when you don't need that, it's for your pleasure.
> Love Isabel

Maude folded the note and put it back into the envelope with the money. "If questions come up." Maude didn't understand the message. She skipped an imaginary stone along the surface of the lake that appeared outside the window of the train. Then her stone became buried in the foothills of the Rockies, along with all the other stones.

"What do I know?" A telephone pole rushed by. In time she said "Maude."

"That's all I know. Maude." She put the package aside and rearranged the blouses in her suitcase. She took out a book that she didn't read. Whenever she looked up there was a pole whizzing by. She said her name.

At the station Isabel had warned her about Stanley. And Maude was afraid of him. When she was a child, she used to watch him from the bushes between the fields. Stanley liked to set traps for birds; he caught them, and probably he killed them. But he hadn't caught her.

Isabel said that Stanley always wanted things his own way, and nothing else would do. He would hold his breath until he got what he wanted, turning red, then blue, until Kathryn would scream and plead with S.D. to give in.

But Maude was a married woman now, who lived far away from home. Why did she need protection? She put these thoughts out of her mind. She was married to Geoffrey. Even though he didn't understand her, he was kind. That was the way it should be.

Maude had her meals in the lovely dining car, at a table with a starched white cloth that someone else had ironed just for her.

The days passed so out of time that she was startled when the porter announced their arrival. She felt quite unprepared, not having settled her mind about what was to come. She hoped her mother would be there to meet her.

Instead it was Lawrence, her father's hired hand. Lawrence had always been old, but he had aged even more since her last visit. Her mother had sent Lawrence in her place. Or maybe S.D. had made him come.

"Well, Maudie. So isn't it nice to see you," said Lawrence, as she stepped down from the train.

They were awkward, not knowing whether to embrace, or shake hands. Their arms sort of tangled and Maude was embarrassed. She held up her suitcase. "I just have this and another small bag."

As they walked down the platform, Maude felt quite light and heady, unused to her feet touching the ground. She reminded herself that she was a married woman. She had her own place in the world. Whatever happened, she still had her own home, far away. She had her husband, Geoffrey, and her sister, Isabel. The scarf hung around her neck.

She carried the overnight case and her black purse. She could afford to lose everything except these two things. As she settled into the family car and arranged her possessions neatly around her, she felt quite secure and defensible.

"How was your trip, then?"

"It was fine, Lawrence."

Maude still felt embarrassed, and looked down at her hands in her lap. She was too shy. She had to look up, look out, the way she had on the train.

The street was old and snared in time. Out of the visible landscape Maude picked those things which were familiar to her: Oskar's Drugstore, Kresgie's, the Plaza Hotel.

"A long trip. All alone. Isabel ain't comin'?" said Lawrence.

"No. No, she couldn't come. She was sorry she couldn't."

Maude hadn't really lived in the town. That's not what she knew. What she did know about this town was the school.

"Would you mind driving by the school?"

"Which school is that now?"

"My school, Elmore School. Just drive by there for a minute, would you?"

"Sure I will."

19

When they reached the brick building the grounds were empty. There were no children playing in the yard. Maude asked Lawrence why.

"It's Saturday. No school on Saturday. Same as it used to be."

"Oh, yes, of course. I forgot." For an instant she had thought that the school was shut down and abandoned. But the silenced voices of the children were still there. The bricks, so solid, had closed around the taunt of "Maudie, Maudie, she's an oddie."

"It looks the same though," said Maude.

They drove by slowly.

"Lawrence, if I went there, when it was open, and walked up to the principal, and told him my name, do you think that he would know me?"

"Know you? Well, he'd know your pa. If you said your name, said Rathbone, he'd sure figure it all out, right there on the spot. Might take him a bit of time, saying, 'Oh, you must be...no, you must be...aren't you...' but he'd figure you out sometime, where you fit. Principal's young, but his old man knows your dad."

"And if I just said 'I'm Maude—Maudie they used to call me,' do you think he would have heard stories, that he'd know anything?"

"No. Don't think so. Need the family name. Then he could figure it all out, figure it high and low, through the family, you know."

"I see."

"Just my opinion."

"Yes, I see." Something had its foot on her throat.

"To Talaru Boulevard, then?" asked Lawrence.

"Yes." Talaru Boulevard. She was confused. "Are we driving to Talaru?"

"Driving by and stopping."

"Staying?"

"That's where everybody is."

"But what about the farmhouse?"

"No farmhouse now. It burnt."

"It burned down?"

"Well, sure it did. Your folks live at Talaru all the time now, not just in winter. Have for a long time. You musta been told the farmhouse burnt."

"How did it burn?"

"Fire."

"Lawrence, I understand that, but how did it happen?"

"It was wood. Not like the Boulevard—and the school—they're brick."

Maude didn't remember that the farmhouse had gone. She must have known that. "How did it burn down?"

"Well, there are lots of stories."

"Tell me one."

"Can't tell just one. Telling one is like telling none. Have to tell them all to get the real picture."

"Well, all right, tell them all."

"Let me say, they ain't worth telling. Farm hand. Accident. Burnt once before a long time ago. When you were a baby."

"I know that, but how did it burn the second time?"

"Stories are a hired hand tried to burn the house down before. This time it burnt right down."

"Are people saying that the hired hand who started the first fire started the second one?"

"People talk. People say lots of things."

"Do you believe that?"

"Believing ain't nothing. The truth swills around like something in a pig's belly. Some day it finally just pops out, like a newborn. Now lots of things just swilling around."

Maude had a slight feeling of indigestion, a kind of cramp around her heart. She brought saliva into her mouth so that she could swallow, but the cramp was still there, a claw, a bony fingered thing that had hold of her. Somehow she felt responsible and to blame.

She didn't want to return home disabled, with a cramp in her chest and bones clawing. She wanted to arrive whole and capable, like a married woman with a place of her own. She needed a drink of water.

"Could you possibly stop here? I need a drink of water."

"Oh, sure. You're tired from your journey. Sure, I'll get you some water." Lawrence stopped in front of the Pioneer Cafe.

She tried to drown the cramp with the water. There was momentary relief. This was the first time in five days that she had stopped moving. The world seemed to tip and return, tip and return.

"People in a dream."

"What's that?" asked Lawrence.

"I've had enough, thanks. Please take the cup back." Lawrence went away.

On the street were people who looked familiar but derivative of even more familiar faces. She was supposed to be home now, and yet the place seconded for something else. Something she couldn't quite remember. Lawrence came back.

"Why didn't I hear about the farmhouse?"

"Maybe you forgot. Old anyway. Wasn't rebuilt so good. They were gonna tear it down."

"Do I look all right?"

"Maudie always looks pretty."

"But now, Lawrence, how do I look now?"

"You look fine. They're just your folks anyhow."

They pulled in front of the large brick house, set back in the trees.

Maude had pins and needles in her feet. Each step hurt as she walked towards the house which was dark and crackling with energy. S.D. was inside that house.

"I wish Isabel were here," said Maude as she walked beside Lawrence on the path.

"Too bad she ain't here. I'd sure like to see her again. She doesn't ever come home."

S.D. possessed this house. As certain as there was a door she had to enter, S.D. was the owner of this house. He would re-possess part of her if she went inside; she would be annexed by him. She stopped. She needed something to make her feel better. She wished Isabel were here.

"Lawrence?" He was behind her now. She wanted to make sure.

"Yes ma'am."

She looked around, trying to find something on which to linger. "Lawrence, that rose bush."

"Yes, ma'am, a fine rose bush."

"I had my picture taken there, when I was a child."

"That's a good place for a picture to be taken."

"It was double exposed. One picture of me was there, behind the rose bush, and another of me, fainter, almost like a ghost, was inside the rose bush."

"I never seen a picture like that. Must be a strange picture."

"I liked it, though."

Having admitted this fact of the picture she felt better. She would have to do that, say out loud the facts that she remembered. About things around her, on the outside.

If Isabel had been there, she would lead the way, pointing out flowers and patches of ground caked in event. Maude would be protected then. But now, to be alone with her family touched old places that had been left to heal, and had not healed.

"The bush was in bloom then, just like now." Maude went and touched one of the leaves. She could barely feel its waxy surface.

Kathryn emerged from the house, wearing white, layers of white cotton. Her hair was pulled back. Standing on the top step, with Maude below in the garden, Kathryn looked tall and imposing. Maude felt diminutive and utterly insignificant.

"Maudie. I'm so glad."

Backed by the impenetrable wall of brick and the darkness of the house, Kathryn held out her arms, waiting for an embrace. Maude moved up the stairs.

"You look well, Maude." Kathryn grasped her hands with thin bony fingers and pulled Maude forward. Maude's head rested on her mother's breast. "How was your trip, dear?"

Maude couldn't hear. She was overwhelmed by her mother's smell: bleached cotton and an associated smell of smoke. She couldn't breathe.

"You look well, Maude." This time her mother's voice carried an accusation, a Rathbone accusation. It demanded a reply or it would be withdrawn.

"Yes, thank you, Mother." Maude thought she was going to faint. "May I have a glass of water?"

"But you're coming in." Her mother's voice was cold like the feel of metal.

Of course; come into the house. She shouldn't ask her mother for a glass of water; she wasn't going to faint. But her limbs were absent and her head floated. Ask Lawrence? Their connection was gone now. "Stick to what you know." She was born Maude Rathbone, now Maude Mason. She was related. She had a husband.

"Lawrence could bring you a glass of water, if you wanted." Her mother softened. "You're tired."

"Would you ask him?" Maude had to be relieved from saying anything more. She averted her eyes so as not to see her mother's face.

"You should come inside. Your father will want to see you." Maude was unconnected to anything but the rose bush. "Your father is inside, Maude," said Kathryn, as though trying to clarify something extraordinarily complex.

"I'll stay here for a minute, and wait for the water." Maude sat down on the upper step with her back to the house.

"Lawrence," called Kathryn. He appeared around the side of the house. "Would you get Maude a glass of water, with some lemon."

Maude waited. She remembered the delicious days of being sick in bed, feverish and cared for by her mother. The men were out sweating in the hot sun while she was inside, being tended, as though she were the most delicate thing, capable of being broken.

She could have stayed there, lost in memory, forever. But the screen door creaked open.

"Maude." S.D. sounded her name like an accusation.

"Yes." I am an adult, she thought. A married woman. She didn't look at him.

"Well now, aren't you going to say hello to me?" said S.D.

"Maude, kiss your father." Kathryn spoke quietly.

Everything was so confusing now. If her mother could have whispered to her, the way she used to, telling her ways to win his favour, to make him be calm and not so big—but Kathryn stood there as his captain now, as his champion.

"Hello, Father." Maude continued to sit on the stairs with her back towards him.

"Yes? Yes?" he said, pressing down on her. Demanding, trying to possess her. Maude stood up and turned on the stair.

She was way beneath him. He would have to bend down if he wanted to kiss her, for she would not raise herself to him or offer her cheek.

S.D. hesitated. He filled his chest with air, which Maude thought prefaced an outburst of anger. She was afraid of his anger. He was all vanity—inexplicable and tangled vanity which masked itself as power. And she did not want to enter his kingdom; she wanted to remain on the step below, in an exaggeration of smallness, out in the open air.

But S.D. didn't get angry. Instead he kissed her on the top of her head, without her consent. She had been fooled by him.

"How was your trip?"

"Fine, thank you."

"Are you well?"

"Yes, and you?"

He hit on his chest with one fist but didn't answer.

Lawrence brought the glass of water and placed it on the stair beside her feet.

"What's this, Lawrence?" S.D. asked. "No, no, come inside now. The whole world will be seeing our goings on. Your brothers are inside. Come in, come in. No sense being out here." And he disappeared back into the house, yelling "Stanley, Clarence. Your sister is here."

"Come inside, Maude, when you're ready." Her mother touched her head, at the same place her father had kissed. The one cancelled out the other.

She was alone. She pressed her eyes shut and red orbs appeared behind her closed lids, orbs of scratched light which spread and widened, and then blossomed again. It was an explosion behind her face, of which she was the centre, spreading and scattering. The colour centred and bloomed again. That picture behind her eyes had always alarmed her. It meant she might be odd.

The loud noises coming from the house upset her and she despised herself for being upset. She stood up and turned towards the door of her father's house. As she did, her foot touched the glass that Lawrence had placed there. It fell over, spilling lemon-scented water on the grass beneath the stair. Maude didn't notice. She went through the door.

She breathed in the odours of the house: cooking entwined with the smell of tobacco. It was Isabel's absence that Maude felt so acutely as she walked into the drawing room alone.

"Maude." Her brother Clarence emerged and hugged her, enveloping her within the scent of wheat chaff. "It's good to see you, Maude." He pushed her out to arm's length.

"Yes, how are you. Nice to see you. Hello, Stanley." Stanley sat across the room and didn't move to greet her. Maude perched herself in the chair near the piano. Her mother brought her some tea. She was home.

Neighbours visited. People asked about Isabel but no one asked her about Geoffrey, she wasn't sure why. The questions were easy to answer. Mainly they required "yes, thank you; fine, thank you." Nothing made very much difference. "Yes, thank you," "fine, thank you." Once more she became automatic, superficial and very subdued. She served tea; asked others if they wanted anything to drink. Her father nodded at her, but did not smile. Seldom did he smile. He, for one, had not asked about Isabel, although Maude wanted especially to tell him—something. Sometimes she imagined saying "Isabel is doing very well." But she wouldn't. She was afraid of his worn, grim face, his rigid unenquiry, his certainty that the only thing which existed was what he contemplated.

Clarence and her mother buffered Maude, making her one of them, becoming almost unaware. But Stanley was not unaware.

Maude was a ripple on the smooth surface of things and it irritated Stanley. There was something foreign going on. He watched her, figuring and calculating. He had been made in the image of his father, and now took the role of the protector of S.D.'s carefully plotted kingdom. Maude was a conspirator against that order.

Once in the house, she entered the slipstream of her youth, where she was directed by the needs of others. She was in a timeless, hopeless state, whose only accent was the hot reality of her father.

On Wednesday evening, all the children were to come for dinner. No other guests or friends were invited or allowed.

The dining-room table was wonderfully set: the linen tablecloth which

25

Maude had ironed in the morning lay beneath the silver cutlery and the china dishes, the special china dishes with the blue trim and gilt edge. The silver peacocks, which were her favourite because their hard, precious feathers fanned onto the table, were placed at the centre, near the candles.

Everyone dressed for dinner.

The men looked elegant dressed in their dark suits, especially S.D. Maude could see the gold watch chain on his waistcoat glitter between the moving folds of his jacket as he walked to the head of the table.

"Maude, please sit here, next to me. Then Clarence. Mrs. Rathbone, you will sit in your usual place. Stanley, that side of the table, please, beside your mother. We have set a place for Isabel to remind us of her absence. If she were here, she would sit next to me."

This was the only time her father had mentioned Isabel. It was a reprimand, positioning her at the table against her will.

Clarence helped Maude with her chair. He was fair and slight for a man, more similar in appearance to Maude than Stanley. Stanley was big-boned like his father. Still, the sun had hardened Clarence and his hands were like gloves.

"The blessing," said S.D. and bowed his head. "For what we are about to receive, Lord, which is part of your bounty..."

Maude lowered her head, but didn't close her eyes. She peered at the others around the table, watching them in their state of grace. She almost sensed that she, like Isabel, was a ghost at the table, circling amidst those who were observed but unaware.

"...thank you for the homecoming of our Maude and for the blessings you have bestowed upon us. Us to your service, amen."

Everyone repeated "amen" except Maude.

S.D. served the food from china dishes placed in front of him by Kathryn. "There you are. Fresh from the garden," S.D. repeated as each plate was served. "No leftovers please."

Maude noticed that Stanley ate like a hungry man; he ate with a dedicated and determined intent. Clarence, responding to requests from others, was constantly passing things and making room on the table. Few words were spoken until the middle of dinner, when S.D. said, "Clarence, we'll have wine this evening, please. The red wine."

S.D. never used to have liquor in the house. Serving wine in the middle of dinner seemed to Maude to be a half measure of restraint, a begrudging festivity.

Stanley looked up from his plate without moving his head; out of his habit of stealth he glanced first at his father and then his mother.

The unusual request for wine quickened Maude from the numbness of the previous days, as though a spell had been lifted. "Yes, I'd like some wine," she said, without being asked. Stanley continued eating.

Maude wasn't hungry any more. The wine was full bodied and its dry, almost dusty taste enlivened her senses. She came to attention. It was as though Isabel was now actually in her midst, having been momentarily absent. Isabel loved parties.

S.D. ordered the glasses refilled.

"Not too much, S.D." protested Kathryn.

"There's no harm in wine, now and then," he corrected. He looked pleased, the way someone with a kingdom is pleased. "My family is here. Even Isabel, in her way. We need to discuss—I choose that we should discuss—the cairn. The cairn will be our memorial, our family's offering. To the land. Our dedication. History is very important." He cleared his throat and undid the top button on his shirt, underneath his tie. He seemed to be having trouble getting started. "We are of the first people to come here and break the soil. You are the next generation. Stanley and Clarence. We should—make a mark. Showing where we have been."

His halting oratory reminded Maude that her father had been a politician. He had been the mayor of the town once, and he must have spoken like this in his campaign. She hoped that she wouldn't be asked to vote on anything. The land had not comforted her and the notion of leaving a mark of one's past took her breath away. She lived in a narrow slit of time.

"We need to decide what will go on the cairn. There will be a statement. Suggestions, please. Clarence?"

Clarence sipped his wine and looked at the ceiling. S.D. lit a cigarette, which gave the signal to the sons that they could smoke.

"Stanley?"

"I think we should say the year you came here. Where you came from. How long you've been here. Then—something else. Some kind of dedication." He flagged.

"What would the 'something else' be?" Her father's patience was extraordinary. Maude had expected him to say "of course, but what?" Instead, he began his sentences with questions and lingered, swirling

27

the wine in his glass. The crystal glinted in the candlelight.

"I think you should write that part," Stanley said, dully.

"Yes, but I would like you to help me. I'm not going to—I won't live forever." S.D.'s voice faltered.

No one spoke. No one moved. To interrupt this silence was to interfere with something that had been forever coming to this moment, as though all the time before was only prelude. S.D. would die. It was now a declared and settled fact. And Maude was half afraid that he wouldn't die. Or that someone—that Stanley—would deny it. But no one did. And the growing weight of silence around the table seemed suddenly greedy for his death. Everyone, thought Maude, wants him to die. To die as soon as possible.

Maude turned to Clarence. "May I have more wine, please," she said quietly. He rose and filled all the glasses.

Stanley spoke next. "Of course it weighs upon you."

And then Kathryn intervened. "You are the pioneer. But we needn't get...you will live for a long time yet."

"It's all right, Father," continued Stanley.

Everyone was suddenly clamouring for his attention.

"I'm trying to tell you something," said S.D. without rancor. "I'm going to die within the next—what's the date?" No one answered him. "What is the date, please?" he repeated.

"July 24," offered Maude.

"Yes," he said, satisfied. "So we must decide certain things—I must decide, and I am asking for your assistance. I don't need to, of course. I can do it on my own. I guess I thought I would live forever. You probably thought that too." He laughed as though a private joke had just come to him. It was a wide, big laugh, full of teeth.

Kathryn got up from her place.

"Mother, sit down. I want to deal with the cairn."

She stopped. "S.D?"

"Please, sit down."

Maude watched her mother retreat to her place.

He began again. "We will say when we first broke this soil. My wife came from the Isle of Man and I came from Londonderry. That should be mentioned. Clarence, pour more wine. Please, keep our glasses filled." The pall had lifted and S.D. seemed excited and patient once again. "Now, someone will have to write that down. Mrs. Rathbone, you will get Clarence some paper so this is not forgotten. Do it quickly." He continued. "I have assembled thousands of acres of land, productive land. I have done this at great cost. I have, all my life, done what I said

I would do. I believe in that. And I have written things down so that there will be no mistake about anything.''

"S.D., you're going to live for a long time," said Kathryn, quietly.

"The doctor said—" he began.

"The doctor said you needed a holiday."

S.D. seemed drunk; he was exaggerated and expansive. Maude couldn't recall ever seeing him this way. Mostly he had been a sharp bladed plough cutting through his life, planting straight rows of seed. Except for her. She wasn't part of the straight row her father planted.

Now, at the dinner table, she felt a sort of kindness towards S.D. He was afraid of dying, and she knew all about that. Death was a withered apple terror under the house, to be kept back only through silence. S.D. shouldn't talk about it, not out in the open.

In telling Clarence what to write for the cairn, S.D. accidentally tipped over his glass, which was almost empty. Clarence stood immediately, picked up the glass, and refilled it.

Her brother's act of service, so tutored he didn't have to ask or be told, was distasteful to Maude. Clarence had grown skilled in his obedience. He was unaware of how he had been sculpted by his father: how definitely he had been shaped to fit the suit his father had made for him, and how quietly he had succumbed.

Stanley had not succumbed in the same way. His obedience was different. When he was a boy, Stanley had set traps for birds, made of delicate twigs. He would sit for hours in the leaves and wait. His will seemed almost to buckle at the moment just before capture. Then he had the impulse to save his victim from what was about to occur. But he never did. He always waited until the very end, until the actual snare.

When Stanley saw Clarence stand immediately, set the glass upright and pour more wine, he wanted to tell his father not to take it, to tell him he'd had enough. But the time wasn't right. Eventually his father would need him, would have to listen to him. In the midst of this thought, he loved S.D. profoundly. He was the only one who really understood him. And Stanley loved this idea of himself, understanding S.D.

"Clarence," said S.D. again, "refill Stanley's glass. We have important things to do." He stood as he said this and reached over to the heavy oak sideboard, opening the drawer. But he could not find the document he had placed there. "Kathryn," he bellowed. She arrived immediately.

"Where is it? Where is it?" he demanded.

"Where is what?"

"The legal paper. I put it here." She looked in the drawer,

found it, turned and went out again.

"Kathryn, I said I want you in here. Stay here with us."

She re-emerged and stood at the doorway. Some said that Kathryn had gone stupid inside this marriage, had become as insubstantial as ash. She protected her children and S.D. split the seams of that protection. Still she translated for him, trying to make him diffused. The effect was that she seemed obscured, as though she were slightly off.

She was tired now and wanted to go upstairs. "What is it, S.D.?" she asked.

"Sit here, near me." He pointed to the place set for Isabel. Kathryn sat down.

Maude was startled. In her sister's place sat her mother, fingering the tablecloth. The others didn't seem to notice. Her mother looked so comfortable there, not realizing what she had done, not remembering that the place had been set for Isabel.

Maude leaned forward and said quietly, "Mother, that's not your place." Kathryn looked up. "That place is for Isabel."

"Yes." Her mother acknowledged the fact as though it was a pleasantry, like the date, or the weather.

"I mean Isabel still has a place here."

"Yes, she does." Her mother was uncomprehending.

"She will sit where I choose." S.D.'s loud voice sent Maude's fears deeper, into the earth. Into the root cellar. Into the dark place left for memory. A small voice emerged. "Where is Isabel?"

"Would you have it that Isabel's place be where your mother's is?"

His logic confused Maude, and she looked to the head of the table, opposite her father, which was empty, and at her sister's place, filled by her mother.

"Tell me what you want," S.D. persisted, sharp and aggressive.

"Now, please don't fight," said Kathryn.

"Nothing. I was wrong," answered Maude. What she could have explained to her mother was gone under the harshness of her father's challenge. Maude thought she might cry. It was an odd sensation that lasted no longer than a shiver. Then she abandoned herself and sat empty and compliant.

S.D. asked Kathryn for his reading glasses. He stared at the document in front of him and began to speak in a monotone.

"I have written my will. I went to the lawyers and they put it all down here, and I signed it in front of two of them. I don't understand it all, but they told me what I want is here." He patted the long heavy sheets of paper, the way he would pat a horse or a cow.

30

Stanley put his elbows on the table and craned his neck. He couldn't discern the words on the page. S.D. hadn't told him about this will, about going to lawyers and writing things down that were final. He could feel the muscles in his neck strain and his eyes dry as he tried to see. The future was written there. Stanley's breath knotted in his chest.

The gossips in the town, who always had something to say about the Rathbones, had probably heard already about this will. They probably knew S.D. had gone to lawyers without consulting his son. They knew it before he did. The gossips were trying to undo him. And S.D. was feeding the rumours by going to lawyers, making a will, leaving Stanley out, encouraging the treachery of gossiping old ladies. His own father.

S.D. was saying, "This paper here that the lawyers wrote says it in legal fashion. My wife will be provided for. The rest of my property will be divided between the four of you, in equal shares. All the farms, four equal ways. When we both go, I want everything divided up, just like this says." S.D. kept patting the paper with his hand.

Stanley had to get control of things. The words on the page were evil and unruly children, bent on undermining him. It was Stanley who embodied his father's wishes, not some lawyers. It was a mistake, an error in judgment. He could use his mother, if he had to. If necessary, he would get his father to change it. If necessary, he would destroy that paper. He could if he wanted to. Destroy the paper.

He sat back in his chair. As a child, Stanley had learned to hold his breath to get his way. He would breathe quickly as if starting a fire, and then hold, floating in a state of non-breathing, drawing attention, drawing extreme concern. From a distant place he would watch his father's worried face. His family would gather around him like flowers he had picked, his mother pleading and his father becoming as red as a rose. But the last time his father had said in a stern voice, "I can hold my breath. If you hold your breath longer than me you'll be dead." Stanley understood completely: his father threatened to endure. Stanley breathed. In the midst of his mother's tears, he yearned to be touched by this man. He wanted to be absorbed by him. He trusted S.D.'s ruthlessless which would dare his own son to die.

S.D.'s voice at the dinner table perforated Stanley's thoughts. "Isabel isn't here, but Maude will tell her what I've done. Four equal ways. The things in the house..."

S.D. was dividing everything into four. This man was not his father. He would have to get his father back.

"...everything will be divided. You will choose lots so that it's fair. Take these silver peacocks." He picked up one of the ornaments and as he did his wine glass rocked but didn't fall. "This peacock. You'd draw lots, each of you. The winner would have this bird. Then would come the next bird." He held up the other ornament. "The person who won the first bird wouldn't draw a lot for the second." As he spoke he jabbed the air with the silver bird to emphasize his words. "Because that person had his chance. So you would draw lots. And on it would go. That's the idea. It's all written here so you'll get it right and there will be—"

Stanley interrupted. "Do you mean everything would be drawn by lots, each fork, each toothpick?"

"Pardon me?" S.D. was defensive, as though Stanley were trying to collapse his dream, his house of cards. "What do you mean?" Meekly at first, the father repeated the question, as the cards tottered but still stood. "What *do you* mean?" His chest filled with air and his eyes widened. "Why are you talking about toothpicks? Toothpicks. Is that the way you see what I've created, slaved over since before you were born. Toothpicks?"

Stanley's only choice was to be more extreme than his father. He sat quietly for a minute. Shame had sunk so deep into his muscles that when he moved his arm the movement contained the shame. He loosened the collar on his shirt because it was choking him.

"Yes, toothpicks." He would repeat the word until it became a sliver under his father's skin. "Do you want us to draw lots, to bid over toothpicks?"

"Toothpicks!" his father yelled back.

"Toothpicks," Stanley said again.

"You idiot. I am not talking about toothpicks." S.D. slammed his fist down on the table and water from his glass splashed onto the cloth to mix with the red stain of the wine. "Boy, you don't know what you're talking about. I should've licked you a long time ago, for such talk."

"Toothpicks," goaded Stanley. He had S.D. hooked, just under the skin.

"Don't you say that any more. Don't say it, you damned fool." S.D. put his fist on the table in an effort to rise. He was shaking.

Kathryn intervened. "S.D., stop it." She held his arm. "Sit down."

"My son will not talk to me of toothpicks."

"Sit down. Drink some water. Calm yourself."

"Don't say sit down. And I won't have any of this foul water. He talks of my life as toothpicks."

"No, he doesn't. Listen to him for once."

Kathryn was an ally. That's right. That's what Stanley had planned.

He had charmed her into his course as if it had been her own. He continued. "What you are suggesting is that everything in your house, down to the very last fork and spoon—and toothpick—should be divided into lots, picked over and bartered on, openly like in the marketplace."

"Don't say toothpicks. We're not talking of toothpicks. I won't hear of it."

"Let him finish." Kathryn ushered Stanley back into the fray.

"All that you have built over four decades, breaking this soil, teaching your sons to live by the land, would be carted off, like cattle to market, where dealers and profiteers would draw lots and bicker over your remains."

"Your sisters and brother are not profiteers. How dare you..."

"That's what you'd turn us into. You'd turn us into grave-diggers picking at your remains. This paper, this stupid paper would destroy everything you've done. You've given me good things. You have taught me the way to live with this land." Stanley was enamoured of his speech, entranced by the sound of his own voice. "I know the value of what you have done. It will live with me each day that I work the land you have worked. That's how you have passed on your wishes. Isn't that right?"

His father nodded.

"You said our mother would be provided for after your death as during your lifetime." S.D. was sipping his wine again, nodding his head, and sipping his wine. Stanley barely knew where his words were taking him. He had lost any plan and was led only by his determination to survive. His teeth marks stayed on the words he spoke.

"It's not right—it's not good to write down what you want for our mother. If your wine spilled on the pages and all the words were rubbed out, your wishes would be done. You know why? Because your sons know what you want—your will, not written by lawyers who don't understand you, but your will as we know it."

Stanley's lust to be secure against the outsiders prickled his vision, the way that a runner sees the road ahead. He was elegant; he was passionate. He had trained for this moment. At all costs, he would get what he deserved. His father's empire was the only thing that would keep him from skidding against the gravel road, against the mean ground that would bite into his skin. The gossips bit his skin.

"What if that paper should be misunderstood? That paper is now the letter of the law. Everything written there, and only that, is what we are left with. These words of the lawyers become your only voice. Nothing else means a thing. What you want doesn't mean a thing. I don't mean a thing. We know what you want. We're your family."

"Yes." S.D. seemed quite calm now.

"We're your family," Stanley repeated.

"No one knows me better than my own family."

"Outsiders would..."

"I don't want outsiders meddling into our affairs."

"No, you don't. If everything's written down by lawyers, people would meddle. They'd pry. It would be like inviting them right into our house, these perfect strangers." Stanley flourished his hand and raised his voice. "Come right on in, sit down, tell us what our father wanted. Tell us what he meant in his lifetime. Let's squabble over the forks and glasses—and the toothpicks. Tell us if we can give a toothpick to our mother."

"Toothpicks, again," said S.D. quietly, and then raised his voice. "No outsider is going to tell me what to do with my toothpicks. If my wife wants a toothpick, she'll have a toothpick, God damn it."

"But what does that paper say about toothpicks?"

"How should I know. Lawyers put it down. Ask them."

"Exactly," said Stanley. "Exactly."

Maude was entranced. She understood toothpicks; they were for teeth. But she barely understood the rest. She was a spectator in a match involving great skill. As the argument progressed her distrust of Stanley increased. She trusted Clarence, but he said nothing and kept his head bowed. Surely her father would look to him for guidance. She wanted Stanley to stop the nattering insistence, the superior gratitude, the condescending acknowledgement. Clarence didn't speak. Could she? "Stick to what you know," Isabel had said. But she didn't know anything. Her sister's words and Clarence's silence didn't help her find her way. She only knew that it was all treacherous, evil-speaking and wrong. Stanley was a snake.

"We can't trust any of them," continued Stanley. "Lawyers take your money. Do you trust lawyers more than our own family? We only trust ourselves. We didn't create these farm lands for lawyers to take. Lawyers are leeches."

"That's right. You're right."

Stanley had him. It was only a question of putting a few more leaves on the camouflage of the trap. "Who knows what they wrote down in that paper? They could have said anything. To make more money for themselves." Stanley picked up the will. "What does this mean, 'per stirpes'? I don't know what that is. I don't even know how to say it." He threw the paper down and leaned over. "But I do know what you want."

"You do. Yes, you do."

"You want us to carry on your traditions, your strong spirit, your fair-mindedness."

"Yes."

"These are foreign words, 'per stirpes.' We can't understand them. We'd have a bunch of foreigners in here telling us how to run our lives."

"I won't let them set a foot in here."

"That's the invitation, that paper. It lets them in. It's their ticket."

"I won't have it."

"Rip it up, then."

"I won't have it."

"Rip it up, or they'll come in here and tell us what to do. They'll come right in, snooping around, looking at everything."

"No they won't." With that, S.D. tore the paper into two, then four, then six pieces. His eyes were bright and fanatical as he ripped into shreds the will which was not his own—the words of the outsiders, the strange language of dispossession.

Even Stanley was amazed. He slumped back in his chair. He was satisfied and almost kind. "That's right. It doesn't exist any more. We know." Stanley's voice was quiet and smooth. "Now, go to bed and sleep, knowing that you've done the right thing."

"Yes."

"Mother, take him to bed," Stanley directed. He was completely in charge now. The will was in shreds and his was the voice of the father.

Maude watched Kathryn and S.D. leave the room, her father humbled on the arm of his wife who seemed strong and steady, fortified by her husband's weakness. They drained the energy from the room as they departed. The noise, confusion and passion of the last minutes lay dormant on the table, the will and testament lying on a bed of purple wine stain.

The children sat without speaking.

Stale air settled on Maude's shoulders. Her hands were limp on the white cloth. She heard the clock chime. One o'clock. Space and time yawned, unorthodox, still and endless. She would never go to sleep and never wake up.

Something else ruled the hour, a confirmed hopelessness, a threat that stalked her. She longed to be set free from this moment that promised only another moment, exactly the same, without a moon and without a sun. She was abroad and lonely: her father banished, Isabel gone,

Clarence silent at her side. Stanley ruled the hour. She was passive and powerless, no day or night to release her.

But Clarence spoke, almost in a whisper, rasping, stuttering, the way he had as a child. "S-stanley."

Maude looked up. Stanley was staring at her. She took her fork and started picking at the tablecloth. She didn't want Clarence to speak now: it was too late for speaking. She lowered her head again and pressed the fork into the cloth.

"S-stanley."

She looked up again. Stanley hadn't taken his eyes off her, but he said in a tone that sounded mean, mean like sticks and stones, "Yes, C-clarence."

That's what he'd always done. They needed to keep hidden from him. Let him look in, but see nothing.

"Y-you sh-shouldn't have d-done that."

"D-done what, C-clarence," mimicked Stanley.

"D-don't make fun of me." Clarence pushed out his chair and stood up. "D-don't make fun of me, you—you b-bastard."

"Clarence, sit down."

"You are a b-bastard, and you treat our father like sh-shit."

"Are you sure?" He tied Clarence to the end of a rope, and twirled him around. "Are you sure? A b-bastard, Clarence? Who's the b-bastard, Clarence, to our father?"

"W-what are you t-talking about?"

"You should know what I'm talking about. Sit down, Clarence. You know what I'm talking about."

Maude stopped stabbing her fork into the tablecloth. She watched Clarence slowly sink back in his chair as Stanley continued to address him while looking at her.

"Some have fathers, and some don't. We're his sons. I'm only helping him." Stanley's tone had become hurt and begrudging. He was a little boy, the same as Clarence, his grand tone reduced to a childhood grievance. "It's not fair. Under that will, we would all take equally. That's not fair."

"But everyone should share," said Clarence.

"Yes. All the children." Stanley was still looking at Maude and his eyes narrowed. "All the children, Maude, so not you." He stood up. "So, not you," he said decisively.

He wasn't yelling. He drew a line that left her out. Not you. Not you, Maude. Why? What did he mean? She had misplaced something, some vital piece of information. She had come to a border, in the middle of darkness, and there was her brother saying she didn't have the right papers. She couldn't cross; she would have to go back. She sat there, searching for it. She was sure she had seen it. She heard children chanting "Maudie, Maudie, she's an oddie." Her parents' voices, loud at night. The clock striking one, next time two. Isabel, at the train station, telling her to say her piece, not to believe them, not to trust them. Not to trust Stanley.

Out of a confusion so deep it had no grounding, Maude said, "Isabel should be here."

"Isabel? Isabel?" Stanley curled the name in his mouth. "Isabel. Do you know who Isabel is? Do you?" He had changed again. His hands were fisted on the table, clenched white as he leaned over. "Do you?"

"She's my sister," said Maude, simply.

"Your sister! You poor thing. Isabel is *not* your sister."

"She is my sister," repeated Maude.

"You fool. Isabel is your mother."

Maude let go. She let go completely. Drifting. It was the middle of the afternoon. Strange, that the side door of the house was unlocked. She pushed open the door, but something was pressing against it, some force, or maybe the hinges had frozen. Against the door was a suitcase. Why had Geoffrey left a suitcase in front of the door? Then she saw a red liquid beside the suitcase. She looked up. Tomatoes and wine and food had been smeared all over the walls. All the food had been pulled out of her kitchen cupboards, and out of the fridge. Slowly she walked through the silent rooms, the couch overturned, her silver gone, every drawer in the house uprooted. Still, nothing moved. Everything in her house uprooted, changed, marked by the intruder. The thief. But nothing moved.

And Stanley didn't move. He stared down at her.

She was alert now. She had left her house idle but she was home now. The invader was there. She had caught him, just in time.

"Stanley, you're crazy. Clarence, take him away. He's drunk. I've had enough of you, Stanley, and your talk. Go home." She wouldn't be afraid of him. She would not.

Clarence didn't move.

"Stanley, go home," yelled Maude.

"I *am* home," he said, his voice full of calm.

"Don't you have a place of your own? You're a big boy now. You don't have to hang on to him. Coming here and ruining everything, smearing everything, making everything filthy with your...."

"Shut up," yelled Stanley. "You go home. You have no right to speak.

You should be grateful to me. You should thank me. Everyone has always lied to you. I'm telling you the truth.''

"Get back. Clarence, take him home," said Maude.

"Don't you move," warned Stanley. "Ask him, Maude. Ask Clarence who your mother really is. Don't you want to know? Don't you want to know who your father is?''

"I know who my father is. He's the man you are trying to destroy just like that paper, with your crazy talk. Haven't you done enough?''

"Why do you think he ripped up the will? Because it wouldn't stand up in court. You aren't entitled to a thing. Why do you think Isabel left home and never came back? You're a bastard. You're illegitimate. Your sister is your mother and your father''—Stanley sneered—"your real father was some stranger, a common farm hand. Tell her, Clarence. The man you call your father is your grandfather. And I am your uncle. And so is he." Stanley pointed to Clarence who sat, twisting his serviette in his hands.

"I'm l-leaving." As Clarence stood, his chair fell back, overturned onto the floor behind him.

"Don't you dare leave. You stay here and tell her the truth."

"You want me to tell her the t-truth?'' Clarence was utterly defeated. ''I don't know what the t-truth is, or who you are, or who I am, or why any of this is h-h-happening." He tripped against the overturned chair as he left the room.

"Don't go. Please, Clarence, don't go," said Maude. But it was too late. There was only Stanley now, the border guard who would not let her pass. Go to sleep. She cleared a place in front of her. Go to sleep. Go home to sleep. She put her arms on the table as a cradle for her head, and closed her eyes.

"Wake up," commanded Stanley.

Maude heard the words, and some of the others which followed, but she had abandoned herself completely. She had quit and gone away.

When Maude opened her eyes she was in a bed. There was a dresser, a table lamp, clothes hung over a chair. Light came in through curtained windows. She heard no sounds.

Strange. She didn't have a name that she could recall. She might have felt empty, except she couldn't remember anything that had gone. She had no past which now eluded her. The objects around her had an unobtrusive presence, as though newly arrived. She was sure she had come through something, to this place, but where she was and who she

38

was were unfathomable. She only looked out. Nothing claimed her. Were the clothes hers? Were there any other people?

There was nothing more to think about. She lay back on the bed and fell asleep.

When she awoke again someone was just sitting down on the bed. She opened her eyes. Kathryn. Holding a cup, giving her a cup.

She accepted it, sat up and took a drink of tea. Kathryn was wearing a mauve dress that rose high on her neck. The sleeves went to her wrists. This woman, she knew, would wait a long time. Already she looked old, the skin loose and lined.

"Good morning, Maude."

"Good morning—" She was about to say Mother, but stopped herself.

"Did you dream?"

Yes, this person always asked her about dreams. Maude liked to tell her dreams, as though she were reporting on the illness of a friend.

"I woke up earlier. It was light. I couldn't remember who I was."

"Had you been dreaming?"

"No, I don't think so. I couldn't remember anything."

"I expect it was the wine, last night."

Last night? A memory of theft. Being homeless outside the world.

"We all had too much wine," continued Kathryn. "Your father is still sleeping."

"My father?"

"He's not used to that much wine. I found Clarence sleeping beside your door this morning and Stanley was nowhere to be seen."

Maude remembered her intense hatred of Stanley.

"Where is Clarence?"

"I put him in the other room."

"He left last night."

"Well, he didn't get very far or else he came back."

"Does he look all right?"

"Yes, why? A bit pale. Green I should say."

"Is Stanley all right?" She wanted to arm her mother against him.

"Why are you asking if everyone is all right?"

"Stanley is odd."

"Odd?" Kathryn paused for a long time, as she swirled the tea in her cup. "He should marry, that's all. He has a new friend. I hope he'll marry her. None of my sons seems to want to marry."

"He was crazy last night."

Kathryn answered quickly, "Whether or not your father has a will doesn't matter. Things will work out fairly. We were supposed to settle the plaque, for the farm. Not the will. Isabel called this morning. Wanted to know how everything was.''

Maude felt suddenly hopeful. ''What did you tell her?''

''I said everything was fine, just fine.''

''Did she ask about me?''

''Yes. I said you were just fine. Sleeping. It would have been nice to have all the family together again.''

''Stanley is a bully.''

''Now, don't talk like that. I didn't want this business of the will brought up in the first place. My father got cheated out of some land because of lawyers. It's better this way. Get dressed. You can help me clean up the mess.''

''Ma—'' She caught herself. ''Do you remember any of the old songs you used to sing to me?''

''Of course I do.''

''Will you sing to me?''

''I haven't sung to you since—I used to make up songs for you.''

''Yes, like that.''

''But you're too old now, aren't you? And so far away.'' Maude moved closer. ''All right then, come up.'' Maude cradled her head and shoulders against Kathryn. She needed to hear the old songs to block out remembering. She wanted to belong to this woman.

''What shall I sing?'' Kathryn mused, as though nothing had changed.

''It was so strange waking up, not remembering where I was, or even my name. Why am I called Maudie?'' It was a dangerous question; she knew that as soon as it was out of her mouth. She couldn't help herself.

''Because there was a first Maude, and then we called you Maude. You know that.''

''Was I named after her?''

''But you've heard this before,'' Kathryn gently reminded her.

''Tell me again.''

''Your father and I liked the name.''

There it was again. She had to stay away from father; she had to focus only on her name.

''Was I named after the first one?''

''Well, no—yes, I suppose. In a way. She was so young when she died. And then you came along. But I would have called you Maude anyway.''

''Even if the first one hadn't died?''

''Well, no, of course not. But you do look so much like a Maude. Soft. Exclusive.''

"Am I exclusive?"

"Yes, I think you are—in a nice way, though."

"Why was I born so late, so much after the others?"

"You weren't, not really. There was Maude, the first. You were the last one. And the last to leave home."

Maude looked at Kathryn and thought that she loved her—and then remembered that she might be her grandmother, instead of her mother.

"I didn't want you to go." Kathryn's voice was feathered and light, caught in a dream.

"Can't you sing to me, please?"

And Kathryn began, with a wavering old voice, to sing the song.

> Sweet Maude, sweet Maude
> You're sent from God
> Come to me
> From far away
> Maude, sweet Maude, my own.

When she was finished, Maude asked her to sing it again, and this time she joined in, the two voices braiding into a long, sleepy plaint. They sang the verse over and over again, singing a quiet sun into the sky.

When they stopped, she was home again, and the things in the room, the clothes on the chair, belonged to her.

"Mother, what's wrong with our family?"

"With our family?" They were sleep-talking, as in the old days, the safe days from before.

"Mother, *is* there something wrong with our family?" She looked up into Kathryn's face, into a slow eternity which could wait forever. The question had come from before, some injunction from before; Maude couldn't think of why she asked it. Something had been wrong. Her mother would make it go away.

"Mother—Kathryn..." The connection was broken, again. Maude was back at the border crossing. This woman in front of her wore a mask of kindness. Motherliness. But she carried a lie inside her.

"Nothing is wrong, Maude. Hush now. Don't get upset. There's nothing to be upset about." Kathryn began to rock her back and forth, back and forth.

"Do you know who I am? Mother. Do you?" Maude began to cry, the tears stinging her dry eyes. She was convulsed with sobs, rocked by Kathryn, who kept saying "hush now, hush now." Maude was indescribably lonely, empty and hurt like the centre of some absolute

41

zero. It was the end of the world.

From Kathryn's neck hung a pendant with pearls set in a golden ring. The pendant swung back and forth, in rhythm with the rocking.

"What's the matter? Don't cry now."

The pendant moved into Maude's line of vision and she touched it. It made a wider arc. She touched it again, and it continued to swing, dumb and foreign to her. Maude asked, "What's that?" She knew it had been in the family for generations. It seemed different now, hardly recognizable.

"It was given to me, by my mother."

"But what does it mean?"

"It's from the Londonderry. It's a symbol."

"Three legs."

"The three legs of Man inside the ring. That's the symbol."

"What for?"

"A symbol."

Maude had stopped crying. The pendant looked like a twisted cross around her mother's neck. She swung it again. The legs on the cross were running back and forth, running, trying to get away. A tickle developed in her throat and built slowly, incrementally, into a laugh. She laughed at the facts: that this woman wore something around her neck; that it had a shape, of three legs without a body; that this woman did not know what it meant; this woman was supposed to be her mother, maybe her grandmother. It was a symbol without a meaning. Everyone forgot. Give me a hint. Kathryn. Pendant. Mother. Londonderry. Facts. The facts, the stupid facts built Maude's laughter into crying. And then crying became laughing, back and forth, rocking, crying and laughing. One inside the other, one creating the other. Kathryn's expression of alarm added to Maude's laughter, to the shrieks of crying and the shrieks of laughing. The three legs of man, without a body, running around the neck of this woman who looked scared. Maude was sobbing and convulsed.

Kathryn shouted, "Maude!" which only endorsed the laughter. "Maude," "Maude." The name running around in every direction. Which Maude, which Maude?

Maude was slapped on the face. Stopped. Struck by Kathryn. Slapped.

"Maude, oh Maude," said Kathryn, clutching, burying Maude's stinging face into her perfumed breast. "Oh Maude, I'm sorry. You scared me."

The air cackled, breathing in and out. Maude didn't laugh or cry.

"I want to go home now, please," said Maude into her mother's dress.

"I'm sorry. You were hysterical."

"I want to go home."

"Oh, darling, don't you know, you are home. You need your rest. There's been too much excitement."

"I'll go home now."

"Maude, please."

The smell of Kathryn's cotton dress. Being held. The smell of smoke. Of panic.

"I hate Stanley. I don't like it here now."

"Never mind Stanley. He was only trying to help your father."

"My father?"

"Of course. You want that, don't you?"

"My father?"

"Yes, your father. Maude, what *is* the matter with you?"

Turning point, thought Maude, turning point, no return, one step more is off the middle ground. Into the danger land where there isn't even a border guard. No border crossing except this, voice of Kathryn gone hard. Apples in a bowl.

"Maude?" Kathryn's voice pliable again. "Have we failed you? Have I failed you, in any way?"

Offer up apples in a bowl? It might be a trap. Maude could hear the trap just a little ways away. This woman was Stanley's mother. Stanley was a trap-man. A border trap-man. This was a real trap which she couldn't avoid, drawing her forward through all the warnings. But the lure of possibility, the excitement of disclosure compelled her. Offer the bowl of apples. Go into the cellar. Bring them up.

Maude couldn't resist. "Sometimes I feel like your child," she said, stepping calmly.

"But you *are* my child."

"And sometimes I'm like a twin that has died."

"I don't know what you mean, Maude. What are you talking about?"

"I mean, I'm different. Different from Stanley. From the others."

"But you're all different."

"You didn't intend any harm."

"What harm have I caused? Tell me. Explain it to me. Don't you know I love you?"

There was another click, closer this time. It wasn't Kathryn's trap, it was Stanley's. Stanley was the one who'd set the traps, not Kathryn. He set them the night before.

Kathryn was—almost innocent. She loved Kathryn and hated Stanley. That's right. Kathryn would understand. Kathryn would remember.

"When I was little, you asked Stanley to help me. I was supposed to take a bath and wash my hair. I was just little. Later, you asked me if I had. I said yes. Then I heard you ask Stanley if I had washed my hair. He said no. I was sitting at the top of the stairs, in the farmhouse. You said to me "don't you know if you've washed your hair or not? Do I have to send you to a doctor so you'll remember?" I didn't understand. I still don't understand. I guess you thought I was lying. But now I think it was Stanley. Don't you see, it was Stanley who did it?"

"But that didn't happen."

"What didn't happen?" Maude was lost. It was supposed to be simple now, everything clear and simple.

"About the bath, and going to the doctor. That never happened between us, Maude."

"Yes, it did." Maude was incredulous.

"No, I never said those things to you."

"But you did."

"I'm worried about you. I think I should call Dr. Graham. You're overtired."

"Mother." Maude raised her voice. "You're doing it again."

"What? What *is* it? Why are you like this?"

"Kathryn, you're doing it to me again. You aren't telling the truth."

"You're upset. You need to see the doctor, that's all. Oh my poor baby, you're so confused. It's been so trying for you."

"There is nothing wrong with me. I am telling you something." Maude placed each word in front of her like blocks of ice. "And now you—you are making me crazy." There was a tiny hair in Maude's mouth. It was caught at the back of her throat and she tried to remove it with her tongue.

"Maude."

Something snapped. It was all, all lies. She had to get out. It was strangling her, choking her. It was the rotten apple face that she had touched; it was all over her hands. The rotten apple death.

Maude got up and quickly put on her clothes.

"I'm getting S.D.," threatened Kathryn.

Maude dressed and stuffed everything in her suitcase.

"I'm getting S.D.," said Kathryn, hurt and bewildered.

"Get him, then, you liar."

"Don't you talk to me like that."

Maude rushed down the stairs with her mother following, yelling, "Don't, Maude. S.D. Clarence. Stop."

Maude got to the front door.

"Please, Maude, don't go, don't go out there. Not yet. Stay and we'll talk this out."

Maude turned the door handle and different air entered the hall. No one else came. Maude wanted to see Clarence, but it was too late somehow. Still she looked back, over Kathryn's shoulder. The long corridor stretched behind her. She was sure Kathryn wouldn't go any farther than the door. She pulled it wide open and then turned again. Her mother had disappeared.

Maude walked back into the dining-room, hoping to see Clarence one last time. There was only the rubble of the night before. On the table lay the bits of paper. She scooped them into her purse, went to the front door and walked out into the hot sun that hurt her eyes. She bowed her head. Down the stairs, past the shimmering rose bush that held her ghost. Onto the sidewalk of Talaru Boulevard. Past all the houses. Unimpeded. To the train station. She waited there, hidden in the ladies' washroom until the train arrived. Then she left the country of her birth.

Maude travelled through sleepless nights. Geoffrey was at the train station waiting; Kathryn had called him saying Maude had run away.

She refused to talk about what had happened. She continued to love Isabel, cautiously, exclusively. She put the bits of paper into a brown envelope and folded it as small as it would go. She wrote a bright, cheerful letter to Kathryn and S.D., thanking them for the visit.

In the end, she made it so that nothing had happened. Geoffrey didn't have to know anything. And she would tell Isabel it had been nice.

She had drawn a line and her life folded back inside itself, brittle, discreet and calm.

1948

The new man came often to see Evelyn's mother. He had to drive a long way to visit them. That's what her mother said. Evelyn liked the puppet that he gave her, and the china doll. She showed them to Elsie.

Evelyn and Elsie sat in the backyard, watching a bee crawl into a hole in the ground.

"Do you think it will sting us?" asked Elsie.

"Dunno."

"What ya gonna call him?"

"Who?"

"Your new dad."

45

Evelyn didn't have any dad. She'd never had one, and didn't want one. There was just Evelyn and her mother. "He's not my dad," she said, poking at the ground with her stick.

"He's gonna be."

"How do you know?"

"My mom said."

Evelyn didn't like Elsie's mother figuring things out about her and her mom.

"How does she know?"

"Will you call him Dad?"

"I dunno." The insect crawled into the hole again and came out. Or another one came out, she wasn't sure.

"You can't just call him mister."

"He's Stanley. That's what I call him." Evelyn closed the subject. "Do you think there's one bee down there or two? Maybe more."

"It's not a real bee." Sometimes Elsie's top lip curled. Evelyn hated that.

"Why not?"

"Bees don't live in the ground."

"Maybe they do. You don't know everything." Evelyn thought Elsie looked like a pug dog, with her lip curled up like that. "Maybe this bee lives underground because it's cooler. See, it's going down again," pointed Evelyn.

"Yeah, but just to explore. Not to live."

Evelyn stabbed the ground around the bee's cave so that bits of dirt fell in. "We could only tell if we put a mark on it. To see if it was the same one that went up and down."

"It might sting us."

"Maybe this is a gopher-bee."

"Never heard of that," said Elsie, turning her head away.

"So."

"So."

Evelyn didn't like being with Elsie any more. She liked her before when they made up names for things. They made up the name "bigeldaws" for women's breasts because that's what the bumps looked like. If one of the mothers had on a party dress for going out, Evelyn could say "bigeldaws" to Elsie, and no one else knew what it meant.

Elsie had a dad but the other kids said they were poor. They lived at the end of the bus route where there weren't any more houses except for Elsie's. It had a door that stuck up above ground and you had to walk through the door to go downstairs into the house which was a basement.

"People live down under the ground. So bees can," Evelyn said. She wanted Elsie to be sorry for what she'd said, thinking she knew everything.

"People don't live underground."

"You do."

"I do not."

"Yes, you do. You even sleep underground."

"So."

"So. Maybe the bee sleeps underground too." Evelyn felt mean, talking about Elsie's house that way. She'd quit if Elsie would. "It's a good place to keep honey."

"My mom doesn't like it where we live." Elsie's voice was low down and quiet.

Evelyn was sorry she'd been mean.

"If you have to keep things there, it's a good place. It's safe I bet."

"My mom wants a real house, above ground."

"Well, yeah, but what you've got now is okay."

"I've gotta go home. This bee is weird. I have to catch the bus."

"Maybe Stanley will give you a ride home. He has a brand new car."

"My mom says I have to catch the last bus. What will you call him?"

"I dunno."

"I bet you'll call him Dad. That's what my mom said you'd call him."

"My mom doesn't say that."

"Mine does. She says it's about time you had a dad. I have to catch the bus."

Elsie went around the corner and was gone.

Something was wrong. Maybe it had always been wrong. Evelyn continued to watch the bee go down into the hole. The only thing that seemed right was the place where the bee had gone, into the dark where secret things could be kept. Elsie was going to her house under the ground. Evelyn felt stuck there on top where people could get at her. They could decide things about her, and make Stanley into her dad.

Evelyn's mother called to her from the house. She pressed her teeth together, threw away the stick and went inside.

Sometimes in the morning Stanley was still there. He ate breakfast at the table in their kitchen. At night she could hear his voice coming up through the floor.

Then one day Evelyn's mother, Muriel, told her that they were going to be moving. They were going to move to Stanley's town.

47

"Stanley is going to live with us," she said.

"Why?"

"Because he's going to be with us and support us. Wouldn't you like that?"

"But you support us."

"It's been decided. We'll have a new house and you'll be going to a new school. Run and play now. You should be thankful. He's a nice man."

Evelyn went up to her bedroom. She sat down on her bed and then lay down. She didn't want Stanley to live with them. And there were things she couldn't think about, things from before. She had to try not to think.

The crack in the ceiling of her room started at one corner and rilled its way across to the other corner, taking turns and jogs around invisible stones. She imagined standing on the ceiling and walking along her stream-crack, looking down on the bed, the table where her books were, the china doll Stanley had given to her and the puppet. She could see the tops of things. She walked slowly along the stream, avoiding what the crack avoided. The ledge above her door was covered with dust, but the dust didn't get into her eyes because things, like dust, fell down and not up. If her mother came in she would see the top of Muriel's head where the hair was thin. Some things had to be avoided. She closed her eyes and went into the forever darkness where nothing could happen that she didn't love.

The car was hot. Only important things could come with them. The boxes and furniture would be brought later in a truck. Evelyn had marked her boxes EVELYN PAUL in thick black letters. She brought her doll's blanket and put her books in it, tied at the ends so it made a bundle like a hobo's sack.

The sky had no clouds for a top, and the road ahead was wavy with heat. It disappeared into the sky. Evelyn looked at her books. And then they were slowing down and coming to a stop on the side of the road. Her mother was getting out of the car. Eveyln could hear a sick sound and then her mother calling, "Evelyn, get me something. Bring me a towel. Quick." The only thing she could find was her doll's blanket. Her mother was leaning over the ditch. She made a horrible sound into the doll's blanket. Being sick.

They got back into the car. The awful smell filled Evelyn's nose. She hated her mother for being sick into the blanket that was for her books.

48

As they drove along the steaming highway, she wanted to smash the glass in the car: the front window that held the fixed and never-ending road, and the side windows that contained her within this stench. She didn't care if her mother was sick. She wanted her to die, right now, so everything would stop.

They pulled into a gas station and her mother left her alone. She tried to curl up on the floor of the car but the stupid hump was in the way. She crouched over and the rug on the floor prickled into her knees. One time she had dropped a quarter into the ledge between the dashboard and the front window of the car; she had pressed her head against the window and tried to look into the crack where her quarter had gone. Now Evelyn wanted to make herself thin, like the quarter, and so small she could slip away from this place.

Her mother returned, with the blanket all wet. She opened Evelyn's door and leaned over. Evelyn could feel her hot, sour breath.

"It will be all right. Come up now. We'll be there in an hour. Don't make it harder."

Her mother's voice, her hand on her back and around her shoulder; her mother with tears in her eyes, showing a crinkled face, all misshapen and ugly. She hid in her mother's sweater so she couldn't see that face.

"Can't we go back?"

"No, honey. Please, do it for me. Please, Evelyn."

She was trapped inside her mother's tears and her ugly crinkled face. She had to look after her mother who was sick. It settled into her, like the dust on top of the ledge, that she had to make things better. It worked into her like a fate as the car drove back down the road.

Evelyn opened her book and started to read to her mother. The doll blanket lay drying in the back seat. There was nothing else to be done.

Stanley bossed Evelyn around. He tried to own her, like she was his. Everything was happening so fast. She was going to go to a new school. She had to meet an old man and woman who were Stanley's mother and father. They had a big house in town with lots of things in it. They were rich.

At night she could hear them talking in words she didn't understand. Secrets were in the house. Her mother and Stanley made these secrets at night when they thought she was asleep. The secrets came up through her floor and collected in the corner near the ceiling. They didn't have eyes. They huddled together like bony things spawned by her mother's wispy voice and Stanley's dark voice. They seemed like things not yet born, way before being born.

A black piece of stick had been on her leg last summer when she came out from swimming. She had tried to flick it off but it still clung to her. The thing looked dead, except it was attached to her and wouldn't come off. The man in the next cabin brought a red hot knife and put it on top of it; the black thing curled up and fell on the ground.

The secrets were like that. They were black and useless as though Evelyn could flick them away, like dead twigs. But they stuck there in the corner, pulling on her, sucking on her. Bloodsucker lies.

When she got up and turned on the light, they were gone. Curled away to nothing.

In the morning everyone pretended. Evelyn wanted her mother to tell her what they had said about a baby, and marriage. But her mother's life after dark with Stanley was a secret world that threw long shadows into the corner of Evelyn's bedroom. In the day, in the light, the secrets were in hiding.

One day, before Evelyn had to start school at the new place, Stanley and Muriel went away and Mrs. Polter came to stay with her. Mrs. Polter was old like Stanley's mother. Evelyn liked the sweet lime freshie Mrs. Polter made. She put it in the adults' teacups, the blue glass teacups with the rills on the side. Evelyn ran her finger back and forth around the outside of the cup to feel the bumps. The sugar swirled in the cup and sank to the bottom where she licked it, putting her tongue way down into the cup.

In the evening it began to rain. Evelyn watched from the front sun-porch, beside the curtains that smelled of dust. Her mother would be home soon. The sun had gone and the street was filled with rain that stayed.

In this new place, there was a piano in the front room, and Evelyn had to take piano lessons. There were black notes on the piano and white ones. The white notes were bigger and easier to play, but she had to reach for the black stick-notes and they always sounded wrong. Sometimes she played them by accident, making a dull, squashed sound. The white notes and black notes were a cage. Every Good Boy Deserves Fudge hid in the cage. Good, Fudge, Deserves. EGBDF. Who is good boy. What is deserve. Black and white. Play your scales. Black, white. Secret world of other secrets. They know. EGBDF doesn't spell anything. Illegitimate. What does that mean. Evelyn felt like the black note touched accidentally and all wrong. She had no words. There was only an endless looking and a dusty smell, the street becoming lakes.

"Evelyn, come in now." Mrs. Polter stood at the entrance to the porch, filling the doorway with her big body and warm bread smell.

Mrs. Polter would tell her the truth. "Where's my mother?"

Mrs. Polter put her teacup on the coffee table. "You know. She's with Mr. Rathbone."

"When's she coming home?"

"Soon as she can."

"What does illegitimate mean?"

"It means … like not legal. Means born out of wedlock." Mrs. Polter's voice was on the white keys at the low end of the piano, where there were heavy meaning sounds that stayed in the air.

"So somebody didn't get married?"

"It means the mother didn't get married."

"So if my mother's not married then I'm born out of wedlock?"

"Yup."

"Illegitimate."

"Yes."

"If I don't have a father?"

"If your mother and father don't get married."

"And do I have a father if I'm illegitimate?"

"Yes. He would be your real father."

"From before, you mean?"

"I guess so."

"I asked my mother once, but she said I couldn't ask any more."

"About your father?"

"Am I illegitimate?"

"If your parents didn't get married. Maybe your father died. Wouldn't your mother tell you that?"

"Does illegitimate mean bad?"

"No, not bad. Now you shouldn't worry about all these words. Nobody pays attention to them if they are happy. It's only if they ain't happy, that's when the word gets to be used. If people want to be nasty."

Evelyn brooded. "Where's my mother?"

"She went out with Mr. Rathbone. You know that."

"But maybe she got sick, in the car."

"It's just the rain, that's all. Don't you worry. You curl up over here, by me."

Thunder rolled across the sky. Outside grew darker.

"Will my mother marry Stanley?"

"I don't know. I expect so, child."

"He has lots of money."

"Yes, yes he does."

"Will I call him Dad?"

"Your mother probably wants you to."

"Should I call him that?"

"You'll do whatever comes to you. Now you go up to bed."

Evelyn wanted to sleep there, near Mrs. Polter. The sounds in her head were all mixed up, the black and white notes coming together with the thunder. "How do you know if people are going to get married?"

"They announce it, tell it."

"And if they don't tell, how do you know then?"

"Well, if they don't announce it then—then I guess they might look different. Or act different. Like they can't tell something."

When Evelyn woke up in the morning, Mrs. Polter was gone. Her mother was in the kitchen making breakfast. Stanley, sitting at the table, looked up.

"Evelyn, how are you," he said. He was grinning.

"Good morning," said Muriel, pulling back another chair at the table. "Sit down, honey, sit down." Her mother's voice sounded pretend. More pretend.

Stanley was in his generous mood. But that wasn't the way he really was. He could give things away when he was in that mood, things that somehow didn't belong to him. She knew that about him. He gave things to her in order to get what he wanted. That was like stealing.

She knew something had happened, something different. Her mother was too attentive and Stanley was smiling and on the alert.

"I'm cooking an egg for you," her mother announced.

The egg arrived with the scummy part still on the yolk, just the way she hated it.

"You didn't come home last night. I waited," said Evelyn.

"We went over to Rosetown. It was late. We got caught in the storm. You had Mrs. Polter here. You were all right, weren't you?"

"Evelyn," said Stanley, "we got you a little something." As he handed her the brooch, she decided to take it and never, ever give anything back to him.

"Can't you say thank you?" said Stanley.

Her mother looked stern. She looked more and more like that since they moved. Since Stanley.

"Thanks. I didn't know where you were."

"We were at Rosetown like your mother said," replied Stanley.

"Now eat your breakfast," said Muriel. "We're going visiting this afternoon. Mrs. Polter will come. We'll be back before dinner."

"Who will you see?"

Evelyn was talking to her mother, but Stanley interrupted and took over. "We're going to see my mother and father. Clarence. Our friends."

"Can I visit Clarence?" Evelyn asked Muriel.

"Not today," replied Stanley.

Clarence was Stanley's brother and Evelyn liked him. He told her things about grasshoppers and the way they could fly. He took her driving through the wheat fields. The wheat was even higher than the hood of the car, and it bent over as they moved, making hushing sounds on the bottom of the car. But she didn't like the old man, Mr. Rathbone, the one everyone called Esdey. People did what Esdey told them to do. He was gruff and sometimes barked, just like a dog. Especially at Mrs. Rathbone. Evelyn expected Muriel to tell Mr. Rathbone not to be so stuffy, who did he think he was anyway. That's what she told her teacher once, at the other place. Muriel could stand up to Esdey and to Stanley, if she wanted to. But she didn't stand up to these people in this place.

Clarence was different; he was kind. He did what Esdey said but Evelyn figured he really loved Esdey. The others were just afraid of him.

Muriel had married Stanley. They did it last night at Rosetown, and that's why they hadn't come home. It was just the way Mrs. Polter said; they were different now. If she asked her mother, her mother might lie. Or tell her to be quiet, and not to ask questions. Bloodsucker lies.

She wanted to crack the windows of the porch where she sat reading. She wanted to break things.

Evelyn went up to her room early in the evening. Her room was blue. She could smell the fresh paint, and in one corner of the window sill the paint was thick and sticky. Evelyn touched it and left her fingerprint there in the paint, in front of the window. There were no cracks in the ceiling of this room, or anywhere.

It was bigger than her old room, big enough for her bed, her new bookcase, a chest of drawers and a chair.

The smell of the paint made her sick.

She never heard the voices of Stanley and Muriel at night any moᵣe. The secrets had crept underneath the paint and gotten inside the walls.

She couldn't go to sleep. She moved her tongue across the roof of her mouth. At the front, near her teeth, it was all ribbed and rilled, the way the beach was at the lake where she went with her mother. Then it arched into a smooth curve. Sickeningly smooth. She moved her tongue back and forth from the rough shore to the arch. The roof of her mouth seemed huge like the top of a sky. Her head was monstrous to contain this arch. But her legs felt small and spindly, like her arms. Then as she moved her tongue over the vaulted ceiling of the cave in her mouth, her legs grew large, like elephant's legs. Her body was distorted, big and small. It was a weird, awful shape that filled the room and then retreated into a tiny dot. She rolled over.

"Please God, please God, make it go away, please God, please God." She lay there, feeling her body changing shape on its own. She had become an awful monster. Something terrible and bad had gotten inside her.

She couldn't tell Muriel what happened to her any more. She knew some of Muriel's secrets, and now she had her own. She kept them in her mouth.

Her mother was rich now because of Stanley, and Evelyn had lots of new clothes. She had the three dresses Esdey had bought for her. She had new shoes and a new coat. She wore the clothes but they didn't really belong to her. She thanked Esdey for the dresses, when Stanley reminded her she had to say thank you. She wore the clothes like a disguise.

On the day before school began her mother took her out in the car. They drove to the brick building called Elmore Public School, Est. 1911 and parked.

"This is your new school. This is where you'll go tomorrow."

"Yes," said Evelyn, thinking how dingy it looked. No one was in the playground.

"When you go to your classroom, they'll have roll call."

Evelyn didn't know why her mother was telling her what she already knew. There was always a roll call.

"The teacher will call out your name as Evelyn Rathbone."

The grasshoppers cracked their legs: the black sticks sounding on the piano.

"That's not my name."

"That's what they will call you."

"Why?"

"Because Stanley's your father now."

"Why? Who said so?" Evelyn felt too hot. The air stuck onto her face.

"It's better this way. We're part of Stanley's family now."

"Are you still my mother?" She should have asked Mrs. Polter. She should have asked more questions.

"Yes, of course I am. I'll always be your mother."

"Will Stanley always be my father?"

"Well, yes…of course. He wants to be. Do it for me. We'll be happy now."

"I was happy before."

"But I needed someone else. You understand that, don't you? Please Evelyn." Grasshoppers snapped their legs and there was no breeze anywhere. Her mother's face was coming undone, the way it had before, in the car, with the smell of sick in the doll's blanket.

"Please, Evelyn."

Evelyn felt chiselled out and separate. The dry grasshoppers were breaking their legs to fly.

"I'm doing this for you."

It was too hot. Something was disappearing into a tiny dot way far away. She couldn't untangle what her mother said.

"Please. Will you answer to Evelyn Rathbone?"

Answer to Evelyn Rathbone? A new person. Evelyn Rathbone. Someone she didn't know.

She couldn't say yes. She couldn't answer to that other person.

"Please, Evelyn."

She was still thinking of the name, Evelyn Rathbone, watching her mother's face becoming ugly, when her voice said, "Yes." Evelyn wanted to stop the word as it came out. Did she say yes? Her mother's arms were around her, covering her face. Evelyn Paul was covered over.

"Evelyn, Uncle Clarence is here, he's brought the bird. Wake up."

Evelyn was pulled out from sleep, like a bucket brought from the bottom of a well. With her came the liquid stuff of dreams, the sweet mossy decay of old and luscious places.

"Evelyn, wake up."

The voice was near. Evelyn opened her eyes. Her mother was sitting on her bed.

"He's waiting for you. He's brought the bird. Get dressed, he's in a hurry."

Uncle Clarence was going on a holiday to see his friend. Her name was round and ringing. Isabel. Evelyn had seen the name in a letter in his house, peeking at it when no one else was looking and the house was quiet except for the sound of the yellow budgie. His Majesty, that's what Clarence called his bird.

Clarence was sitting at the kitchen table, his large brown hands holding the blue rilled tea-cup. His Majesty was in the cage beside him.

55

"There she is," he said. "You're a lady of luxury, sleeping late on such a morning."

Evelyn went over to the bird and whistled; the bird whistled back.

"How do I feed him?" she asked.

"Some of this bird seed, every two days. And water. Keep the cage clean. I expect you'll have him talking by the time I get back."

"Will he talk?"

"He's not supposed to, but who knows."

"Where are you going?" She wondered if Clarence would tell her. He wouldn't lie, but no one in his family ever said very much about what they were doing.

"I'm going to the coast. To the edge of the country."

"Is it nice there?"

"Don't know. Never been there."

"Who will you see?"

Stanley interrupted her. "Evelyn, sometimes you ask too many questions. That's enough."

Now Stanley could tell her what to do, just like Muriel did. "I just wondered."

"I'll be back in two weeks," said Clarence. "Where shall we put the bird?"

"In my room, please."

Clarence carried the cage upstairs.

"Right here on the table, please. It won't be as nice for His Majesty as in your house."

"He'll get used to it."

"What if he doesn't like it?"

"Well, you'll just have to talk to him and explain things. You've got everything here to provide for his material comfort."

"What's material comfort?"

"It means food, water, that kind of thing."

"But not other things. Like having you here."

"No, that's right." He kissed her on the forehead and was gone. She could hear his footsteps down the stairs, Stanley talking and the front door closing.

"He's gone, now, His Majesty. He says he'll be back. He's gone to see Isa-bel at the edge of the country. I'll get you some water." Evelyn lifted the plastic siding, the way she had seen Uncle Clarence do, and went to the bathroom, filling the tray with water and returning it to its place. "There now, you've got lots of water, and…I'll get you food." She repeated the procedure with the food tray, dumping out the almost

56

full container of bird seed and replacing it with new seed.

"Now, you see, you have lots of material comfort. You have everything you need. You should eat now, His Majesty, so you'll be happy." She whistled. "Eat, His Majesty." The bird sat on its perch, flicking its head from side to side, its tiny pellet eyes not looking at her.

"Good-bye, His Majesty. You have all the material comfort you need."

Evelyn walked down the stairs. She had the bird to look after. She'd done what she was supposed to do, giving him new food and water. She had talked to the bird, telling him to be happy. Right now the bird was singing.

At night, Evelyn covered the cage with a towel so it was dark inside, like a cave. Then she decided to let His Majesty sleep in the mornings, with the towel over the cage to make it dark. When she arrived home from school at noon she would go up the stairs, whistling two long notes, and one short note. On every fifth step she called out "His Majesty, wake up."

She took the towel off the cage. Always His Majesty was sitting on the perch, flicking his head, not looking at her with his blank eyes.

"Sing, His Majesty." The bird didn't seem to be eating the seed. "Eat your food, His Majesty. Drink your water." She noticed that the food had bird droppings in it, and the water was stale. There were briny edges in the holder where the water had been drunk or had evaporated, she wasn't sure which. "You have to eat all the food before I give you any more."

After a few days she lifted the plastic sidings on the cage and tried to coax him to come out, whistling and calling his name. He just sat on the perch, anxious in his eyes.

"Are you lonely, His Majesty? Do you want to go back to your real home at Uncle Clarence's? I can't give you any more food until you've eaten all this other food. Come out. You could fly around this room if you wanted to. Sing."

The bird shuffled back and forth on the perch with its long curved nails. It looked so helpless there, and sort of stupid. It wouldn't come out. She put the towel back over the cage, but left the sides open and the door to her room open. She wouldn't clean out the bird droppings until he ate the food.

"Here's a dark cave for you. I won't bother you, His Majesty. And you can come out, if you want to. Eat your food. Do it for me."

His Majesty never sang to her the way he did at Uncle Clarence's.

She thought something was wrong with him but she didn't feed him, because he had the food from the first day. She continued to whistle the song she had made for him and let him sleep in the darkness, with the door open.

On the eighth day, Evelyn whistled on the stairs and called his name. When she took the towel off the cage, His Majesty was leaning against the bars. When she touched the cage, the bird fell off the perch and lay still on the waxed paper beside the bars.

"His Majesty, wake up. It's time to get up." The bird didn't move. Evelyn reached into the cage and lifted him out. She had never held him before. He was so little and cold. She put the towel on the bed, and placed the bird gently on top of it.

"His Majesty, don't you want to wake up now? Uncle Clarence will be mad that you didn't eat your food. Try to wake up please. Do it for me." The bird was like something detached now, like a hand that had been cut off, or a foot. He was still. The air in the room was still. Evelyn felt calm, almost satisfied that it was the end of something. Nothing else could happen to His Majesty, except he'd have to get buried. Then it would be even darker, inside the earth. No sound would enter.

"Evelyn." Her mother was calling her. "Evelyn."

Her name was getting closer. It cracked the air. His Majesty couldn't hear. He didn't eat his food. It was too late. Tears blurred her vision of the bird.

"Evelyn, where are you?"

"Good-bye, His Majesty." Her mother was at the door.

"What is it, Evelyn?"

"Oh, Mommy, His Majesty died."

"How did…" Muriel stood beside her and touched the bird. "Oh dear."

Evelyn buried her head in her mother's shoulder and started to cry. She couldn't tell why she was crying. It was all a tangle, a fisted tangle that she had grabbed and couldn't let go.

Her mother rocked her. It was just everything. Uncle Clarence would be sad. His Majesty had escaped. No one else would know what she had done.

"Mommy, what will Uncle Clarence say? What will he say?"

"Now there, it's all right. Don't cry. He'll get another bird."

"No, no he won't. He can't." Evelyn was struck with horror at the thought of another bird, another repetition of the same thing, His Majesty being replaced with another bird that she would have to look after. It might not be finally finished. "No, he can't. He can't get another."

58

"Don't cry, it's all right, don't cry. Come away from here." Her mother half carried her, half pulled her to the door of the room where she slept with Stanley.

"No, Mommy, no, no."

"Evelyn, just lie down here."

"No, Mommy."

She lifted Evelyn inside the blankets. Evelyn was screaming. Muriel mixed some brandy, lemon and honey in a glass with some hot water and made Evelyn drink it.

"No, Mommy. No."

"Shh, there now, there now." Rocking, rocking everything away. Evelyn drifted. Nothing ever finished, always new things. Get another bird.

She could hear her mother on the phone saying, "Yes, she's very upset. She loved that bird. Of course, it could have happened at any time. Poor Evelyn. We must get another bird, she's so upset."

Evelyn slipped into the dark place of secrets.

1950

It was six o'clock and Evelyn wasn't home for dinner. No one remarked on her absence.

Muriel fed Ida in the kitchen and then went into the living room where Stanley was reading the newspaper. She took a section from him and started to read. Then she put down the paper and said, "Who shall we call?"

Stanley looked at his watch. It was seven o'clock. "She'll be home."

He continued reading his paper. She should have been home by now. Evelyn was difficult. He had tried everything with her: discipline, kindness—he'd even given her presents. But they didn't take. If she didn't come home that was Muriel's problem.

Stanley went into the kitchen. Ida had finished her dinner and he picked her up. She was his own, his first born child, but he didn't know quite what to do with her. For perhaps the hundredth time since her birth he was shocked by the tiny fingers on her small but perfect hand. There seemed to be too many of them. Five. That was right, five fingers. She was so impacted; there was too much possibility contained in her.

He carried her into the living-room and set her down on the rug. He tried to play with her the way a father should, but kept thinking Muriel was watching and criticizing. When Ida was sleeping he was the most comfortable. He could scrutinize her in peace, looking to see if her face resembled his own. She was a Rathbone. Her husband, if he was good enough, would also be a Rathbone. Their children would have to inherit the family name, if they were equal to it.

He wished, then, that he'd had a son; it was so much simpler with men. You couldn't count on women. Ida might decide to become part of her husband's family. Lost to him. What would he know of his own daughter—she'd be grafted onto people he didn't like. Competitors. People who would try to find out things about him and his family. That wasn't right. He wouldn't consent to that. She would have to get his consent, and he wouldn't allow it. But with Evelyn, she didn't even have to ask; she wouldn't ask. She'd do whatever she wanted to. Not coming home for dinner. She would run away with some jerk who'd knock her up and leave her, and then try to get at Stanley and take his money. Blackmail. This guy, any guy, would try blackmail. And the town would back him. They'd rally around him, all those people who had so much to say about the Rathbones, the gossips sitting on the bench outside Felmar's store, whispering and lying. When he walked by or stared straight at them, they hushed up. The men, the old farmers with their hands gnarled around the memory of their sins, grunted and coughed. But it was the voices of the women that got under his skin. They were mincing and confidential, nodding at the end of each little intrigue as though to clinch what they had said. He'd catch them in the middle of a nod and they'd go dumb. But when his back was turned, they started in again just where they'd left off. Their mean hearts were excited— "don't tell anyone"—"well I'm only guessing but"—"they say that." Their meanness confined him, wove him into the fabric of lies they spun. Knit one, purl two. Their sackcloth scratched and chafed his skin. S.D. thought he could stop them, but they never even dropped a stitch. On they worked. Evelyn was part of it now. She prompted the gossip. And what could he do if she was pregnant? That was the thing about women. They'd get pregnant. Babies would be born. Everyone would make a claim. How could he control it? How could he control her? And all the gossips.

He stopped bouncing Ida on his knees and she started to fuss. He hated it when she cried. He curled his toes into the carpet and bounced her rapidly, hoping to shake out her distress, rattle it out of her.

"Stanley, stop it," said Muriel. She came over and took the child. "You're too rough."

Too rough? What did she mean? He was trying to appease Ida. He was not too rough. Muriel was wrong. He couldn't even play with his own child.

He needed some air. Go for a walk. Visit his father. Ida was screaming. He hated the sound of her screaming.

"I'm going out," he said finally.

Muriel was pacing with the child on her hip, trying to comfort Ida, who gradually calmed under her influence.

"What about Evelyn?" said Muriel.

"Evelyn?" What about her? Surely he didn't have to deal with her, too. He had already failed with Evelyn. Wasn't that enough for Muriel? Or did she want more; did she want him to grovel and confess his inadequacies? He wouldn't confess. If she wanted a confession she'd have to get it from somewhere else. Let her try.

"I'm worried," said Muriel.

"So, call around."

"Who shall we call?" .

It was impossible. He was being hooked in by her questions. "I don't know. How should I know?"

"You're her father."

He was, now, her father. That's what he'd wanted. But it wasn't working. "I'll go out. I'll look for her. I'll find her," Stanley said.

"Where will you go?"

He put on his coat. "Never mind. I'll find her."

"Let me phone Helen's house. She may be there."

Muriel passed Ida back to him while she went to the phone. Stanley waited. He couldn't remember who Helen was, but he wouldn't ask. He was ready to move now and he hated this waiting. He stared hard at Ida. Did she look like him? Maybe Muriel had tricked him and someone else was the father.

"Are you mine?" he said into the baby's face. He was imploring now and he hated that. But Ida only smiled like a baby, her knowledge locked up and separate from him.

Muriel came back. "She isn't at Helen's house. They haven't seen her. I don't know where else to look."

"Clarence?"

The suggestion visibly annoyed Muriel. "I suppose that's possible."

Her voice sounded putrid, the way it always did when he mentioned Clarence. He tried not to smile. "I'll go over to Clarence's." Stanley handed Ida to Muriel and left the house.

He hated going out, even if it was only to his brother's house. But he was supposed to find Evelyn. His daughter. Adopted daughter.

He liked the open fields at the farms and sometimes stayed overnight there, sleeping in the back of the truck or in the barn. Muriel was stiff and angry with him when he did that, so that it was hardly worth all the trouble it caused between them. This town was too crowded for him, especially tonight. He smoldered within it. Evelyn wouldn't be able to run away if they still lived on the farm. But Isabel had. She'd left and never come back. If Evelyn got knocked up, she'd leave and he wouldn't be able to stop her.

He decided to take the car so that he wouldn't be so visible. He liked his car, a 1950 Oldsmobile, and felt pride of ownership as he opened the door. It was big and comfortable inside.

The seat in the car had been moved forward so that he was squashed into the steering wheel, his knees against the dashboard. God damn her. Muriel had her own car, why did she have to interfere with his? He pulled on the lever and pushed the seat back. He was humiliated. The radio blared out as he started the engine. He never turned the radio on in his car.

The air began to press against him like a cushion stuffed with needles. Everything bristled with his annoyance. He abruptly shut off the radio and stepped on the accelerator. The car spun on gravel left over from winter. So what if the neighbours came to their windows to peer at him. He didn't give a damn.

A light was on in Clarence's house; he parked the car. If Evelyn wasn't there, he didn't know where else to look. Who was Helen? Who were any of Evelyn's friends? Maybe she had really run away this time. She might go to Clarence first, but it was unlikely. She'd just go. Disappear. And he'd be left not knowing.

If she were inside they'd be in the living-room, and he'd be able to see them. But the only light came from Clarence's study and the light over the door on the side of the house. Stanley moved the gearshift into drive and edged forward to watch the side of the house. As he did, Evelyn came out of the door. Stanley moved forward again, directly in line with the walk, to block her way. But she was going in the other direction, away from him; she was disappearing into the dark.

He drove around to the back alley but waited on the street, thrumming his fingers against the steering wheel. He didn't know which way she would go, towards his house or away from him. He turned off the car and hunched down beneath the dashboard. If she passed in front she was going home.

But she would recognize the car. So what if she did? She wouldn't see him unless she came over to look inside. Otherwise he could deny being here at all. But if she did look inside he would seem like a fool.

He hated her then and wanted her to run away forever, and keep running. Right to the edge of the world, out of his life. She was trying to humiliate him, the little bitch. He sat up.

Just then Evelyn came out of the alley. He looked at her, ready to stare her down. But she didn't notice the car. She walked straight ahead and entered the next alley.

She was a back alley cat. Slouching, skulking in the dark. He should have guessed. She had two more lanes to go and she would be at his house.

When she was out of view, he started the car but didn't turn on the lights. He slowly moved down the street parallel to the lane, and watched her emerge again into the light, her shadow growing beside her until it was again enveloped by the alley darkness.

Stanley was satisfied. He stepped on the accelerator, turned the corner and parked in front of his house. He had beaten her at her own game.

He walked slowly towards the house, his heel hitting the concrete first so that the shot of pressure went up his leg to the ramrod of his back, up his neck to the top of his head, until the next heel hit the ground. The deliberate movement satisfied him completely. It captured the rhythm of a funeral march.

As he entered the house he called out clearly and distinctly to Muriel. "She is coming."

Muriel looked worried. "Where was she?"

"At Clarence's." He handed his coat to her. "Hang this up, will you?" He was pleased with himself.

"Why didn't she come back with you?"

"I saw her but she didn't see me. I followed her from Clarence's. She was trying to hide, going down the back alley."

Muriel was frowning. Stanley ignored her and went into the living room. "I'll handle this," he said, opening the paper.

Evelyn came in the front door. Muriel started to get up but Stanley put out his hand. Evelyn stood in the doorway.

"Hello," she said.

She didn't even sound guilty. What an actress, trying to cover up with that phoney empty voice of hers. Stanley turned the page of the newspaper and said nothing.

Evelyn repeated, "Hello." When no one answered, she said, "What's the matter with you guys?"

Stanley abruptly put down the paper. It crackled like things in a fire. He got up and walked toward Evelyn. She backed away from him.

"Stay where you are," he said, towering above her. He wouldn't touch her; if he touched her he would squeeze her, grab her arm in his hand and squeeze the life out of it. "Stay where you are," he repeated.

Evelyn had backed up against the wall and started to slide away from him.

"You know what time it is, don't you? You know what time we serve dinner in this house, don't you? Answer me, yes or no."

"But, I..."

"Yes or no."

"Yes, but I..."

"Don't be late, ever again." Stanley turned.

"I left a note," she blurted out.

Stanley stopped, but didn't turn. "I don't care. Don't ever be late again."

"Mother." Evelyn was left alone, almost slumped against the wall.

In the living-room Stanley held his hand up against Muriel's attempt to answer.

"I left a note," Evelyn said again.

"Go to bed. Now," said Stanley.

Evelyn went slowly up the stairs. When she got halfway up she screamed, "I hate you" at the top of her lungs. Stanley started to lurch out his chair but it was Muriel who stopped him. "Let it be."

When she thought it was safe to speak, Muriel asked, "Did you see a note?"

"Of course not. She didn't leave a note. She's lying."

1953

Evelyn thought maybe she was crazy. She felt odd, the way the black notes on the piano sounded. Clarence was odd too, but in a different way. He was more like the insides of the piano, an actual touching of the strings, of the tight wires that made the sounds.

Maybe she didn't belong to any of them, not even her mother, who seemed like someone she didn't know any more. Maybe she'd been fooled, or had made a mistake, gotten mixed up the way crazy people do. Sometimes she wasn't sure about anything.

Every Good Boy Deserves Fudge. Boy Deserves. Every Good. She wasn't Good. Fudge. Fudge-it. Hide.

She had moved out of the blue room, where the paint always seemed sticky and smelled acrid. She now stayed in the basement bedroom, off the den; she liked it better down there, away from Stanley and Muriel. Ida lived in the blue room. Stanley liked Ida.

Stanley was like a stone on the road she wanted to kick.

She thought of Muriel and Stanley as M and S, they were so much of a unit now. Sometimes she would add other endings to the initials: she would call them Smarty and Marty or Marty and Farty.

M and S put in an electrical system so that when they wanted Evelyn they could press a button upstairs in the kitchen and it would buzz downstairs in her bedroom. She was always startled when the buzzer went off. She put a pillow over it to pad the sound. And she would wait a long time before buzzing back. If she waited too long she would get buzzed again; timing was very important. It was a kind of malicious game of shuttlecock. Buzzlecock. Buzzlecock to you, Martyfart.

Stanley never said much to her any more, since he'd gotten what he wanted. But if she stepped out of line, he'd raise his voice and yell at her until she was small to disappearing. And that sound shocking through her head, that buzzing, he could do any time. She hated Stanley especially for that; it was part of the house he had built.

She regretted having accepted Stanley's presents in the early days. They'd become his trophies; he owned her because she'd taken them. She gave them to Ida. She didn't much like Ida, but Muriel said Evelyn was good to share her things. She could think whatever she wanted.

Muriel was really two separate people now, one inside the other. There was Marty, who had married Stanley. The other had never married; she was still alive in the past. Evelyn tried to keep this mother true to the honour of the old days when things had been better. Sometimes the only sign of life in her mother came from the one who hadn't married; it came like a beam of light, revolving past her, flicking her face. Memory hit Evelyn's face, like an insult.

No one else remembered the real Muriel. They only knew the one who had given up everything to become Stanley's counterfeit wife.

Marty's big idea was to be happy. She always said how happy she was, especially if she'd had too much to drink. She would stop Evelyn in the hall and say, "Evelyn, I'm so happy. You're happy too, aren't you?" And without waiting for an answer, Marty would say, "Of course you are. I've really lived, you know. I've really lived." Evelyn would nod and go downstairs to her room. She figured her mother wasn't so happy if she had to drink all the time, but then she really didn't know. Maybe Ida would grow up knowing this new mother. The most Evelyn knew was the slap of light from the old days creasing her face.

One night a man came to dinner, someone Evelyn had never met before. Muriel asked Evelyn to join them for dinner, instead of eating with Ida in the kitchen. The man didn't have a farmer's line on his forehead, the sky-earth line of brown and white skin, like Stanley had.

"Evelyn, I'd like you to meet Mr. Rainer. This is our daughter, Evelyn," said Marty.

He held out his hand. It was soft. Stanley's hand, by comparison, was like a foot.

"May I get you a drink, Phillip?" Marty was at her best. She sort of purred at Mr. Rainer, as though it would make her happiest if he would just stroke her hair.

"Sherry, please, if you have some."

Stanley, when he drank, had hard liquor, which was sickly coloured and smelled like something for painting.

Phillip Rainer turned to her. "What grade are you in, Evelyn?"

"Grade 7."

"Do you like school?"

"Some subjects. I like English. I hate maths."

"Same with me when I was at school. I enjoy reading enormously."

"Enormously." The word had open arms and wide space around it. It was a generous, welcoming word. Mr. Rainer was interested in her, even after he got his glass of sherry and lit a cigarette. Under his fingernails the skin was clean.

When dinner was over, Evelyn sat close to Phillip Rainer on the couch. If he moved to town, he could be Clarence's friend.

But Marty made her go to bed. She wanted to stay up and talk to him. They could have talked about books. As she lay in her bed, she fingered the events of the evening as though they were new and brightly coloured crayons. He had asked her questions; he was interested in her, like she was important. Marty called him Phillip; she liked him too.

Maybe he knew her mother from the old days. He had come to visit the real Muriel, the one from before. And he was interested in Evelyn because she was the child from before. He didn't ask much about Ida. And Stanley wasn't very friendly to him. He was definitely more like Muriel's friend. He might even know something, from before, that he couldn't tell Stanley.

He could be Muriel's old boy-friend, from a long time ago. And Stanley suspected it, so he was especially mean. Maybe they'd been lovers for a long time and gotten separated. Maybe, even—maybe he was Muriel's first husband,—maybe, maybe he was her father—her father come back—come back to find her and make sure she was all right. Was it possible? Could he really be her father? He was interested in her, as though he really cared. Where did he come from? No one said. Did he look like her? He had dark hair, too. But he was handsome and she was ugly. He was sweet and she was sour. He couldn't be her father, just turning up like that, without warning. Where had he been all these years? He didn't give her any sign, not like he really recognized her and wanted to take her away with him. It wasn't like that. That's what her real father would do. He would want to take her mother away from the pretend she was under, capture them both and take them back to the real place where people told the truth and didn't despise everything the way she did now. Her father would recognize her. He would know. Phillip Rainer didn't press her hand or give her a special look. He mainly asked questions, nodded, and asked another question. Like a doctor asking about a stomach-ache. As though there were something wrong with her. They didn't call him doctor. But maybe his job was to find out things without her knowing. All those questions. He was very skilled with his list of doctor questions; he asked every one of them, setting her off guard. Marty had put him up to it. Probably Stanley didn't like it because he had to pay for him to come and eat his food and drink his sherry. She'd been fooled again. The bastard. Pretending that he liked her. Pretending that he was someone else, like maybe her father. She'd found him out. She'd go upstairs and tell him that it was all a lie, and she knew it was a lie.

She got out of bed. Her feet were cold on the floor. She couldn't find her slippers in the dark.

She'd tell him, the bastard, pretending to be someone else and drawing her in like that. She opened her bedroom door. He'd be sorry. Trying to figure out if she was crazy. That's why he was there. During the day he wore a white coat and sat behind a desk putting people into two piles, a crazy pile and a not-crazy pile. Which one would she be put in? She stopped mid-way up the stairs. She could feel the rug bristle under her feet. Which one would he put her in, especially if she went up and called him a liar. Which one? The crazy one, if she called his bluff. She slumped on the stair, and put her head against the white wood of the bannister. He'd put her in the crazy place if she didn't go along with him, play good girl, sweet girl, does well at school especially in English, has some trouble with maths. That's what he would write, if she fooled him and pretended she didn't know his real game. If she told him, he would be like the others, he would hate her knowing and put her in the crazy pile.

She got up and went back to bed, pulling the covers way over her head, trying to make a nest.

Muriel was drunk again, slurring her words. She raised her voice at Stanley until he said, "I'm not talking to you any more" and went to bed. Then she sat alone, clouding up the living room by smoking her cigarettes, one after the other.

When Evelyn went upstairs for a glass of water, she called, "Evelyn, are you going to bed?"

"Yes. Do you want something?"

"Freshen up my drink for me, will you? Just a little rye and some ice, okay?"

Evelyn took the smelly glass to the bar and emptied the rest of the bottle into the glass.

"That's a good girl. Sit down and talk to me."

The light in the room was shadowed and amber, as though diluted through the silky liquid her mother was drinking. Marty looked strange, dark around the eyes, like a bandit. But she had a big clown's mouth: full, red and ambivalent, like a clown.

"Stanley's gone to bed," she said.

"Yes, I heard him go up." Evelyn waited. She wasn't going to talk. She never did. She only listened and waited while her mother brooded. An idea would move across Marty's face and then come out of her mouth. Her bandit-clown's mouth.

Evelyn waited for the old flick of remembered light, the ancient light from the forgotten years. If and when it came, as it seldom did now, Muriel's brooding would change to acknowledgement and recognition. Skin that was raw to the touch, Evelyn's skin, could heal.

She was conscious of winging above her mother now, and looking down on her, waiting. Heaven and earth could possibly join if the old Muriel emerged. When it had happened before, Muriel looked straight at her and wasn't all pinched, the way she was now. Muriel wouldn't look at her now.

"So, Stanley's gone to bed," Marty repeated.

"Yes, I guess so."

"Good for him. He was tired. He gets that way. Tired."

"Uh huh."

"He had to see S.D. tonight, and Kathryn. Always S.D. and Kathryn."

"Mm."

"They want something from him."

"Mm." Evelyn knew that her participation wasn't really needed, that she could agree or not speak at all. It didn't matter. Her mother was mainly talking to herself, leaning against Evelyn with her voice.

"My parents. Weren't like that. Proud, but they didn't have money. Parents demand things if they have money."

Evelyn had heard this before. If Marty was brooding and Evelyn asked, "What were your father and mother like?", Marty closed up. Evelyn wouldn't ask Marty for anything.

"Mother never had money," Marty continued. "I never asked for money. I won't allow my children to ask for money. So who asks for money? Do I? Does Stanley? Do you?" She turned and looked at Evelyn, but there was no light behind her eyes. "None of us do. Anyway, S.D. has too much money. He keeps it under his mattress. Hidden everywhere. Doesn't trust the banks. Can you believe it? Not even the banks. He probably has it stuffed in his pillow, or in Kathryn's pillow, so she doesn't sleep well. He sleeps well. Maybe he stuffs it in his ears, and that's why he's going deaf. He has it hidden in his teeth. In his gold caps. Or in the hooves of his horses. Money. They don't know what it's like to live without money. They'd eat their young for money. All of them."

Marty's mouth puckered, as though she had just tasted something bitter. She took another drink.

"And how are you?" Her dull eyes turned to Evelyn and her gaze leaned forward.

"Fine."

"Are you, really?"

Evelyn hated this part. "Sure."

"Happy?"

"Sure." Marty's questions were like the click click of the shoes of a drunken tap dancer. Evelyn kept her distance.

"Really happy?"

"Sure." Then after a long silence Evelyn said, "Are you?"

"Me? Ask me no questions, I'll tell you no lies." She took another drink, draining the glass. "Get me another, would you, honey?"

Evelyn cracked open a new bottle of rye. On her way back from the bar she had an idea. She would try to get her mother to talk about Evelyn's real father.

"I had a dream last night."

"Did you?"

"I dreamed you were in a boat, a row-boat, with two men." Evelyn was lying, but lying to get the truth was all right.

"Two men?"

"Yes, older men. About your age."

"What happened?"

"They were trying to row the boat."

"What did they look like?" Marty was now focussed on the conversation.

"They both had dark hair, like yours."

"My hair isn't dark any more, it's salt and pepper grey. What's that?" Marty cocked her head. "Is that Ida awake?"

"What do you make of the dream?"

"Dark hair. Nothing. I think that must be Ida. I should go up." She drained her glass. "Good night. Sweet dreams. I do want you to be happy, dear." Marty gave her a dry kiss.

Evelyn turned off the lights and sat in the empty room. Did her real father have red hair, then? Or maybe blond? Probably red hair. Her hair was dark, but had a tint of red in it. That was probably it. A redhead who couldn't stand the hot prairie sun. Mr.—or Doctor—Rainer had dark hair. Would Mrs. Polter know? She hadn't seen Mrs. Polter in years. Maybe she was dead now. If she caught a bus and went to find Mrs. Polter, would she be at home, drinking lime freshie, knowing everything if only the right question could be asked? A blanket wrapped around her legs. Mrs. Polter would say, "Yes, dear, that's right. I expect he did have red hair. The colours are in your hair, too," rocking in her chair, as calm as Evelyn was urgent. Green freshie, sugar silting down like dust from stars. Nothing matters. Stir it, it swirls again and settles. You can lick it with your tongue.

Evelyn, hopeless in her desire to get through the camouflage that surrounded her, tasted nothing.

She went downstairs to her room. She could hear footsteps above her head, and the slam of a door in the kitchen. More footsteps. Then silence. Her mother getting up, going to bed. Mother Marty, her creamy happiness slept off, sloughed off like the layered thickness from too much rye and too many cigarettes. In the morning she would be abrupt and grumpy, wanting quiet, going back to bed before noon.

Evelyn couldn't sleep. She wanted to see Mrs. Polter. Or go back and find Elsie. To catch the bus, right now. They would come after her, though; Stanley might even hit her. He'd grabbed her once, pinching her arm above the elbow where the flesh was soft, digging his dirty fingers into her skin. He would probably lock her in her room, in the dark where the only sounds were from inside the house, buzzing and footsteps overhead.

Evelyn got up from her bed and moved her hand along the wall until she found the light switch. The light was unkind. She got dressed. She had to get out.

Light from her room illuminated the dark hall that led to the stairs. On the right was the cedar room where Marty kept the suitcases. Evelyn never went into that room. Maybe the old clothes had money in them she could use for the bus. She opened the door. The strong smell was like her mother's sticky breath the morning after she had been drinking.

There was a rack where Marty's summer clothes were hung, the large flowers on the dresses blared out their colours. On the floor were empty suitcases, trunks and boxes. On some of the boxes, in large awkward printing, were the words she had written, EVELYN PAUL. She hadn't seen these boxes with her old name on them since the move. She stared at the childlike lettering and the foreign name. She was still more like Evelyn Paul than Evelyn Rathbone. Evelyn Rathbone was pretend. She picked up a small blue suitcase. The metal handle was cold. The tag said "Muriel Paul, R.R. #1, Kindersley, Sask. Ch2-5479."

The old Muriel. Evelyn snapped open the clasp. The sound muffled against the cedar walls, but she still looked up, waiting, listening for an intruder. This room existed beneath all that she had done, beneath the surface of things.

The suitcase she opened was packed with papers and envelopes. She picked up an unmarked, sealed envelope and carefully opened it, prying up the gummed flap. There was a picture inside, a black and white photograph of a man. He was smiling at her, leaning against a brick wall. Wearing an old style dark hat. Smiling; almost winking. His arms folded across his chest. Handsome. Looking at her.

Evelyn put the picture back in the envelope and shook it so the picture fell to the bottom. Then she held the envelope up to the light and saw the picture as a dark object in the corner. She folded the envelope and put it in her pocket, closed the suitcase and turned off the light.

She went back down the dark hall to her room and placed the envelope under her pillow. She wouldn't leave tonight. Not yet. She had her father's picture now.

In the morning, she took a razor blade and slit the plastic lining of her pencil case, just wide enough so that the picture would fit inside. Then she went upstairs and left for school. No one else was awake. It was still dark outside.

During class she took out the case and made sure the picture was still there. She could see it like a shadow under the cloudy surface of the plastic. She couldn't make out his face, or his hat.

At recess she put the case on the bench in the playroom. On top she placed her silver bracelet as a decoy. It would seem as though she didn't want to have her bracelet lost or broken. A thief could take the bracelet and leave the case.

When she got home, she went down to her room and looked at the picture again. The light was made harsh by the darkness all around her. It wasn't Phillip Rainer in the picture. Did her father have red hair? She couldn't tell. It wasn't black hair—more like the colour of his hat. Darker than his shirt. He looked mischievous. Like a trickster. Someone who would play jokes on her.

She put the picture back underneath the plastic. It was refracted, like something under water. She went upstairs. Now she, too, had another secret. An enormous secret to match all of their secrets. She had something to hide.

She felt kinder towards Muriel and Stanley because they were connected to her through the secret she had against them. She almost felt sorry for them because they didn't know what she had. And if she acted nice to them they would never suspect. She wouldn't have to tell anyone. It wasn't lying, it was just not telling. Even if her mother noticed the picture was gone, what could she do? Ask about it? Evelyn would say ''what picture?'' and her mother couldn't answer. She was a thief who had stolen from another thief. ''What picture? Whose picture?'' She practised saying it innocently in the mirror, with her mouth full of toothpaste, the water running to drown out the sounds. She tried it accusingly, sternly, wiping the toothpaste from around her lips. Concerned, frowning, sympathetic. ''What is it Mother? You're worried about a picture?'' She was satisfied. She couldn't possibly be detected.

Evelyn's one friend was Helen. Helen played the flute and called herself a flautist. The word sounded sissy, even for a girl, but Evelyn liked it. None of the others were friends with Helen, only Evelyn. Helen had clammy hands, like wax candy with sweet red liquid inside. She had bony knees, like Evelyn, that everyone could see in gym class.

Helen was standing in the cloakroom at school the next day. The others had gone into the classroom. Evelyn decided to take the chance. She opened her pencil case and took out the picture.

''Helen, I want to show you something.'' She held the picture behind her back in case Helen might want to touch it and make it sticky with her skin. ''I want to show you a picture.'' She held it up.

Helen leaned forward. ''It's too dark. I can't see it.''

Helen reached out to take the picture but Evelyn drew it back. ''Okay, come over here.'' They went to the window at the far end of the cloakroom. ''See? Who do you think he looks like?''

"I don't know."

"Come on, do you think he looks like anybody you know?"

"You?"

"Yeah."

Helen looked at the picture, then back at Evelyn. "I don't know. The nose, I guess, is—but there's a shadow from the hat. Because it's a man it's hard to—his face is round, like yours."

"Is my face round?"

"Of course it is. You've got a moon face."

"Nobody told me that."

"Well, you do. Just like him. He's got a moon face too."

They were huddled over the picture when they learned a stern voice say, "What *are* you doing?"

Evelyn turned her head so quickly she crinked her neck. Miss Cloves, their teacher, was standing at the doorway. In two steps she was in their midst and snatching the picture from Evelyn's hand. She didn't look at it, she just took it.

"I suppose this little discussion is more interesting to you than your lessons. Be that as it may, we would appreciate it if you would join us in class—if you would be so kind." With the picture in her hand, Miss Cloves extended her arm and pointed to the door. Helen followed the indicated path.

Evelyn felt sick. Miss Cloves was bending the picture as she held it. She made it into a funnel that was draining everything from the room. She stared down at Evelyn, who didn't move.

"Evelyn, if you would be so kind."

Miss Cloves always spoke like that, as though she was big and important instead of a stupid little teacher in a stupid little town. Evelyn continued to stare at her.

"*Evelyn*, if you please."

It didn't matter if she raised her voice, or even shouted. Evelyn hated her for catching her, for stealing what was hers.

"Can you hear me, or have your ears turned to stone?" Miss Cloves looked like a witch. Her eyebrows were so arched they almost touched her hairline.

That was her picture; Miss Cloves had no right to take it and bend it. That was the picture of her father that Cloves was using as a pointer, standing there in Evelyn's way.

Evelyn started, grabbed the picture from her teacher, and ran. She ran through the classroom, past all the other children sitting in their places. Her hand slipped on the silver knob as she opened the door and ran down the hall, down the green corridor, past all the other closed doors. She smacked the bar on the "emergency exit" at the end of the hall. The alarm clanged as she ran into the cold blast of winter air and sun, bright and shocking. She had the picture. Her shoes slipped on the icy sidewalk. She ran into the field where the old snow had a frozen layer on top that couldn't support her weight. The ice grabbed at her ankles. Hounded by the bells ringing, the snow snapping at her legs, she didn't look back. Couldn't look back. She was chopping her way through the snow, clutching the precious picture that no one must take. Not ever again. She had to hide his face. Save him. Save him from them.

At the end of the schoolyard she dared to look back across the white distance she had travelled. Other people were coming. Miss Cloves was coming. The snow glinted in her face. The picture was curling up. She had to get it away.

Across the street there was a rest home where the old people stayed. She ran between the buildings to the back. Quietly, she opened the door. It hushed closed. No bells. Sudden calm.

Time and the chase had stopped. The smell was a hospital smell. She looked at the picture; he was still smiling at her, winking. She put it in her shirt pocket, next to her heartbeat. As she leaned against the wall the cold sweat inside her shirt trickled down her side. She would have to find a place to hide. The sound of the alarm bell from the school was faint, like water spattering.

She knocked on the door numbered 107. No answer. Putting her ear against the door she could hear that someone was inside, shuffling and moving about. She knocked louder. Still no answer. She couldn't wait. She opened the door. A man was standing there, a tall man with his back to her.

"Excuse me, sir." He didn't turn or speak. She closed the door behind her. "Excuse me," she repeated, placing herself in front of him.

"Oh." He saw her rather than heard her. "I didn't know you were here."

"Sorry. I knocked."

"What?"

"I knocked. May I come in?"

"What?"

She put her mouth to his ear. "May I come in?"

"Yes, yes, you're in."

"Am I interrupting you?"

He paused and then said, "Oh, no. Please, sit down." He looked around and there was nowhere to sit, except on one of the two single beds in the room. "Yes. Over there. This room is too small."

Evelyn sat down on the bed that seemed least used.

"Do you stay here by yourself?" she asked. He didn't answer. She was afraid of raising her voice for fear someone might hear. She moved her face very close to him, and mouthed the words big, so he could read her lips. "Do you live alone?"

"Oh, yes," he said softly.

He didn't seem surprised that she was there. After a few minutes her heart stopped beating so quickly and she settled into his solitude. He couldn't possibly hear the bells, or even a knock on the door from Miss Cloves.

The room was cluttered with pictures, books and papers. It was so different from the space and luxury of her mother's house. The man sat opposite her on the other bed. It looked too small for his long shape. He had thick white hair.

"I should tell you how I got here," she said.

"Here?"

"Yes."

"Oh, no, not very well." He smiled, sweetly and humbly.

She began again, making the words big with her mouth. "No, how I got here, to this place. I ran away."

"Did you?" He was like the catcher on her baseball team, with a huge soft mitt where all her words went. "Oh yes, you ran away."

They continued to look at one another. He smiled, and rocked slightly, back and forth, back and forth, wearing a big woollen sweater.

"You know why?"

"No, why?"

She thought of the blue light inside the teacups when Mrs. Polter stayed with her. The sun through his window was sweeter than the sugar settling to the bottom of a cup. There was no hurry any more. She was safe.

"I found this picture."

"Oh, a picture. That's nice."

"I had it hidden, so no one could find it."

"Yes, that's a good idea."

"But when I showed it to my friend my teacher took it. It's the only picture I have. I took it back and ran. So they came after me. I had to break out. They're coming after me."

"Yes."

Her heart started to beat fast again but slowed with his rocking affirmation of everything that she said. Back and forth. Still, quiet. Blue, calm.

"Did you get away with the picture?" he asked.

"Yes." She reached inside her shirt pocket.

"Where is your coat? You're shivering."

"At school."

"You shouldn't have left your coat at school."

"I had to get out in a hurry."

"Oh yes, so you did. Now, let me see." He took the picture and put on his glasses. She didn't mind that he touched it. "That's a fine looking man. Is that your boy-friend?"

"No. It's my father."

"Oh, yes. Very nice. Would you like some tea?"

"I don't drink tea."

"No, of course not. I don't have any anyway. I don't have a kettle in here." He handed the picture back to her. "He's very handsome, your father. Young and handsome."

It was all so simple. So clear. "Well, it's an old picture, so he's not that young now."

"Oh, no, probably not."

"No."

"What's your name?"

"Evelyn."

"Yes, that's a good name. You can call me Rudy. That's my name."

"Will anyone come here?"

"The nurses come."

"I mean will anyone find me?"

"Not if we don't want them to. What's your last name?"

"Rathbone, that's the name I have now. It's not my real name, though."

"Where do I know that name from?"

"My real name is Paul."

"Paul Rathbone. Never heard of him."

"No, my name before was Paul."

"Paul Rathbone. Must be related to old S.D. I know him. You're S.D.'s daughter?"

"No, the man in the picture is my father."

"Don't look like S.D."

"No, that's my father. Paul was his last name. I got adopted because I was illegitimate."

"So, you must be Maude."

"Maude?"

"S.D.'s illegitimate."

"I don't know Maude."

"Didn't know he had two. S.D. Mean old bastard. He should be in here with me. Serve him right. Doesn't serve me."

"S.D.'s my grandfather, sort of." There was a loud knock on the door and a woman called, "Mr. Rudy." Evelyn jumped to her feet.

"Rudy, there's someone at the door."

"What?"

She moved close to his ear. "Someone's at the door."

"Mr. Rudy, may we come in? Are you decent?"

Evelyn whispered, "I'll hide. In the bathroom."

The door was just opening as she slipped into the bathroom and behind the shower curtain. There were short white hairs on the sill of the tub.

"Mr. Rudy, sorry to bother you. We have two guests to see you. This is Miss Cloves and Mr. Hunter. They want to ask you some questions."

"Is it tea-time?"

"No, Mr. Rudy, it's past tea-time—we always serve them tea first thing in the morning—Mr. Hunter is the principal of the school, you know, across the field, and Miss Cloves is one of the teachers."

"Teachers? Bridge?"

"No, Mr. Rudy—I'm sure he's not going to be of any help to you, he wouldn't have heard a thing. These people are from the school. Across the field. They want to ask you some questions, whether you saw anything or heard anything—he never would have heard anything. Go ahead, Mr. Hunter."

"Mr. Rudy—"

"Beg pardon."

"Mr. Rudy," began the principal again.

"His real name is Truman," interrupted the nurse. "We just call him Mr. Rudy, his first name."

"Yes, Mr. Truman, did you see a young girl here a short while ago? Dark hair, round face, freckles across her nose."

"Short girl."

"No—did you see a little girl around here? She would have been wearing a blue blouse."

"Wearing a house?"

"Blouse, wearing a blouse." The principal was yelling. "A blouse. You know. A shirt."

"A hurt? No, not today." Eveyln, crouching in the tub, listened to Rudy Truman playing the deaf old man for his guests.

"It's no use," said the principal. "I see what you mean. Thank you, Miss Hamilton. Miss Cloves, we should press on."

"Let me try," said the teacher. "Mr. Truman, my name is Mildred Cloves. Let me write that down for you. May I use this paper?"

Evelyn's heart tripped at the sound of Cloves' voice. She checked her pocket for the picture. It wasn't there. That bitch. Evelyn's knees started to ache.

"Oh, I'm sorry, it's a picture. Is this yours?"

"What?"

"Is this picture yours, Mr. Truman?" Miss Cloves had on her accusing voice.

"Of course it is. This is my room isn't it? This is where they put me, didn't they? Whose bloody picture do you think it is? Eh?"

"I'm sorry, Mr. Truman. There's no need to raise your voice. We didn't mean to upset you. We were only looking for a little girl who ran away from school without her coat, into the cold. It's just a coincidence—just one of those things—that the incident happened to centre on some picture or other. Do you mind if I look at this?"

"Eh? Look at it. Sure, go ahead. It's me, as a young man. Helluva lot younger than I am now. Helluva lot smarter, too."

"Yes, very handsome. The girl's name is Evelyn Rathbone. Will you tell Nurse Hamilton if you happen to see our young friend? We're very concerned about her."

"Sure."

"Thank you, Mr. Truman."

"No thanks to me."

Evelyn heard the door close. She waited and then drew the curtain aside. The old man was standing at the door. In a hoarse whisper like an ancient growl, he said, "Young lady, I have to use the facilities."

"Oh, sorry." She got out of the tub. "Sorry."

"I locked the door. You close the drapes. Don't want that teacher peeping in the window. She's a peeper if I ever saw one."

Mr. Truman made a loud noise in the bathroom, like a horse pissing.

Evelyn was scared. She wanted to be small, to be the space between things, like the empty place between the old man's table and his bed. That space. That emptiness. Thinner than a quarter. It wouldn't matter if people walked through you because it wouldn't hurt—there would only be a slight pressure, like fish bumping one another accidentally.

Mr. Truman came out and sat on the bed.

"You in trouble I guess," he said.

"I guess so."

"Don't look like me in the picture."

"Does he look like me?"

78

"Hard to tell. I haven't had so much commotion in this room since they put me here."

It was dark in the room. Rudy turned on the lamp between the beds. "You want to see a real picture of me when I was young?"

He pulled out an album from beneath a thick stack of papers and sat beside Evelyn on the bed. "I have one here of S.D. and me, when S.D. was mayor."

Evelyn envied the album of pictures; she didn't have any photographs of the old days before Stanley.

Rudy showed her a picture of six men in front of City Hall. "That's S.D. there, in the middle. And that's me behind him. See that?"

Evelyn looked deep into the photograph and squinted. The faces of S.D. and Rudy in the picture carried a dusting of how the two men looked now. "Yes, I can see that."

"Long time ago. Funny you should turn up now and there I am in the picture, standing behind your grandpa. Picture has a lot of memories. I got into trouble about then—seemed big at the time. A fellow tried to ruin my reputation. Started spreading lies about me." The old man went over to the dresser and turned on the radio. "Can't hear me if there's a lot of voices." Then he paused. "You wanta hear this story?"

"Yes, I do," said Evelyn; and she nodded yes to be sure he would know.

"Well, this man—Sutcliffe was his name—he was running for City Council against me, in a by-election. He called me a liar right out in public. S.D. was mayor—did I tell you that—so I asked him what to do. He said to forget it. Well, I couldn't do that. So I sued him. I charged him with slander. Was a big case back then, with a jury and all. Came in specially for the trial."

He kept on talking as he took off his big sweater and put it around Evelyn's shoulders.

"So, I got this lawyer. Young but smart. Never forget him. Charlie Enright was his name. Dead now. Killed in the war. When my case started Charlie was getting harassed by that judge, right in front of all them people. I remember it like yesterday." Rudy was caught in a full pocket of time, and he stared straight ahead as he spoke.

"Charlie had all his books and papers spread out on the table—and the judge says to him, 'Are you going to be calling so-and-so evidence'— can't remember what it was. But he asks him. Charlie stands up and says, 'Yes, My Lord, in due course.' Nice as pie." Rudy Truman grew more excited as he talked.

"So that day finishes, and the next morning this judge—Judge

Wetmore—starts right in bugging Charlie. 'Mr. Enright, what about this—what about that.' So Charlie, a bit haughty himself, says, 'My Lord, in due course.' He knew what he was doing. So the morning finishes and we start again in the afternoon. The judge asks right off, 'Mr. Enright, if you please, when might we expect to hear this aspect of the case?' Fancy talker that judge. Charlie gets up, walks away, then turns and says, 'My Lord, as I have told you before, and as I will tell you again, in due course.' Well, Judge Wetmore didn't like that at all. He turns to the jury and he says, 'Perhaps, gentlemen of the jury, you are entertaining doubts as to whether Mr. Enright's client has any real case to bring. I certainly am.' I was shocked. Everybody turns to Charlie, who was leaning against that bannister they got in court. He looks real calm. He doesn't say anything. Everybody's watching Charlie. Charlie starts to move forward—and I'm thinking he's going to slug the judge, the way I should have slugged Sutcliffe—but no, Charlie puts his brief-case on the big table and slowly starts putting all his papers and books into his brief-case. He snaps it shut, turns and walks out of the courtroom. We're all pretty pole-axed by that. I don't want to be left there, so I follow him out. He's walking slowly down the hall. I catch up to him just as he's turning into the room marked 'barristers,' but I follow him anyway. He sets down his brief-case, undoes his lawyer's vest, puts his feet on the table and lights a cigarette. I'm about to ask him what's happening, when the door flies open and there's the court clerk—with the same black robes—sayin', 'Mr. Enright, Mr. Justice Wetmore would like you to attend in his office.' That's how they talked. Charlie just puffs on his cigarette and blows a stream of smoke into the air. Then he says, 'Will you tell His Lordship I would be most pleased to attend in his office if he withdraws his remarks in front of counsel for the defendant'—that's the other lawyer—'and in front of the jury.' So this clerk leaves, and Charlie is just smoking away. I ask him, 'What are you doing, Charlie, what are you doing to my case?' I remember this— he said, 'Your case is about truth and fairness. It's being tried right now.' So we waited. I had a smoke too. Then the clerk comes back and says, 'Mr. Justice Wetmore has asked me to tell you he has already withdrawn his remarks to counsel for the defendant.' But it turns out the judge didn't because the other lawyer came in and Charlie asked him. So Charlie sits back down again, puts his feet on the table and lights up a fresh cigarette. When the clerk comes back all impatient, Charlie says, real quiet, 'Please tell His Lordship that he has lied to me, and I will not attend in his office.' Well. The clerk's eyes nearly bugged out of his head.'' Rudy stared for a long time.

"What happened?"

"That judge had to apologize in court, in front of everyone."

"Did you win?"

"We won. Truth and fairness. That's what it was all about. We just had to stand our ground." Rudy closed the album and looked at Evelyn. "Don't let that teacher push you around. She's a big talker too, I bet. Tie you in knots with all her words, just like that Judge Wetmore."

Evelyn wanted to hear more stories. "What did S.D. say?"

"Don't remember." He sat quiet, as though he had spent all his words.

"And so you were elected then?"

"Yup, that's right." Rudy Truman leaned forward and looked at Evelyn. His eyes were heavily lidded as though all he had seen was slipping down over his face. "Now, I'm going to call you a cab. It will come to the back door. Here's ten dollars. You go home now. You can come back and see me sometime if you want. Now you should go home."

"I don't want to go."

"I know, but you gotta face them. Stand your ground."

The old man picked up the phone and dialed. "I have a young lady here who is going to"—he cupped his hand over the phone. "What's your address?"

"71 Crease Street."

"To 71 Crease Street. She'll be waiting at the back. No need to honk or come in. Come to the old folks prison on Weir Crescent. No. 5 Weir Cresent, at the back."

Evelyn stood up. She was still scared.

"Take your picture. And my sweater, to keep you warm. That way you'll have to bring it back. Don't forget your picture."

She put the picture into her shirt pocket. "What shall I tell them?" she asked.

"I don't know." He led her to the door, leaned over and kissed her on the cheek. "Tell them what you want. Make them do what is fair. They can't take anything from you if you won't let them. Best to stand up to them, you know. Like Charlie."

Evelyn sat in the back seat of the taxi, just the way a fancy lady would.

"Excuse me, sir, but what time is it?" she asked the driver.

"Eleven-thirty."

"Do you know where we're going?"

He looked back and then to the road again. "71 Crease Street."

"How much will it cost to get there?"

"About three dollars."

"Could you drive around until there's ten dollars used up?"

81

"If that's what you want."

"Yes, please. Could we go somewhere pretty?"

"That's depending on what you think is pretty."

"Well, with a forest and water."

"Don't know about any forest. We could go down near the river."

"Yes, please."

They drove a long way from the school, to the outskirts of town where she'd never been. She decided that she always wanted to have enough money to take her away from where she was. She wanted to be able to hire a cab and ride like a queen in the back seat to somewhere else.

There were trees near the river hanging low and heavy with white frost. The river was frozen to a narrow channel between the ice.

Rudy Truman wouldn't tell her what to do. He just told her a story that she liked but barely understood. The adult world was complicated and yet Rudy Truman was simple and kind.

"So, there's your river. And some trees," said the cab driver, as he pulled away and entered territory that she recognized.

"Do we have to go back now?" she asked.

"Used up ten dollars already," he said.

As they stopped in front of her house, Evelyn handed him the ten dollars. "That's all I have."

"Sure. You'd better hurry, it's cold."

She went up the front walk and rang the doorbell to see if anyone would come. No one did. She opened the door and went to the telephone. She called the old folks' home.

"May I speak to Mr. Rudy Truman."

"One moment please."

Rudy answered.

"I'm home now." She hung up not knowing if he had heard what she said.

She went downstairs into the cedar room. All the suitcases were in disarray. Marty had probably gone through everything and knew Evelyn's secret by now. She went upstairs. The clock on the stove showed 12:10. Afternoon. She would just wait for them. The house was so quiet.

No one came. She went back into the kitchen, looked at the time, and then took her old coat from the rack and put it on over Rudy Truman's sweater. She didn't have any other boots, and so she wore her shoes out into the snow.

She took her regular route to school. Mid-way down the last alley she saw Helen, and called to her.

Helen stopped. "Where have you been? Are you going back to class?"

"Yes."

"So, they'll catch you after all."

"I'm not running away from them."

As they entered the playground, the other children in her class gathered around her, not speaking but following closely behind her into the school.

Miss Cloves entered the classroom. When she saw Evelyn all her movements stopped.

Evelyn pulled a book out of her desk and opened it.

"So," said Miss Cloves, putting her fists on her desk and leaning forward. Evelyn thought she looked like an animal trying to use her forelegs for arms. "So you have decided to come back, have you?"

Evelyn didn't answer.

"You will come with me to the principal's office." Cloves leaned farther forward on her fists.

"No, I won't attend at the office," said Evelyn, using the fancy words from Rudy Truman's story to give her confidence.

"Do you mean to say you will not go the principal's office, Evelyn? Is that what you are saying?"

"Yes." Evelyn turned a page of her book.

"All right, Evelyn." Cloves stood erect. "All right. I shall report that to the principal."

When the teacher left the room, the children gathered around Evelyn.

"Hey, way to go."

"That's telling her."

They slapped her on the back and pounded their fists on her desk. She looked across the room at Helen, who shrugged her shoulders and looked away.

When Miss Cloves returned the children scuttled back to their places. The teacher frowned and looked down on them. The principal was with her. The two of them stood at the front of the class.

It was Mr. Hunter who began. "Evelyn, you must understand we have been very worried about you, and your parents have been worried. They will be here momentarily. Please come with me to meet them." He cracked the knuckles of his hands as he spoke. He was breaking himself apart underneath his skin.

"No, thank you."

"I beg your pardon?"

The children in the class tittered and held their breath.

"No, thank you," she repeated. Mr. Hunter's bones were creaking and his jaw stuck out. "I went home. My mother wasn't there. I came back."

83

"Well, yes, that's fine, but I would like you to come with me," he said, snapping his knuckles again.

"No, thank you. That won't be necessary." She was standing her ground.

Everyone in the class stared at her and then at the principal. Evelyn turned the pages in her book.

"Evelyn Rathbone, I am ordering you to come with me," Mr. Hunter said, letting his thick hands fall to his sides. Evelyn tried to concentrate on the words in the textbook. "You refuse? What then do you intend to do?" His voice had become high and squeaky.

"I'm going to read my book."

Someone in the class laughed.

"All right then." He turned. "Miss Cloves, please continue." Mr. Hunter closed the door behind him with exaggerated firmness.

Evelyn was scared again. The white page of her book seemed too white and the words scattered on the page.

Miss Cloves sat behind her desk and stared at the students as though at things unspeakably detestable. The children began to fidget.

"I suppose all of you are in on this, is that correct?" said the teacher. No one moved. "You must be proud of yourselves," she said. "I suppose you will conduct yourselves as adults the way you conduct yourselves now: taking other people's concerns, legitimate concerns, and turning them into objects of your contempt. That doesn't surprise me about some of you." Her speech seemed too complicated to Evelyn. It blurred in and around the fast beating in her head.

Miss Cloves rose from her desk, slowly and deliberately, like a gathered fist. She walked down the aisle and stopped near Helen. "That does surprise me about you, Helen." She put her hand on Helen's shoulder and pressed her fingers into the bony knobs of Helen's back. She continued down the aisle, gathering strength. "And Robert." She put her hand on the top of his head. "I had higher hopes for you." She released his head and it bobbed like a toy head on a spring.

The next person she claimed was Louise. "You are ruining your parents' hopes for you, their high hopes. Pity." She spat out the word "pity" like a God curse which rippled through the skin of the children. Then she moved to Frank, laying her white hand on top of his hands, enveloping them. "I know your mother and your father. They would be so upset that you had consented to this vicious display of—"

The classroom door swung open. Miss Cloves withdrew her hand, like a serpent its tongue.

Mr. Hunter walked into the room followed by Evelyn's mother. She looked shrunken standing there in a winter coat that seemed too big for her. Stanley was beside her, large and full, his face all red.

"Evelyn." Stanley's voice rolled over the heads of the children and caught Evelyn around the throat. In her surfaced an equal charge of rage. He had used her name as an insult. She took the spleen clotted in her throat and hurled it back at him like a fireball. "Stanley," she yelled.

She saw her mother's arm shoot out and grab Stanley who had started to press forward.

"Evelyn, we're glad you're safe," her mother said quietly. She came slowly down the aisle. Evelyn hated every step she took. Her mother's upper lip trembled. She looked like Muriel, from the time before.

Muriel stopped. She seemed almost distracted. "Helen, will you help me?" she said in a voice that was milky, pathetic and urgent. "Would you get Evelyn's coat for me?" Evelyn couldn't look at her friend. "I could get it myself, but I don't know where it is." Muriel's smooth voice was mesmerizing. It was like a children's game: fisting the hand, squeezing, and then letting go. The soft touch of her mother's voice made the hand open, involuntarily. Helen stood up. It was all over. Muriel took Evelyn's arm and gently raised her, drained of strength, from her chair. Muriel placed the coat over her shoulders, as a blanket over a sick child, and led her down the aisle.

"We're sorry, Miss Cloves, that we disturbed your class," she said, as she continued to move Evelyn towards the door. "We apologize, boys and girls, for this interruption."

Evelyn was ashamed, being led back down the long hall that echoed with their footsteps. She was limp underneath the heavy weight of her coat, over Rudy Truman's sweater.

Muriel opened the back door of the car and got in beside Evelyn.

"Thank you, Mr. Hunter. There will be no further trouble. You may phone him now, please. He's expecting the call."

Dr. Gemmel was waiting in the living-room, where they took Evelyn.

"You've had a long day, Evelyn," said the doctor. As he came towards her, his eyes had the look of a knife. He was unkind. "Sit down, please."

"Stay away," said Evelyn. But her strength had been sapped. She tried to wriggle into the corner of the couch.

"You are upset, Evelyn." She was cornered. "Perhaps I'll give you something that will help you to relax." He swabbed her arm.

"Leave me alone." But he was too big for her. He removed the coat and sweater. They dropped onto the floor. Evelyn felt the prick of the needle, but she didn't see the glare go out of his eyes. A numbness enfolded her into a blank.

85

When she awoke darkness pressed against her open eyes. She turned on the light. She was in her room downstairs, her clothes neatly folded on the chair. But Rudy Truman's sweater was gone. Evelyn checked the pocket of her shirt. The picture was gone.

She put on her dressing gown and went upstairs. It was still dark outside, and artificial light spread through the kitchen with a seedy familiarity.

"Good morning, Evelyn." Her mother was at the stove, smiling at her. "Did you sleep well?" Voice full of pretend. Smile full of teeth.

Yesterday had been scoured clean like a kitchen pot. Not a trace. Eggs were placed before her on the table.

"Please, dear, before they get cold."

Evelyn swallowed the first mouthful and felt her stomach turn. She swallowed the next. And the next. She could only eat by creating an absence around her, emptied of this moment, like a glass of water spilled.

"I'm glad you were able to eat."

"Pardon?" Evelyn couldn't quite hear.

"Eating. I'm glad."

Evelyn looked down at her empty plate.

"Stanley will take you to school this morning."

"Why?"

"Because, we are worried about you and—"

"What did you do with the sweater?" Evelyn felt groggy, and had difficulty focussing. "And my picture."

"Don't worry about anything. Everything's taken care of."

"The sweater wasn't mine. It belonged to Rudy Truman." She was defeated; everything inside had collapsed.

"Who's Rudy Truman?"

"At the old folks' home. He'll be wondering."

"We'll look after that. Please, Evelyn, don't worry."

"He'll want to see me."

"No, dear, you're not allowed to see him. You were very upset. It's all over now. Stanley will take you to school, and pick you up. Get ready now, please."

"I hate you." Evelyn felt cold and angry. She had the impulse to pick up her plate and throw it against the kitchen window.

"Evelyn, that's enough." It was Stanley. He grabbed her arm with his huge hand and he hurt her. "There will be no more talk like that. Do you hear me?"

Evelyn looked up at him. Maybe he would kill her. Maybe they wanted her to die.

He released her arm. Evelyn put her head down on the table and leaned against the window that was shut. So what if she died.

1956

Muriel often thought of how poor Evelyn had been marred by her early years, and the years without a father. She was lop-sided. No one else could see it, of course. Muriel had hoped that Evelyn would be happier when she married Stanley. But it wasn't so.

Then, with the incident at school over the picture, Muriel had a sense of satisfaction. At last this deformity, the shadow child contained within Evelyn, was visible. It gave Muriel stamina and a edge of energy to meet, face to face, the crisis that had lain buried for so long. Finally she could act. Stanley, of course, had to be restrained so that his embarrassment didn't erupt into anger. Muriel knew what to do. Evelyn was, after all, her child. Her first victory was in the schoolroom. The rest followed: destroying the picture; returning the sweater; driving Evelyn to school every day. Steady, certain. Now Evelyn was happy, just as Muriel was happy. She was coming along now. There had been and would be no repeat performances. The episode was part of the past, locked securely away.

Miss Cloves wrote Muriel a note:

> Dear Mrs. Rathbone:
>   As I will be retiring soon, I wanted to write this personal note to you in the midst of my reflections on my long, and I might say satisfactory, career in shaping the youth of tomorrow. I feel compelled to commend you on your extraordinary accomplishment through the troubled times that now lay behind us. Your daughter seems well on her way to becoming a model pupil, and, I should add, a model citizen of our community. I grieved with you over the incident with the picture—and although I admired your conduct, I was sure that 'we were in for trouble'. The 'way has been smoothed,' due to your diligence, and, I am sure, your forbearing.
>   I will always remember you and Evelyn with a sense of accomplishment.
>
> Yours truly,
Mildred Cloves

Muriel's face burned with pride. She hesitated to show the letter to Stanley, fearing it might start the old argument again. He thought Evelyn should go away to school. He couldn't deal with her; she didn't fit with his idea of the family any more. Ida was his own; she fit.

Muriel knew she was right to oppose Stanley. Evelyn couldn't just be shipped away, like someone else's problem. Besides, S.D. wouldn't approve, not that she cared if he did or not. S.D. liked Evelyn, in a way. Why did he like her so much? He was peculiar. They were all peculiar. Distorted. Evelyn's father was part of it, part of the crooked life that had created Evelyn. Why had she kept that photograph of him? She always threw out things like that, old clothes and letters, photographs. She insisted on a new house when she married Stanley. She never even kept left-over food in the fridge. Why had she kept that one photograph? Of course Evelyn would have to find the picture, sniff it out, like a dog. She had a knack for rooting out things that should lay buried. Was there anything else? This fixation Evelyn had for the past had to be destroyed. But somehow Stanley's solution wasn't the right one. What would S.D. say if Evelyn was sent away? It would prove she had failed. Of course it wasn't the right thing to do. Evelyn was happy now. She was doing well in school—even Miss Cloves said so.

But was she keeping Evelyn, as she had kept the picture, out of a bad habit? Stanley had insisted on the adoption. He had wanted Evelyn to be raised as his child. But Evelyn never fit in to the new family; she refused to call Stanley her father. And Stanley wouldn't bring himself to treat her as his own. It was against his grain. So he wanted to send her away to school. Should she have gone along with him?

The questions bobbed around her, and she had no answers. The more she pushed them down, the more they bounced back, like apples, bad apples.

But the arguments with Stanley had diminished; gradually and by degrees she had won him over. This letter could seal her victory, if she played it right.

As Muriel and Stanley sat in the living room after dinner, Muriel decided she would try it. "This came in the mail today." She handed the letter to Stanley.

He read it slowly, too slowly. His eyes had that sly look, moving back and forth across the page. She was sure he didn't really trust the words. He would have to be managed. He would have to accept it, the fact of her victory. After all, without her, Stanley would be a lonely and brutal man. She had rescued him from that, and he didn't appreciate her enough. The thought tugged at her sleeve and made tiny pinches in her skin. At least Miss Cloves recognized her abilities. As Muriel gently stroked her arm, she grew kind remembering this recognition.

Of course, Stanley had grown up in a misshapen world. She would just have to explain the letter so that he felt he was important in the success that had been achieved. He was probably calculating his response instead of understanding what the letter said. That was it. She understood him. She would have to unseat the claim the letter made on him. He hated publicity of any sort; he would think this letter was too public a statement, and he would be threatened.

"I'm so glad—" she began.

"I'm not finished yet."

"Well, you get the sense of it."

"Not if you keep interrupting me."

"You're so slow."

Stanley looked up quickly, as though to ward her off. It was always a risk, telling Stanley he was too slow, or too fast. He took everything personally. His ancient suspicion would be on the attack if she wasn't careful. And so she smiled extremely, trying to make her kindness and caring get to him through her eyes.

"I want to talk to you, that's all." She squinted her eyes at him.

It worked, as it always did. He slumped his shoulders.

"Okay, hold on, I'm almost finished."

Muriel continued talking in order to distract him. "Miss Cloves really doesn't understand us."

"She sure doesn't," he said, hunching again over the letter.

"All along, we've only done what's best for her."

"Hmm."

Maybe he hadn't really heard her. "You've always wanted that. Right from the beginning."

He looked up. "Wanted what?"

"What's best for Evelyn."

"No thanks to this Miss Cloves," he added.

Muriel was contented. "You've wanted her to be happy. And now she is. She is quite happy." He accepted it. He recognized her achievement as his own. "So how was your day?" she asked.

"The only thing is—" he began again.

Muriel thought the matter was closed; they had said enough.

"—Clarence talked to me the other day."

Muriel turned away. She didn't want to hear about Clarence. She didn't like him. Not because he tried to have any control over her; on the contrary, he seemed indifferent to her. But there was something oblivious about him. He was more like Kathryn than S.D. He was slightly stupid. It was just that stupidity which kept him out of reach, almost untouchable. She had tried with Clarence. Especially after the incident with the bird; she had wanted to bring him in over that. But he wouldn't come. He was unresponsive to her, like someone absent. She liked a man's man— Stanley was a man's man. Clarence had agreed to talk to Evelyn about the bird but he had never told Muriel what he'd said. That was foolish to leave her out. Evelyn had been so upset. It might even have led to the February crisis—who knew how these things could get a start? And Evelyn wouldn't talk. Oh, no, she wouldn't talk any more. Poor Evelyn. That bird was such a loss to her. What had to be controlled in Evelyn was the fact that she dwelt on everything; things grew in that child's imagination. It would be like her to imagine that she was responsible for the death of that bird. Stewing, her distorted notions festering. Well, all that was past, not to be thought of.

Oh yes, Stanley was loyal to Clarence. Very loyal to what he thought of as *his* family. She'd rather deal with S.D. any day, the old goat, than have to deal with Clarence. She wouldn't let him get under her skin.

"What did Clarence have to say for himself?" She smiled, trying to sweeten the bitterness in her mouth.

"He said the life had gone out of Evelyn."

"Oh, come on."

"I'm only telling you what he said." Stanley opened up his face in that annoying way he had when he knew he'd said something contentious.

Muriel turned away. He was just trying to goad her, to get his own way. "Everyone has their ideas I suppose." She tried to find a milky tone of voice.

"I still think we should send her away to school."

She looked at the letter in his hands and it calmed her. He would not contort this victory into a defeat, no matter what. "Yes, I know you do. I think it's so fortunate she's doing well in school. That's the most important thing. If she was failing it might be the time to make a move." Evelyn had skipped a grade. She was smart. Smarter than his clan.

"Mm." Stanley folded up the letter and handed it back to Muriel. "Miss Cloves is a bit too fancy for my taste."

"Not any fancier than your father is, when he gets going." As soon as she said this, she regretted it. It was like waving a red flag.

"He can afford to be fancy. She can't."

Muriel didn't want to fight about S.D., or about Evelyn. Or about Clarence. What did Clarence know about anything? He hadn't married. He didn't have any of his own children to deal with. He'd always had

90

lots of money and not many problems. That was the trouble with him. He acted quiet and shy, but inside he figured he was cock of the walk—trying to tell her what to do with her child.

"I'm not sure that Clarence knows anything about this whole situation anyway," she said, finally, scratching her arm.

"He likes Evelyn," said Stanley.

Muriel tasted the bitterness in her mouth again. So what if he likes her. Does that make him an authority?

"Why don't you get us a drink. I'll have rye, thanks." She needed something to take this taste away.

Stanley brought back one glass.

"You're not having anything?" she asked.

"Nope. You drink too much."

"And you don't drink enough," Muriel shot back.

They seemed to be reaching out for the sore points, lighting all the tapers on their old disagreements.

"I like Evelyn, too," she added. Their discussion was like a kindergarten exercise, each of them marking the boundary between them with primary colours, one on top of the other, generating other colours, with acid tones.

Stanley's face was open, like a set trap. He didn't believe her. The bastard didn't believe her.

"I *do* like Evelyn," she insisted. No, she mustn't protest. She didn't have to convince anyone.

"Clarence figured that Evelyn was better off before."

That was it. The trap snapped shut and she was caught in it. She put her drink down heavily on the glass coffee table.

"Before what, Stanley? Before what?" Stanley sat there, his face reset into the wide openness. He looked like an empty pail she wanted to throw slop into. "Before Ida came along? Before Clarence came along? Before *you* came along? Just what 'before' is he referring to, exactly?" She picked up her glass and took a drink.

"I dunno," he said, slovenly, shrugging his shoulders.

"Well, why don't you know?" Muriel was on her feet. "You should know before you start telling me how Clarence says I should raise my child."

Now Stanley was on his feet. "Nobody's telling you how to raise your child." They were nose to nose, like two ancient combatants.

"Least of all your brother."

"Why least of all?" Stanley challenged her, stepping over the acid boundary between them.

91

"Just least of all." Muriel wanted to let it go now; but Stanley was on her ground. He had set his trap in her territory, and all her mellow tones had gone.

"Why least of all? You just tell me about 'least of all'."

He always defended Clarence, or used Clarence against her. She would not be bullied. Not by this family. They put themselves above her, figured they were better than her. Above her? They shit from a high place. That's what they were about.

"You think you're so superior. All of you do. But I know, you can't fool me. You fake it. You're all faking it. Deep inside"—her lips wormed out the words, and she moved her finger toward him, snaking it into his stomach—"deep down inside, you know."

"What are you talking about? Know what?" His face narrowed and the trap tightened.

"Don't you speak to me like that. You're trying to sound like S.D. Don't you dare. I am not Kathryn and you know very well what I'm talking about."

"You just tell me, then." His face closed in contempt, as though it was all he could do to utter the words. "You tell me, then."

She wouldn't be treated in that way, damn it. "I've heard. I know about your family." She made her voice snake into him. And then she was scared. The shadows in the room were harsh and angular. She had to get him back. She had to absorb him into herself. She didn't know where she was going. "Look, let's forget this."

"No, let's not forget it. What do you mean?"

"It's nothing."

"You started this. Keep going, God damn you."

He had never sworn at her before. He was cursing her. She had to make him understand. "When I first met you, and when I agreed to marry you, I told you everything. I told you…" Her voice was shaking and tears came to her eyes. Stanley watched her from a distant place. "I told you about Timothy. I told you about my parents. And you, you told me nothing." She looked up at him. He was a wall of stone she was hitting. "You didn't tell me the things I've heard since—"

"What have you heard?" he snapped.

He was asking for it, then. Her tears dried instantly. He deserved what he got. "All right, what about the sister you never talk about? You never talk about Maude, do you—and I know why."

"What about Maude?"

"She was in a fire. You saved her." Maybe she didn't have to say everything; maybe she could just hint at what she knew and he'd back off.

92

"Is that what *they* say, is that the cheap talk you hear? The cheap gossip you get in the streets?"

"You bastard. You saved Maude because she was your brother's child. Clarence got your sister pregnant. The illegitimate child is Maude. And that's why you don't talk about her. Clarence doesn't talk about her. But she's what everyone *else* talks about. That's how high and mighty you are, you and your God damn family thinking you're so..."

"Shut up. That's a lie. You slut, that's a God damn lie." Then his voice bladed. "Don't you ever say that again in this house or I'll—I'll leave you. I'll leave you just the way I found you." He turned, marched from the room and slammed the front door.

Muriel sat still, as the house echoed with the sound of his leaving her. She poured herself another drink. The yellow liquid swirled around the ice cubes, filmy, serpentine, almost like gasoline. God damn Clarence. God damn him.

All there was to lose: Ida's future. Living again in a rotten house, creeping along. She wanted better things than that. She wanted a real home, without disgrace. She finished her drink and refilled her glass. The rye steamed on the ice cubes. Hissed. Mocked.

Where had Stanley gone? He wouldn't come back. Then what? Her life was about to slough into the past. Splits creased deep into the air. Why? She wasn't guilty of anything. She only said what she had pieced together from the gossip that neighbours were all too willing to tell her: illegitimate child, Isabel sent away, Kathryn following and coming back with a baby they called Maude, Clarence not marrying. The scandal hushed up. Probably with money. She had figured it out. The proof was in Stanley's leaving, slamming the door, telling her never to speak of it.

She was wrong to have spoken. That's what happened when old ghosts were unearthed. She'd only wanted to get back at Clarence, to shut him up. She poured herself another drink.

Old ghosts should never be let out. So what if the neighbours talked? They probably talked about Muriel, too, with their evil tongues. Why did she want the approval of people like Miss Cloves? Who were they anyway—people who had their own ghosts. People who had their own Maudes and Evelyns somewhere to remind them of things gone wrong.

Maybe Stanley had the right idea. She loved Stanley, didn't she? Didn't she understand him completely? Evelyn should be sent away. Was Evelyn really happy now? Who could be happy now? When Stanley came back— if he ever came back—he'd never walked out on her before—if he did come back, she would agree. That was the best thing. They'd still take care of Evelyn. They'd send her to a good school, a very good school.

In fact, she'd get better teachers if she were sent away—better than old Cloves and skinny old Hunter. What could they teach her child? Nothing, zero, zilch. Evelyn was smart; she had a future. She was better off to go to school somewhere else.

She poured herself another drink. The front door opened. He'd come back. She put down her glass, this time gently on the table. "Stanley?" She called him forward. "Stanley, I think you're right. Evelyn should go away to school."

"I don't want to talk about it any more. The subject is closed."

"Please, Stanley, I'm sorry. You're right about Evelyn. Can't we talk about Evelyn?" It took all her courage to try to win him back. If he left again, if he wouldn't talk to her, it was all over.

"As far as I'm concerned, Maude is dead. She died in the fire. Don't you ever"—he moved towards her as though he was going to strike her—"don't you ever speak of her, don't even think of her again."

Muriel could have taunted him, she could have ridden him into the ground. Maude was not dead. Kathryn talked about her, even S.D. wrote her letters. But she had to leave it alone. Let him win. She could let him win this once.

"But Evelyn. We should talk of Evelyn, and where she'll go to school…"

Evelyn waited at the top of the stairs until she could hear them finally go to bed. The circle was drawn, and it included Clarence, Timothy and someone called Maude. Illegitimate child. She said the names over and over, re-arranging the order. "Clarence, Maude, Timothy, Evelyn. I'm the last one. I'm going away." She looked out through the window that had been painted shut; their names paraded in a circle front of her.

She went down the steps, each one lettered E, G, B, D, F, E, G, B, D, F. She stepped over the stairs that creaked, like the black notes. As she fell asleep, she was in the company of others.

1957

Evelyn wrote to Helen, describing her new school and her life in Winnipeg. When Helen wrote back, Evelyn could envision all the people and places she talked about. But Helen didn't know about Evelyn any more, she couldn't really understand.

> Mostly I'm glad to be here. The teachers are okay—better than the ones we used to have, anyway. Better than Cloves— they put her out to pasture just in time. I have an English

teacher everyone calls Spin—short for Spinster. She teaches all the grades. Lots of teachers here aren't married, but the name fits her best. Her real name is Miss Holgate. They say she was here first and they built the school around her. She's the best one, reads a lot—but she's kind of twitchy. She gets very excited about the books she has us read and I think the other kids get embarrassed sometimes, because it's like her whole life. She's the only lit teacher. I like her.

The other girls are mostly stuck-up and rich. My room-mate's name is Marsha. She really bugs me. Her deepest thought is whether her boy-friend at home still loves her. Can you imagine? I'm going to ask for a room by myself.

It's kind of strange eating and sleeping and studying all in the same building with the same people. Sometimes it feels like prison, or a big public indoor swimming pool with no exit doors. Bright and noisy. Constant. I guess sometimes I get lonely.

As the months passed, there was less and less to say in letters to Helen. At Christmas, Evelyn called Helen when she went back home, but didn't go over to visit. Then she stopped writing altogether. She couldn't explain anything to Helen any more. She wrote another letter to Rudy Truman at the old folks home, but it was returned marked "unknown." She guessed Rudy really was dead by now.

Evelyn was called a loner by the other girls.

In the evenings when it was mild, Evelyn escaped from the incessant noise of the dormitory and went down to the river. She sat on a rock near the water's edge. The river always surprised her; she half feared that it would dry up between her visits and become only a cracked tracing which marked a vanished life. But it was always there.

The sun slipping down the sky and behind the water filled her with indescribable longing. Her life didn't make any sense unless an answer came to her. It was as though she had lost someone she needed. And so she waited, as one waits for someone who promises to return. She tried to find words to fill up her longing. "The grass grows around me and covers the rock on which I sit. When will you return? When will you, long absent, return? I wait. Sometimes I think I can hear you coming. Are you coming? Sometimes I think I can hear you coming."

The words carried the rhythm of her blood, as nostalgia turned urgent, and hope turned into excitement. The light was dying. "Are you coming? I think I can hear you coming." In the trees, by the river, expectation stirred the leaves. "Are you coming?" All the world defined this absence, and she was at the very centre of it, waiting. She was as attuned as a lover when there is no appointed hour for the return. And what she was waiting for she could never have said.

Her task was to wait for something, some answer or hint of recognition. It could be discerned only by its thin absence which she carried in her, the way a brooch carries a gem.

The ending of the day marked the deep descent of her waiting, its ritualized retreat. The fading light was the last light that would ever be seen in the world, the last knowledge of something that might never happen.

There was nothing about her that was angry. She didn't struggle. And she felt, with an attention that gave her purpose, that there was no end to the waiting. She had a certainty that was like a scar for the absence that she could only shape by this longing.

When she was with other people, she lost the sense of it. She lost the expectation of an answer to her loneliness. The world was cluttered then, airless and suffocating. She wanted to be alone and private. There was nothing that could assuage that need; there was no idea that excited her except the anticipation she felt when she was near the river. Otherwise everything was flat and it pressed against her like a hand. The lines around her eyes were the old lines that a tortoise has, from too long looking; in the company of others she had old tortoise eyes in a soft head and a hardened back.

On the way home she stopped underneath the railway bridge. Other people had been there before her and left their marks on the huge concrete walls which held up the bridge. FUCK YOU ASS HOLE FUCK SHIT. The words didn't have any particular meaning; they belonged to her journey to the river. They were like fingers moving inside her, as tactile as the absence she contained. They held dangerous earth smells, the soft "f" sound and the hard "ck". They were part of her excitement when the night was on and the lover might return. Fuck. It was the sound she made in her mouth as the train screamed overhead. The sound was the dark part of the dream, when the waiting had gone under and rolled inside her.

Evelyn held the telegram in both hands.

> S.D. passed away 7:38 a.m. today stop funeral Wednesday
> stop fly home tomorrow first flight ticket waiting Stanley.

Something had happened to them. S.D. had died. 7:38 a.m. The tittering laughter of young girls in the hall seeped under the door. Evelyn kept perfectly still, like something in marble or stone.

Voices shouting, "Okay, Marsha, you're going to get it." "You're a nerd, you're a creepo nurd." The sound nudging against her, like the nose of fish against a bowl. "I couldn't care less, Marsha." "Shut up you guys I'm trying to work." Nothing was connected to her except this paper and S.D. being dead. "Betty, get your dirty socks out of my room."

Having to go back. She was five months from graduation. Then she would go somewhere to university—somewhere away from this cold place.

She felt relieved, as though it were a blood relative who had died, some lineage of which she was a part. As though a hat she had worn was removed, sounds were clearer, her head was lighter. She was unencumbered.

Something had happened to them. To Muriel and Stanley. Everything was changed.

"Marsha, creepo, guess you think you're smart, eh? You're just dumb."

Even the voices of the girls in the hall were almost bearable. She didn't have to feel sad any more that she wasn't connected to them. Whatever the other girls were like—and she couldn't say she knew—she was now related to something different that had happened. S.D., dead. At 7:38 a.m.

She felt sorry she didn't have anyone to tell.

S.D. had meant very little to her. He was only an ogre in a long line of ogres, of brutal men. He couldn't buy her a new dress for her graduation, the way he bought her clothes when Muriel married Stanley. He couldn't do anything any more, except bring her back on the plane for his funeral.

What if she didn't go? They'd make her go. They'd call the principal or send her mother in after her. She had to go. Others were in charge now instead of S.D.; Stanley and Muriel were the new king and queen.

She felt powerless, thinking of them.

If she was relieved about S.D.'s death, Muriel would be dancing right out front, and so would Stanley, except he wouldn't dance. Everything would come to the surface.

And then Evelyn felt so sad, like an empty well. All her tears had drained away. There were only stones left on top of barren ground.

As she held the telegram, it seemed that she had been numb for a long time. Even her fingers and hands were numb. They could hold things but only the way a cup holds things, a stone cup. Someone had placed the telegram there in her hands. Holgate had given it to her, after dinner. It said S.D. passed away. Dead.

"Would you girls please settle down." Lid on a jar. Knock on the door. Opening.

"Evelyn, are you all right?" It was Holgate. "Bad news?" Evelyn couldn't speak. "Good news?" Still Evelyn couldn't connect with her voice.

Evelyn noticed for the first time how Miss Holgate's face jumped around as she talked. There was a battle behind her face. "Evelyn, are you okay?" Jumping face, like cats in a bag. Moving towards her.

Evelyn held up the telegram.

"Oh, my, I'm so sorry. Who—was S.D. someone you were close to?" Holgate's cats fought over the words.

"No." No one understood. She hadn't tried to explain anything to anyone for a long time.

"But someone you knew?" The words had a dry texture, like finger-nails scratching a mirror.

"My grandfather, sort of."

"I see."

"He'd been sick. Put away."

"You mean he was too sick to look after himself?"

"He'd been put away."

"You mean in a hospital?"

Holgate was pressing in on her.

"In a place to die. Stanley did it and my mother. Clarence was against it."

"Stanley and—you mean Stanley, your father?"

"Step-father."

"I see. It happens that way, in families, I suppose. Not everyone agrees with the best interests of—"

"My mother was glad." Evelyn wanted to be left alone.

"I'm sure she was. I'm sure she was glad that S.D.—your grandfather—was going to be well looked after."

Evelyn felt envenomed by her teacher's platitudes. "She didn't care about that." There was no one she could talk to. Her eyes felt tired.

"I'm sure your mother went to great efforts to assist your grandfather."
Out of the corner of her eye, Evelyn could see Miss Holgate's hands
resting on one another, like two dead birds. Only her face was alive with
contradiction.

"My mother doesn't like old things."

"That's a big generalization. There are lots of old things in the world."

"She doesn't like them."

"Well, you're very upset now. You shouldn't try to talk until you've
had a good rest."

The black note sounded. It collapsed the air. Evelyn sat up straight.
She'd been off guard. She wouldn't be forced into sleep. Not by Holgate
or anyone. "I'm not upset, Miss Holgate, and I don't need to rest."
Evelyn's fear sliced her words into neat packages with sharp edges that
made paper cuts on Miss Holgate's bag face, tiny bloodless paper cuts.

"You misunderstand, I was only suggesting—"

"I can sleep just fine, thank you."

"All right, Evelyn. There's no need to be hostile."

"I'm not hostile, Miss Holgate, and I'm not upset. You assume too
much."

"Most people would be upset." Holgate's cats hissed.

"I don't care about most people." Evelyn turned away. She wanted
to cry for this stupid, wasteful battle she was having with Holgate. None
of it mattered. Holgate didn't matter. She wouldn't fight with her.

"Listen, I came here to find out if you were all right, not to argue
with you." The cats relaxed and rolled under Holgate's eyes, trying to
soften them.

"I have to see about a plane."

"All right, that's fine, that's fine." Holgate retreated and then said
coolly, "If you want, you can call from my office."

"All right."

Evelyn went with her teacher down the long empty hall. She was edgy,
like a bear in a bear pit. S.D. was dead. That had nothing to do with
Holgate who'd come barging in, uninvited.

"I wonder why Mr. Rathbone, your step-father, didn't call. Instead
of sending a telegram."

"You don't tell things like that over the phone. At least not in my
family."

"Really? That's unusual."

"I guess you'd say that wasn't like most people." Evelyn felt mean.
She tossed the sting into the air, as a leftover.

"You have a sharp tongue, Evelyn."

Her teacher kept walking but Evelyn stopped. The hall lights glanced off the shiny walls like light inside a can. Evelyn was angry. And then she felt tired. She wanted to sit down right there and not go any farther. But she resumed walking, dutiful and defeated.

Holgate looked injured. "I'm sorry, that was probably uncalled for. Do you have enough money, to get home?"

"Yes, thank you."

The office was at the top of the building where the floors were carpetted and footsteps didn't echo. Miss Holgate unlocked her door. A lamp spotlighted a clear, clean desk with only an ink blotter and a pen.

"May I call the airport for you?" Holgate's cats purred inside her voice.

"I can call." Then Evelyn recanted. "Okay, thanks, you call."

Evelyn sat on the leather chair at the student side of the desk. Holgate's voice was teacherly, clear and efficient as she made the arrangements.

"Now, that's fine. You're confirmed on the first flight tomorrow. I'll send a telegram—to Stanley, Mr. Rathbone—your step-father—in the morning to ensure that someone is there to meet you. I can drive you to the airport, if you'd like."

Evelyn was grateful to her. Holgate's cats had gone to sleep. "Thank you," Evelyn said, although it was hard to say thank you. It could mean she had asked for help, which she hadn't.

"You're most welcome. It's really the least I could do." Holgate paused. "I apologize for my awkwardness earlier. It's difficult, talking about death."

"That's okay." None of the other teachers ever apologized. She liked Holgate for that.

The teacher moved around the desk to a cabinet across the room. "Because this is a very unusual situation, as we have noted, I propose something unusual." She took out a wad of keys from her full skirt and unlocked the cabinet, taking out a bottle and two glasses.

Evelyn was surprised. Was Spin a tippler? Students could be expelled for drinking. Evelyn sat up straight; she had to be careful.

"Would you like to join me in a drink?"

"But I don't drink."

"All of you girls drink, I know that."

Evelyn was out of her element. She knew how to get drinks for her mother, how to pour them exactly right. And she knew that most of the other girls in her year drank at parties, or whenever they could get it. But Evelyn had never tasted liquor.

"I've never had a drink," she said flat out.

"Oh, I see. Well, then....It's time you tried it." Spin held up the bottle and her face glowed from the reflected light inside the bottle. "I save this for—well, for special occasions. We've never had much opportunity to talk, you and I."

"No, I guess not."

Evelyn sipped the sherry.

"S.D. was Irish. They drink a lot when somebody dies, like in a wake," she said.

"They do, that's right. Do you like it?" Spin was very gentle and intent.

"Yeah, it's good. I'll have more."

"It's odd you don't drink. I thought all the girls drank." Evelyn was silent. "It can be pleasant, in measured amounts."

The sherry was sweet and warm. Evelyn felt as though her eyes were set back in her soft head.

"I guess this is your coming of age," said Spin. "Better that it should happen under the proper auspices, rather than in the uncertain corridors with your peers." Spin was starting to make long sentences, high-blown sentences the way she did in class.

Evelyn liked listening to her now. All her own words had been ploughed under. Her teacher's voice nicely filled the room. Holgate would call the airport, drive her there, call Stanley, pour the sherry. She would take care of things.

"Were you close to your grandfather? He was your grandfather on your mother's side was he?"

"No, Stanley's. I guess I didn't know him that well. He was hard to get close to. Nice sometimes."

"I see. It must be very hard for you." Spin touched Evelyn's shoulder. Evelyn recoiled.

"Oh, I'm sorry, I—"

Holgate had left a hand print on her, like a scald.

The teacher withdrew to the other side of the desk, far away now. "I didn't mean to alarm you."

Evelyn's hands were thick lumps of dough, incapable of defending or protecting her. She wouldn't speak any more. "Evelyn, have I hurt you somehow, or offended you?"

Evelyn sat still. She was a soft furred animal that had been stabbed by a stick. She curled up into a round limbless ball.

"Evelyn, please."

The teacher was coming around the desk toward her. She might be touched again. Slip away and disappear, thin and slipping away between the shapes of things.

The voice was searching her out. "What's wrong? I don't understand." The teacher had shrunk. She had become small and her voice tiny. She was squatting on her knees right in front of Evelyn.

Holgate wanted something from her. Needed her to do something. Wanted her to give in. 'Please, Evelyn, do it for me.' The teacher might cry and Evelyn would have to come back. She'd have to say yes, and then would have no place to go, no privacy.

The teacher got up and returned to her chair behind the desk, her fingers tented in thought.

"Evelyn, you're a very intelligent girl. You will graduate at the top of your class." Holgate paused for a long time but kept looking at her. "I'm just going to keep talking, because I don't know what else to do. I must say I have taken a great deal of pleasure in teaching you, because you have an appreciation of language and of literature—you can leave any time if you wish. It's difficult, being a teacher, because most of the students don't give a damn. But you seem to care; I've seen it in the essays you've written. But I don't know very much about you—not like the other girls. You keep to yourself. And I respect that. I respect your solitude and your isolation. It must be very painful for you, because it's a hard path. But it's also easy in some respects, if the isolation becomes automatic, a neat response to everything. What you write is often—you have an affinity for—what shall I say—the dark side. I suppose that's it. That's what you are exploring. And I have worried that you don't seem to like anything; you don't like people, in a way. You probably don't like me. You're a model student, but I wonder what's beneath that. What are you hiding? Why are you afraid of me? Why are you afraid of—a mere touch?" Spin undid her hands and leaned forward. "It's only me, here. It's only your teacher, another person—someone you know."

It was all too late. Evelyn couldn't hear this now. There was no hope; there hadn't been for a long time. Her teacher's words burned into her.

"Where are you now? You won't answer. I have a hunch that the only thing you cherish, what you are holding on to now, is your own sadness and isolation. Nothing can interfere with that. Isn't that right? Is that how you feel? That you are bound to be unrecognized and unacknowledged? Well, I recognize you. Look at me, Evelyn. Look up. I'm out here. I'm another one, over here. I'm the same as you—I'm not a monster and neither are you. I'm right here, looking at you, wanting you to look at me."

Holgate moved around the desk and placed herself squarely in front of Evelyn. She held out her hands, both hands, palms up, in front of her student. Her voice was very soft and slow.

"It's not so hard, you know. If you want to. I'm not taking anything from you." No one had ever spoken to Evelyn like that. Wasn't it too late? She slowly looked up. There were no cats behind her teacher's face. She was only a pale woman, in her fifties, with hatch marks under her eyes and folds of skin under her chin. She was squatting down again, directly in front of Evelyn, unavoidable.

Evelyn was slightly unfurled, but she longed to retreat. She longed to be only waiting and expecting. Left alone. The presence of the teacher hurt. Her hands were only cups. She was stuck. She couldn't move.

"Try. Lift up your hands even if it's to ward me off. Hold them up."

Evelyn couldn't do it. She couldn't do what she was asked. How to bridge the impossible distance from here to there. How to move out, towards Holgate, when all her limbs were stone. It was impossible.

And then she heard a kind of chant. An absurd rhythm on the white notes. Holgate, in front of her, was almost singing.

"Paddy cake, paddy cake, baker's man." The teacher slowly clapped her hands together and patted the air, clapped her hands and patted the air. "Bake me a cake as fast as you can." Solemnly, like the high priestess of an important mystery, she incanted the childish words. Her hands fisted, her arms rolled, and then she put the air cake into the oven and started all over again.

"Paddy cake, paddy cake, baker's man." Evelyn was fixated, watching the arms roll, the B marked in the air. Her own fisted hands were lulled awake, and started to match her teacher's actions in the air between them. Their hands touched, making cake. Paddy cake, paddy cake, baker's man. Their voices joined together in the song, getting faster and faster, wobbling out of control. "Bake me a cake as fast as you can. Pad-it-and-roll-it-and-mark-it with a B an puddit in the oven for baby 'n me." They started all over again. Suddenly and halfway through, Holgate stopped. She held her hands out flat, parallel to the ground. Evelyn followed and placed her hands on top of Holgate's, palm to palm. Quickly, Spin withdrew one hand from underneath and slapped the top of Evelyn's hand.

"Ouch."

"So. Fight back."

She did it again.

"Stop it."

"Fight."

This time Evelyn jerked her hand back and Spin missed. "Two misses and I'm out." They were both standing. Spin missed again.

"Your turn," said Holgate.

They reversed roles with Spin's hands on top. Evelyn scored a hit. "You're too slow," Evelyn accused.

"Come on, just try me." Evelyn struck again. "You're vicious."

"It's your game."

The sting of the hits was exhilarating; it was intoxicating. Evelyn's hands were alive, top and bottom. They burned from striking and being struck. Her legs took root and she planted herself against Holgate's attack, ready and alert. Then she struck, quick and hard.

Finally Spin yielded. "All right. You win. Uncle."

"Grandpa. Say grandpa."

"I won't."

Evelyn swacked but missed. She tried again and hit. Hit twice in a row.

"Okay, grandpa, grandpa." Evelyn ignored her and struck again. "Grandpa, I said grandpa. What do you want?"

"You take S.D's name in vain. Repent." She tried and missed. Tried again and scored.

"Okay. I repent. I repent. Stop."

Evelyn stopped. The air prickled with energy. Evelyn's hands were stinging. "My God, it's hot in here." Both were sweating.

Spin filled the glasses. "I propose a toast, then."

"A toast," said Evelyn, and held up her glass.

"To paddy cake."

"Paddy cake."

They both downed their sherry and Spin re-filled the glasses.

"You have been very cruel to your old teacher. You could have let me win."

"Humbug," said Evelyn and laughed. Her hands tingled with a thousand nettles.

Her teacher had grown serious and reflective. "I take pride in my work here at the school. I don't know why, I'm probably foolish and dotty, like an old school marm."

"We call you Spin, short for Spinster." Evelyn wanted to say things, to tell her teacher things.

"I know. I probably can guess most of what you call me." Spin took a drink of her sherry. "Let me tell you something. Everything that happens comes out of the blue. It's unadorned. If you think too much about doing something, you never will. It'll die on the vine. You just have to do it. It's a question of being practical, or not even that—of attending to what is right in front of you. Like a slap on the hand. My guess is that you don't know, yet, if you want to be involved—maybe you were once, and you got hurt. So you got hurt? So what? You're young. You can take it. When you're old like me you'll be full of regret that you drifted and never got hold of anything. You can retreat; but if you do it's because you're stubborn and wilful. You think you're a good girl. But you're not. No one will thank you."

"You think I'm wilful then? Not goody two-shoes?"

"Goody two-shoes?" Her teacher smiled. "No, no I don't."

"What then?"

Spin moved forward and stood in front of Evelyn, pausing to sip her sherry. Evelyn had to crane her neck to see her properly. She wanted to hear more, she wanted Holgate to come closer with the words.

"You've spent a long time in a kind of darkness. My guess is—to extend the analogy—that the light will hurt your eyes. But the light is of your own making. It's what's true about you. There will be plenty of time for the dark." Holgate knelt down in front of Evelyn and placed her hands on Evelyn's knees. This time Evelyn didn't withdraw. She wanted Holgate to press down hard. Her limbs wanted to grow.

"I've been watching you. Maybe you didn't know. I've wanted to tell you this before. You can take courage. Be courageous." Her eyes were shiny, wet with tears. Evelyn felt strangely blessed.

She put her arms around Spin's neck, and used her shirt to wipe the tears. As she leaned over, Spin raised her head and Evelyn kissed her on the cheek. A shock of energy went through her body. Ancient air stirred and moved, in her legs, up through her thighs and into her hands. She hugged the grey tangled head of her teacher and rocked her, close to her new heart, close to a spreading web of delight. As she rocked, the room tipped this way and that with her movements.

Spin lifted her head and Evelyn grinned down at her. "I feel like one of your cats," said Evelyn.

"My cats? I don't have cats."

"You do, sometimes. Behind your face."

"Behind my face?"

"Goodnight," said Evelyn. "The sherry has gone to my head. Thank you for the cake." She pushed back her chair slowly, half afraid that Holgate might fall over without support. But her teacher stood up. Again Evelyn said goodnight. There was no answer.

Finally Spin said, "I was just in the middle of a speech to you about light and dark, about how I see you."

"You can tell me again. You can tell me lots of times."

"All right, that's enough light and dark for one night."

105

Evelyn tiptoed down the long corridor, rubbing her fingers across the surface of the shiny walls. The walls were pebbled and bumpy to her touch. The roughness of the wall was pleasing to her, as though she had never before felt anything at the end of her fingertips. The feeling vibrated through her body. She started to giggle. "Is this drunk?" she asked aloud, then quickened her pace, running with her fingers against the wall, her thighs rubbing together. She ran with her hands hitting the sun-barred slats of a picket fence. Slapping the sun, teasing and slapping the light and dark.

When she got to her room she sat down and leaned against the outside of the door, with the laughter hot in her belly. She didn't want to go to bed, oh no, never, never go to bed. Maybe she'd find Spin again. She'd left too soon. Maybe she'd—have some more sweet, sweet sherry, for S.D. She was lonely out here, in the hall. She would stay awake until it was time for the plane; sit up in the chair in Spin's room, sipping sherry until the funeral parade started. Spin loved her. Now wasn't that something. She'd been watching. She knew her and she wanted to talk to her. Take courage, she had said. Running down the hill. Running.

"Evelyn."

She opened her eyes. There was the old face of her teacher in front of her again.

"Evelyn, what are you doing here?"

Evelyn stared around her. She was leaning against the door of her room. Her neck was stiff and her throat was sore and dry.

"You have to get ready."

Holgate helped her to her feet. "It's almost 7 o'clock. Take a shower, and I'll pack your clothes. You have to wake up."

The water was spiders through her skin. She was back in the hideous world.

Holgate got her packed and took her to the airport.

"Why don't you come with me," Evelyn asked.

"Don't be silly."

They parted at the gate.

"Paddy cake," said Evelyn out loud as the plane pressed into flight. She still felt groggy. She was conscious of the sharp shadows around things, thrown by the sun. The speck of darkness on the ground was her plane moving over the snow fields beneath her. She slept. Then the pilot announced they were about to land. Evelyn looked out. They were still quite far from the ground. And then the ground was there the bump, and the landing. Death would be like that—a long way off, and then smack underneath her, like the sudden landing of a plane. Without any more time, then. No more time to live her life.

Muriel was waiting for her at the airport. Outside, it was cold; it hurt to breathe the air.

"Do you want to go and see S.D.?" asked Muriel. Evelyn didn't understand. "You can, if you want, but you probably don't. I'm not sure I'll go."

"Where is he?"

"At the funeral home. The coffin is open from 7:30 to 9 o'clock tonight. But you probably don't want to go. It might be upsetting."

Evelyn did want to go but felt wrong about her curiosity. She didn't look at her mother. "I'm not sure. Do you think I should?" She looked down and saw that her hands were fisted.

"No, I don't think so. Your last memory of him should be when he was alive." Marty looked straight ahead at the road. Evelyn could see from her mother's jaw that she was pressing her teeth together.

Evelyn unfurled her hands. "Maybe I will go, to pay my respects."

"I'm not stopping you," Marty said.

In the evening Evelyn went with Stanley to the funeral home. It was in a huge converted house that had been painted white and green. A tall man came to the door; he had a small hairless head and a thick body covered in a dark suit. He seemed tipped backward, as though leaned against by an enormous wind.

"Mr. Frank," said Stanley, "this is my daughter, Evelyn." Evelyn shook his hand; it felt as soft as an uncooked sausage.

"You have come to see Mr. Rathbone, have you?" said Mr. Frank and continued without waiting for a reply. "I thought you would come tonight. Miss Rathbone is here already."

"My mother?"

"No, no." Mr. Frank folded his arms over his chest, and smiled kindly. "Your sister. She's with him now." Mr. Frank stretched out one of his arms and swept it across his dark body. "In there."

Stanley followed the direction but stopped at the door of the room. "How did' you get here?" he said, accusingly.

He blocked the doorway so that Evelyn couldn't see. She slipped around him and stood facing a huge oak casket with its lid raised; S.D. was inside, surrounded by white satin. In front of the coffin was a small woman, elegantly dressed with a black hat and veil. Her gloves were limp in one hand and the other hand rested on the rich oak of the coffin. Her skin seemed whiter than S.D's, as white, almost, as the soft satin which surrounded him.

"Hello, Stanley," the lady said. "This must be Evelyn. How do you do, I'm Mrs. Mason." Evelyn took her hand. It was delicate, with soft feathery skin. She seemed much too gentle for Stanley's rough presence.

"How did you get here?" Stanley repeated.

"I flew in this afternoon." Her answer didn't meet the challenge in his question. She turned away from him. Evelyn had never seen Stanley so thoroughly ignored. She wished she could do that, ignore him instead of hide from him.

The lady stood at the coffin, her back to them. Evelyn moved foward a few steps.

"Why are you here?" Stanley demanded.

"I came for the funeral," the lady said, simply, without turning around. "I've never seen him so peaceful. More peaceful in death."

Stanley's ribbons of rage had been precisely snipped. He seemed lost and bedraggled, unable to go forward.

S.D's black glasses had been positioned on his head. All the lines and creases of his old age had been smoothed away. He looked quite beautiful, lying there in his crib of satin. The room was heavy with the laboured smell of roses.

Stanley was silent, and the minutes collected around them, cloying with the burden of death. S.D.'s stillness seemed a masquerade. But he couldn't wake up any more. There wasn't even a dream of sleeping and waking. There was only an absence which filled out his immovable dead shape.

Evelyn watched in amazement as the lady reached over and pulled back the cuff of S.D's jacket. The pasty white liver-marked flesh of his arm was revealed above the solid line on his wrist, marking the work of the undertakers. They had covered up the dead hands with a thick coat of pink make-up. Evelyn's breath caught in her throat.

The lady whispered, "The farmer's tan line." Then she turned again toward Stanley. "I'll be seeing you tomorrow." She walked by him, her long black dress almost touching his legs. Stanley followed her out.

Evelyn turned back to S.D. and adjusted his cuff so that it covered his mushroom-coloured skin. His mouth looked neutral, not as downturned as it used to be. His lips were dry. She remembered then that the corners of his lips had always been moist, so that he had to lick them to remove the spittle.

She had a sudden impulse to touch him. The impulse twitched in her hands. Stanley's thick voice was far away. She put her finger on S.D.'s hand. It was cold, full and hard, the way that marble in a warm room is cold. He had gone to stone. She touched his forehead, furtively, and

108

then placed her whole hand on his head, as though she could warm him. Against a brutal coldness she felt her own vitality, her full-blooded being. Her hands could touch. They could pick up things, and put them down or drop them. She had been withholding her life from her hands and now wanted, yearned desperately, to bring something to life through them. But it would take a thousand years for his hands, cupped in hers, to be warmed.

The voices stopped.

"Evelyn."

She quickly withdrew her hand and felt ashamed at what she had been doing.

"Evelyn." He was coming. "That's enough. Let's go."

As Evelyn turned away, the image of S.D. lying there, the bony skull beneath the bloated and pretend skin got trapped behind her eyes. She was angry at the stubborn refusal of the living to let the dead look dead, and ashamed for her part in hoping to insinuate warmth into him. He had been mean and stubborn and his son carried on that legacy. She felt unforgiving towards both of them, the living and the dead.

In the car, Evelyn asked about the lady behind the veil Mr. Frank had called Stanley's sister. Stanley would only say, "It's my business and none of yours."

"We've come to pay tribute to a man who was born of this land." The preacher's voice sounded dusty, the way his black suit looked dusty. The huge box at the front of the chapel contained S.D., its lid closed forever.

Evelyn sat between Muriel and Stanley; Ida hadn't been allowed to come to the funeral. Stanley had his fingers pressed into the crooks of his eyes. He always did that in church. S.D. used to sit that way too. Muriel was stiff and straight, holding a white handkerchief.

When Evelyn looked across the aisle, she could see, from beneath Stanley's chin, the veiled profile of Mrs. Mason. She was old-fashioned in her mourning, her face shielded behind a dark veil. Her figure loomed in the crowded chapel amongst S.D.'s survivors. There was something exotic about her; she might have been a rare tropical bird happening by mistake into this frozen place. Evelyn kept peeking at her. She, too, clutched a white handkerchief, but sat immobile through the service; not rigid like her mother or studying a pose, like Stanley. She was a mystery, called Stanley's sister. She was part of what was happening to Stanley and Muriel now that things had changed.

"Sean De'Ath Rathbone loved this land, and fathered it, as he did his children: with discipline and with care..."

So his name was Sean De'Ath Rathbone. Evelyn had never before heard his full name—had never thought of a name other than S.D. He had often been kind to her, but so distant, the way a king is kind. But he'd become weak and he'd fallen into their hands through his illness. And now another daughter was here, Mrs. Mason. And Stanley hated that.

The minister drew in air and exhaled the words. Evelyn wondered if she would cry. The funeral was set up for crying, everyone ready with their handkerchiefs; but she heard no sobs and felt no sadness. She imagined she could see through the oak of the coffin, could see S.D. lying there, pious and satisfied, the way he always looked. She remembered her first meeting with him, when she was taken by her mother to the brick house on Talaru Boulevard. S.D. had looked old, even then. An old king. He had never said very much, but everyone always listened intently when he spoke, and obeyed him. The next day two new dresses had arrived. Muriel had been furious, but she had made Evelyn wear them anyway. It was one of the things that Muriel talked about, late at night. Muriel said how she had been insulted by S.D. Evelyn imagined that for Muriel even his death was a kind of retribution to make up for past wrongs. Marty would use anything as her agent.

But the dark lady was there, too, as an agent of some kind. Stanley's reaction to her guaranteed it. Evelyn was excited.

"We will now commit his body to the earth from which he came." An assistant emerged from the shadows. As the minister spoke, his helper fingered earth onto the coffin in the shape of a cross, the way she had seen her mother spice the food.

Evelyn whispered to Marty, "Don't they put him in the ground?"

"Shh. Too cold. The ground."

But the ground wouldn't thaw until spring. Evelyn didn't understand.

"May his soul rest in peace," intoned the minister.

The assistant positioned himself at the front of the aisle and nodded to Stanley. Kathryn and then Stanley left the pew. Evelyn stood, staring at the coffin with its earth cross. Muriel nudged her, "Go on, follow Stanley."

Stanley was many steps ahead of her. Evelyn flushed with embarrassment. Her hands were fisted at her sides. She unfurled them and spread them out on her thighs. Like Holgate's cats. Her hands were cats, yawning and stretching, rubbing their necks against the black wool of her dress. She liked the sensation of the fabric. She was now at the front of a line; she was queen of this parade. If she stopped the others would have to stop. She was being looked at. And her hands were like cats.

Stanley was standing beside his mother in the foyer. The others filed in, putting on their coats, shaking hands with Stanley, embracing Muriel. Evelyn stood to the side, watching. Clarence walked towards her.

"So, he's gone," he said, putting his hand on her shoulders. His touch came through the woollen sleeve of her dress and onto her skin. She was afraid he would say something unnatural, ask about school, or talk about the weather. She wasn't sad, but she couldn't bear the idea of ordinary talk.

"Who is Mrs. Mason?" she asked. She was sure Clarence would answer.

"Mrs. Mason? Let me introduce you to her."

"We've met."

"Ah," he said, "so you've met her." He paused, as though gathering in old, forgotten information. "She is my sister."

"That's what Mr. Frank said. How could she be? I've never heard of her before."

"No? I guess Stanley doesn't talk about her very much." It was so much an understatement as to be deceitful. "Would you like to speak to her? I'll take you."

"But aren't they going to bury him?" Evelyn was conscious of the unfinished business involving S.D. His coffin was still inside the chapel.

"On Monday."

"Why Monday?"

"Grave-diggers charge more on Saturday. Stanley thought, since the ground was so cold that—" Clarence seemed suddenly perplexed and his sentence trailed off.

Evelyn understood this wasn't the day of S.D.'s burial at all. It was pretend. The outside doors of the chapel opened and closed, breathing frozen air onto the crowd.

Evelyn followed Clarence. Faces loomed at her and nodded, large faces with coarse heavy features, big noses and lips, whispering "hello, how are you," "how are you Evelyn," "still at school, Evelyn." She nodded at them, but didn't reply.

"Maude, I believe you have met our niece, Evelyn. She wanted to talk to you." Clarence stepped back.

Evelyn was blank. She had nothing in her mind to say. Clarence had said, "our niece" and linked her with Mrs. Mason. She was related to this woman. Her face grew hot. Maude Mason was so serene and self-contained. Evelyn felt coarse and heavy like the others, with their big faces and thick lips. This intense discomfort grew until Evelyn blurted out, "I didn't know we were related. I mean, last night. I didn't realize. Until now." The silence around her stumbling speech seemed enormous and pressing.

Finally Maude Mason spoke. "I didn't suppose that you knew who I was."

Evelyn was so grateful for the words, it wouldn't have mattered what she'd said. She repeated the sentence in her mind, squinting hard to gather in all the meaning. She glimpsed it just disappearing beneath the surface of things. She had to get her to talk again.

"Why didn't you suppose I knew?"

"I've been away a long time." There were islands around what Maude said. "Stanley doesn't really like me, I suppose."

Clarence moved forward a step but didn't speak or interfere.

Evelyn felt her hands tingle again. They were thawing out. Her hands were enlivened. Maude Mason was somehow unadorned and truthful, right there on the outside.

"I don't think he likes me either," Evelyn said out loud, urged to meet the truth that surfaced. She turned to see if Clarence was listening, but he had gone.

"No, I wouldn't suppose that he would like you."

The sentence stayed there, lingering amidst the other voices. Evelyn wanted more. "Why?"

"Because he's that way. He doesn't like outsiders."

Everything Maude said was unexpected. "Am I an outsider?"

"I think so. Don't you?"

"Yes, I guess."

"Yes," said Maude Mason, and then a shadow came over her face beneath the veil, a further darkness.

"Well, and how are you, Maude?"

It was Muriel. Evelyn stiffened, mirroring her mother's rigid back.

Muriel had sensed their connection from across the room, the scorched smell of something too hot. The way that a householder knows the common smells and the uncommon ones. The smell of something wrong; not a fire—before a fire: the smell of too much energy.

"Yes?" said Maude, as though she couldn't quite hear where the sound was coming from.

"We've never met. I'm Mrs. Stanley Rathbone." Muriel placed the name out in front of her, like a prickly crown.

"Oh, yes," said Maude.

"We were so surprised you were able to make it. You must have had very short notice."

"Yes. The Rathbones bury their dead very quickly."

"I'm sorry?" It was Muriel who now seemed dumb.

"The Rathbone family buries its dead quickly," Maude repeated, in the same tone of voice: quiet, unassuming, factual.

"Do they?" Muriel said sarcastically, and turned to her daughter. "Evelyn, did you give your respects to your grandmother?"

"No, I..."

"You should have. Do it now. No one is around her."

"Yes, in a minute."

"Now, please." And Muriel left, taking the cold shadow with her.

Evelyn didn't want to leave. "Mrs. Mason are you...are you coming over to the house?"

"To your house?"

"To Stanley's. Everyone is going there afterwards."

"I hadn't been invited."

"I would like you to come."

"I don't know where you live."

"Oh, it's not very far. I'll write it down." Evelyn scribbled the address on a piece of paper she got from her purse. "Where are you staying?"

"At the Plaza."

"Please come." Evelyn turned away, as though turning from a smoldering warmth. She went to her grandmother.

Muriel had redecorated the living-room once again since Christmas. The chair on which Evelyn sat had peacocks this time. Evelyn thought it looked gaudy. She waited on the peacock chair for Maude Mason.

No one had arrived for over an hour. Everyone at the funeral party was drinking and some people were drunk. Muriel was drunk. Even Stanley was starting to confuse his sentences.

Kathryn sat across from Evelyn in the other peacock chair, drinking tea. People went up to the widow and talked in low, respectful tones, but soon there was nothing more to say and they lapsed into poses around her chair, until excused by other mourners. Stanley moved through the room, serving drinks.

"Stanley," Evelyn called out as he passed. "Could I have a sherry, please?"

"No, you can't."

"I'm almost old enough."

"When you earn enough to buy the sherry you can drink it."

"Come on, Stanley," chimed in Mrs. Philmore, a neighbour from the next farm, "this is a special occasion. Don't be such an old grump. Bring a sherry for me, then." She turned to Evelyn. "I hate sherry. Bring me a rye, too," she called after Stanley. Then she leaned over and said in a confidential tone to Evelyn, "Stanley can be a bit tight with the booze, don't you think? I don't mean tight as in drunk, if you know what I mean." Mrs. Philmore winked at Evelyn. "It's okay, dear. I'll pull the booze for you. Stick with me."

Stanley brought the drinks and Mrs. Philmore handed the sherry to Evelyn, who drank a silent toast to Spin. Spin would like Maude Mason.

"He's a chip off the old block, don't you think?" said Mrs. Philmore, still leaning sideways. "That's what I've always said, a chip off the old block. S.D. was tight—if you know what I mean—with more things than the booze. A corker of a bash would have done him a world of good—it would be good for Stanley, too. Loosen him up a bit. They say the old man used to hide his money in the farmhouse—nearly got wiped out when it burned down the first time. He ran back into the house to rescue the money he had stashed in there—threw it out of the top floor of the burning building. Risked his life to save the money. That's what they say. Bet you never heard that story before."

"No, I haven't," said Evelyn.

"Yup, that's what they say. Bet S.D. never told you that one."

"No, he didn't," said Evelyn, turning to see who was at the front door. The party was thinning out and Muriel and Stanley were at the door, saying goodbye. Still Evelyn waited.

"Well," sighed Mrs. Philmore, "I'd better collect my husband and slip away. I guess Stanley's in charge of the realm now. Goodnight, dear."

Clarence moved to Evelyn's side. "I see you've become a lady now, who drinks sherry," he said.

"Only on special occasions."

"Oh, I see."

"I'm afraid Maude Mason isn't going to come."

"Did you expect her?"

Evelyn felt slightly light-headed. "I invited her."

"Oh, you did."

"She's your sister. Don't you think she should be here?"

"I guess you're right. I didn't think about it."

Evelyn had never spoken so directly to Clarence. She was fed up with him. He was being too passive, and thoughtless.

Mr. and Mrs. Philmore were standing beside Kathryn. They had lapsed into idiocy, looking out in the same direction as the widow. They were the last of the outsiders. "Mrs. Rathbone, may we take you home?" Mr. Philmore asked.

"Yes, that would be nice, thank you."

Everyone paid their respects to Kathryn and she left with the Philmores.

Evelyn went to the phone in her mother's bedroom. She had to get Maude Mason to come to the house, otherwise everything would be the same as before. She called the Plaza Hotel.

When Maude answered the phone, Evelyn spoke quickly. "Aunt Maude, you're not here yet so I sent Ron, the cab driver, over to get you, so you wouldn't have to walk. He'll be there any minute, so you should go right down."

Maude Mason sounded flustered when she started to speak but Evelyn wouldn't let her finish. "He'll be right there to get you." And she hung up and phoned the cab.

It was just a small lie. It didn't count, as long as Maude Mason came.

And then she waited. When the doorbell rang, the sound twitched through her. She knew she had done something that might cause trouble. She got up. Her mother was opening the door.

"Yes," said Muriel. Evelyn knew from Muriel's face and voice that it was Maude Mason. "May I help you?" Muriel said.

"It's all right, I asked her to come." Clarence stepped in front of Evelyn. "Come in, Maude, it's very cold out there. Come in, you've just missed Mother. Too bad. You'll see her tomorrow." Evelyn hadn't counted on Clarence taking a part.

Muriel gave Clarence a dark, frayed look and then withdrew. Evelyn was sure she had gone to get Stanley.

Maude Mason wasn't wearing her hat and veil. She looked exposed without them.

Evelyn went forward. "Hello, Aunt Maude. May I take your coat?"

"Yes, thank you." She turned her back and Evelyn touched her shoulders. She had tiny bones beneath the thin coat.

Muriel returned with Stanley. He placed himself in front of Maude Mason. "May I help you," he said. His jaw was set and his chin stuck out.

"Stanley, Maude's just come to be with us," said Clarence, under deliberate calm.

"Why?" said Stanley as blunt as an axe-handle.

115

"Because I asked her to," said Clarence.

A rush of blood went to Evelyn's face at the repeat of the lie. Her hands rested on Maude Mason's shoulders, like lumps of dough. She moved them, tightening her grip. She had to stand her ground. Rudy Truman had said that.

"I see," said Stanley, looking around him as though there was a conspiracy in the air and he couldn't quite discern all of the traitors.

Everyone stopped talking and moving. The old clock in the hall dropped seconds in their midst, sounds that bristled, like the blood in Evelyn's hands. Evelyn brought her hands to action, and continued to remove Maude's coat.

Stanley turned his full face to Maude. "There is nothing here for you," he said, each word creasing the space in front of him.

Everything was strangely bloated—the way Muriel's fingers were after she had been drinking, tight and filled with toxins.

"I'm not sure what you mean," Mrs. Mason said. "I don't want anything from you." Her arms went rigid and she twitched her shoulders so that the coat pulled away from Evelyn's grasp. Maude started fixing it around her. "I will leave if I am not welcome."

"I think you had better leave," cut in Muriel.

"Maude, please, I invited you..." started Clarence.

Maude squirmed under the tug-of-war over her coat. Then she stopped and turned around to face Evelyn. "No, it was you who invited me," she said simply. "You sent the cab."

Stanley and Muriel pulled their heads in unison to stare at Evelyn.

"That's—that's right. I did. I invited her," said Evelyn, putting her hand back on Maude's shoulders. This time, because Maude faced her, the gesture was more intimate than functional.

"You invited her?" said Muriel. "You sent a cab for her?"

"Yes, I did." Evelyn was standing her ground. "She has as much right to be here as I do." She became more confident as she spoke. "And I think all of you are acting like pigs. Just like pigs. Her father died too, you know."

"I'm not so sure about that," said Stanley, and a smirk appeared on his face.

"Clarence and I want you to stay here and visit. I'll take your coat." Evelyn was challenging Stanley outright.

"Sure, Maude, stay," said Stanley, his tone sick with condescension. "No problem. But you should know one thing. You're not entitled to a penny. So, come on in. I'll even give you a glass of wine. Let me help you. I'll even help you with your coat," he said in a sickening tone.

116

Stanley lurched at Maude and almost pulled her coat off. "Hanger, please, Muriel."

"Oh, my," issued from Maude. She rocked slightly, closing her eyes, and then spoke, as calm and quiet as before. "I'm so sorry. I didn't understand. You're worried about the money. Of course, the money. I should have known."

Stanley wheeled around, the coat in one hand and the hanger in the other. He spat out the words, "Don't you tell me you have come here to pay your respects. You sure as hell haven't come because you were devoted to S.D. Don't give me that bull."

Evelyn was stunned at Stanley's violence. "Stop it. Stop it right now," she shouted.

"Don't you dare talk to your father that way," said Muriel.

"He is not my God damned father."

"Evelyn," Muriel yelled.

"Forget it. Just forget it," Evelyn shrieked. She grabbed the coat from Stanley, took her own from the closet and almost pushed Maude out the door. "You're a bunch of assholes. If she isn't wanted, neither am I. Come on, Mrs. Mason." Evelyn grabbed Maude and banged the door shut behind them.

Finally, and certainly, she held out Maude Mason's coat, and helped her put it on. "Let's go." She guided her down the steps and onto the sidewalk.

A meringue of snow covered the earth. Shards of cold pressed down from the moon.

"Where are we going, Evelyn?" asked Maude, querulous and confused.

"I don't know."

They kept walking. Maude still had her boots on, but Evelyn could feel the leather on her shoes start to stiffen. Her intention had taken them only to the street. She was without plans, and felt guilty for exposing Maude Mason to Stanley's rage. She had set it up. She was responsible. "I don't know, where do you think?"

"We could go to my hotel."

"That's a good idea." The two of them could make choices, could decide things. "That's a really good idea. We'll phone Ron at the cafe. Do you...do you have money?"

"Yes, dear, I have money. Despite what Stanley thinks."

They began to walk the two blocks to the cafe in silence. Evelyn was excited again to be with Maude Mason. But as they approached the first corner, Evelyn could hear the sound of tires packing down snow on the road behind them. The sound was hushed and harsh at the same time, the heavy groan of snow being squeezed from a great weight. Headlights caught them. It was Stanley, bearing down on them.

"This way, Aunt Maude." Evelyn gently pulled her off the sidewalk onto the front lawn of the corner house. She guided them between two houses and into the dark. "We'll wait here. Lean against this house." Evelyn pushed her flat against the building. "He can't find us here."

"What is it, dear?"

"It's Stanley."

They were talking in strained whispers that seemed more natural to Maude than to Evelyn.

"Maybe it's Clarence," suggested Maude.

"Clarence wouldn't bring the car. He'd come on foot." They watched the blue Oldsmobile lumber past, its searchlights groping on barren ground. "Nope, it's Stanley."

"But we're not afraid of him, are we?"

The question made Evelyn pause. "No, I guess not."

"Then why are we hiding?"

The question was so obvious, but Evelyn couldn't think of an immediate answer. "I guess because he'd make me go back."

"I see."

"This way." They walked between the houses and down the alley until they reached the main street and the cafe. Evelyn phoned for the cab. When it came, she got in the front seat, and Maude in the back.

"Hi, Ron. Could you take us to the Plaza?"

"Sure. What are you doing out and about?"

"I'm with my aunt. We're going to her hotel."

"Sure. I saw you earlier," Ron said, looking into the rear-view mirror at Maude.

Evelyn watched the streets for Stanley's car.

"Sorry about your grandpa," said Ron. The snow on the main street had been worn away along two black tracks which directed them.

"Yeah," said Evelyn.

"Guess his time was up."

"Yeah," said Evelyn, keeping her lookout.

"How old was he anyway?"

"Really old," said Maude from the back seat.

Ron again looked into the rear-view mirror at Maude. "So, you must be his daughter, then, from out of town. Vancouver is it?"

"Yes. I used to live here."

"Oh, yeah, for sure. A long time ago."

"Yes, that's right. Before your time."

"Yeah. But I heard of you."

"Yes, I would assume so," said Maude in a weary voice.

Mrs. Mason paid Ron and they went into the hotel. She told the desk clerk, "My niece and I are not to be disturbed, please, under any circumstances. In fact, you may tell callers that we are not in." Her voice sounded quiet, but confident, and not unkind. Not the way Stanley talked to people.

The light above the desk in her room was on, and the sheets on the bed were turned down. The room was neat, as though Maude Mason barely occupied it. There was an unopened bottle of sherry on the table.

"Are you old enough to have a drink of sherry with a maiden aunt?" asked Maude Mason.

"Sure."

Maude Mason was trembling slightly as she poured the sherry. "I'm sorry we only have these horrid water glasses. I always think the container makes a difference. I suppose we could ask for others to be sent up. Do you think we should?"

"I guess they wouldn't have any others here."

"No, I suppose not." Maude Mason handed her a glass. "Shall we have a toast? To S.D., I think."

Evelyn raised her glass and sipped the sherry. She felt suddenly shy and awkward, afraid she wouldn't have anything to say. "I was sure surprised to see you at the funeral home."

"Yes, I expect so."

"Did you like him?"

"S.D? Well, yes of course I did. But he was what you might call— how can I say this nicely—a tyrant I think."

"People figure Stanley is just like him. He's a bully, too. Pushes people around."

"Except your mother. I don't expect he pushes her around."

"They take turns, I guess. How come they're so awful to you? And Stanley never talked about you before."

"The family's divided up. There's another sister as well. Isabel. Have you never heard of her?"

"Isabel? No, I don't think so." The name was vaguely familiar to Evelyn. It stirred memory in the shape of a circle. Maude's name was part of the circle. "Is that Isa-bel? Sure, Isa-bel. That's what I called her. I only saw the name written, a long time ago."

"Isa-bel. That's interesting." Maude looked way past Evelyn, and seemed to take distant pleasure in the new name.

"I think I did hear about you before, one night."

"Isabel would enjoy that. Isa-bel. I must tell her."

"Isabel is still alive?"

"Oh, yes. I live with her."

It was as though Evelyn had found a whole new set of rooms in a house that had been too small. "Why didn't Isabel come for the funeral?"

"I guess she's smarter than I am."

"You're not married?"

"My husband died. Two years ago. Then Isabel moved in with me."

"And is she married?"

"No, no she's not."

Evelyn had so many questions now, questions which she could barely formulate. Vast permission had opened around her. "How come everyone's divided up?" she finally asked.

"Splits happened in this family, from a long time ago. It's more obvious now that S.D. is dead."

"Why did you come back?"

"Why? That's a good question. I haven't been here for a long time. Not for a very long time. I'm the one who comes back, I guess."

"Not Isabel?"

"No, no she doesn't. I thought I'd make one last visit. See my mother, pay my respects." Maude leaned forward with an air of confidence. "You know, I am part of this family. So is Isabel." Maude leaned back again and looked past Evelyn. "He thought he'd gotten rid of me."

"Stanley?"

"Yes, Stanley."

"Did you think you'd shake him up then, about money?"

"He doesn't like to see me. I remind him of bad things, I guess. He's always been worried about money."

"Because he thinks you'll take S.D.'s money?"

"I don't know. I won't make a claim, of course. But he's nervous about me." Maude's thin mouth was turned up at the corners, ever so slightly. It gave her an abstract, sinister look.

"What would you claim?"

"Nothing, really. I only wanted to remind him that I'm part of this family. So is Isabel. And I wanted to see my mother again."

"Stanley has enough money, that's for sure."

"No, I don't think Stanley can ever have enough money. Never enough." And she drifted again, her mouth as thin as the pencil line on her eyebrows. Evelyn thought that her lips looked sealed.

"They went to the lawyers yesterday. Did you know that?"

"Mm."

"They went to the lawyers," Evelyn repeated.

"Yes, the lawyers. S.D. always hated lawyers."

"So does Stanley."

"Yes, that's right."

Evelyn decided that Maude Mason would only confirm the truth, she wouldn't reveal it. Evelyn would have to guess first.

"They probably talked about the money with the lawyers. They probably talked about you. I guess that's why it was on Stanley's mind when you came to the house."

"Yes, that's right. I expect they did."

"It seems unfair, that you shouldn't be part of it—that you wouldn't get something. You and Isabel."

"It doesn't matter. This is enough." Maude seemed to wake up slightly. "I didn't want to go to the house, but then I didn't really expect such a to-do. But never mind. Now I've met you, which is very pleasant. And you need more sherry." Maude took the bottle and filled the glasses again.

Evelyn had to bring her out, encourage her to talk. "You know," she said, "I always thought S.D. was kind of miserly. That's what my mother said. But sometimes he did nice things. When we first moved here, he bought me some new clothes."

"Yes, he would do that. He was fair, in his way. He was always fair in the long run."

Evelyn realized she wanted to hurt Stanley and Muriel, and not just let them win. She would be Maude's champion. But Maude was so neat and timid, taking such small steps. Evelyn wanted her to punch out, to use her hands.

"How do you know that he was fair in the long run?" she pressed.

"I know he was fair."

"Nobody else knows that. Stanley's just like S.D. He always gets his own way."

"Oh, that's all right."

Anger suddenly fronted in Evelyn. A snowball cracked on the cold glass. Maude Mason would let everything go on just as before.

"But you've given up. You've quit. He's rude to you. He's glad 'cause he beat you."

"No, I don't think he did, really. Not really."

"But how do you know? You've got nothing to prove it. Stanley wins."

"Oh, I don't think so. I know. I can prove S.D. was fair."

"How can you prove it?" Evelyn prodded.

"I have a piece of paper."

"You've got a paper—you've got something written by S.D.?"

"Actually I have many pieces of paper."

"Lots of paper. That's what we need." Maybe they could get back at Stanley and Muriel with lots of paper that proved they lied.

"Just little pieces, though. Small pieces." Maude was starting to move now.

"Have you got them here? Couldn't we see them?" Evelyn felt the full excitement of a kind of revenge.

"Yes, we could. We could. Just for fun."

Maude got her purse and brought out a sealed brown envelope. "It hasn't been opened," she said with great secrecy. "It's been sealed."

"Do you know what's inside?"

"Yes. I sealed it."

"But did you just get this, because of Stanley?" Evelyn was half afraid she had gone too far again, and would be stopped.

"Oh, no. I have it with me all the time."

Just as Maude started to open the envelope the phone rang, a sound that was like a tearing through the room.

"I'll get it," said Evelyn. It was the man at the desk. "Someone is coming up, Aunt Maude. The man couldn't stop him. He took the register and saw where—"

There was a loud banging on the door.

The two of them froze, Evelyn with her hand over the receiver, and Maude with her hand inside the envelope.

"It must be Stanley," whispered Evelyn.

Maude put down the envelope and said in her natural voice, "Yes, I expect it is Stanley." She had composed herself, but still she didn't move.

"But what will we do?" said Evelyn. She hung up the phone. She was scared. He would take her back, the way he had before. She'd be repossessed for the last time.

"Let him in. Go to the door, please."

"Couldn't we just pretend we're not here?"

"No. Please let him in."

Evelyn went to the door. Her knees were tight and only thin wires connected her to the ground, stretched wires that could snap.

"Who is it?" she asked through the door.

Stanley's voice bellowed, "You know damn well who it is. Open up."

Evelyn turned the handle which released the lock. He pushed the door open. His face was huge and bloated. He cleared Evelyn out of the way and entered the room.

"What do you mean by this? Telling the desk clerk you weren't here, making me ridiculous in front of him. I've been out on the streets looking for you." Stanley gnarled and soured the air. But Mrs. Mason sat calmly in the milky light.

"Stanley, you are not in your own home. Please lower your voice. If not, you may leave." Stanley deflated as though he'd been stuck with a hat pin. It took him a minute to recover, to puff himself up again.

"I've come for my daughter," he said.

Evelyn flinched. It was all wrong. Stanley was all wrong.

"She can come or go as she pleases. Ask her, don't ask me."

Maude Mason wouldn't protect her. She had to stand her own ground. But she was repulsed by this man.

"I'm not asking anyone, I'm telling," Stanley shouted.

"Oh, I don't think so Stanley. You'd better quiet down." Still Maude Mason was calm and purposive.

"Look, I know what you're up to. You can't fool me. You leave my family alone."

Evelyn looked at him from behind Maude Mason, who was still sitting at the desk, the brown envelope in front of her. Maude Mason rose from her place. She rose like a slow sun, until she was high and bright in the room. And then everything narrowed to a thin blade, to a needle point.

"You stay back. You stay out of here," she said. "Stay out or I shall call the police."

"You bitch." Stanley's fists were clenched. "The police? We'll see who will be calling the police."

He stepped forward. Evelyn moved towards him and held up her arm as Stanley's belly pushed against her, fat and soft.

"Get out of my way." Stanley wiped his arm in front of him, knocking Evelyn against Maude Mason. The door slammed, and he was gone.

Evelyn's arm carried the imprint of her step-father.

Maude Mason sat with her head in her hands, slumped over and tiny. "It's okay, Aunt Maude." Evelyn poured her a glass of sherry. "Here, drink this."

"We were having fun," said Maude, despairing.

Evelyn could barely make out the words. "Please, drink this." She put her hand on Maude Mason's head, awkwardly, trying to comfort her. She didn't know how to touch her.

"We were having fun," Maude said again.

"Yes, we were."

"Spoiled. Like a rotten apple."

"I'm sorry?" Evelyn leaned over to hear the words.

"Rotten apple. In the bag. Spoiled. Everything spoiled and ruined."

"Not ruined," said Evelyn. "He can't spoil everything. Please."
Evelyn was desperate to comfort, desperate to keep Maude Mason from defeat.

"Spoiled dead..." She seemed to have collapsed.

"I can't hear you, Aunt Maude," Evelyn whispered.

And then Maude raised her head. Her face was contorted and ugly.

"I'm bad," Maude said. "Rotten. Bad." And then she shrank again, covering her face.

"I don't think you're bad." Evelyn touched Maude's hair and pushed it back from her forehead. It was thin and dank.

"S.D. hated me." Again Maude looked up, but this time she seemed vicious, like a mad dog.

"Stanley hates me. He hates me because I'm born of sin; I'm from the devil."

Evelyn thought Maude must be hysterical. "The devil..."

"The devil. I'm not his sister. I'm from another place."

Evelyn sat down.

"My sister is my mother."

The snowball hit Evelyn squarely on the face.

"Isabel is my mother."

"Isa-bel is your mother?" Evelyn's urgency dissolved into confusion.
It was an enormous puzzle. "Isabel your mother. And Stanley is... your uncle, not your brother." She couldn't figure it out. "And Stanley's not my father. He's never been my father." She hesitated. "Your father is your grandfather. But it's all so—mixed up." Now it was absurd.
Evelyn started to laugh. It was a dull tickle just at the back of her mouth where she couldn't reach it with her tongue. It was a hoax. A joke. "Isabel is your mother. But who is related to who? Who are we all?"
Everything was upside down and backwards.

"You're laughing," said Maude, her face wide open and white.

"It's a wise child..." said Evelyn from within her suppressed laughter.

"Wise child?"

"It's a wise child who knows her own sister. Is that how it goes?"

"Wise child? No, it's a wise father who knows....Oh, I don't remember." And they both started laughing, slowly, something breaking up. And then they were laughing hard until Maude was crying and laughing.

"Stop. This happened before," Maude said.

"Before," laughed Evelyn, as though the word was the punch-line of a great joke.

"No, no I can't. Stop. I don't know if I'm laughing or crying."

And they laughed again until the string on the yo-yo reached the end and started rewinding, laughing up to the top, crying down to the bottom.

"What shall we do?" Maude Mason was sober again. She brought Evelyn down.

"Yes, what shall we do?" Evelyn tried to be serious. "Who was your father, then?" she asked, getting back inside the puzzle.

"Who knows?"

"I don't know who my father was either."

"You don't? No, of course you don't."

"Of course I don't." Evelyn unconsciously fingered the envelope and then turned it upside down. Tiny bits of paper snowed out. "More puzzle."

"Puzzle," echoed Maude, with a tiny splutter of laughter.

Evelyn began to turn the pieces over. Maude started to help her.

"This is our proof?" asked Evelyn in disbelief.

"Mm."

It seemed pitiful. "Where did you get this?"

"It's S.D.'s will."

"His will?" She had to contain herself from the riot of laughter. "How did you get it?"

"One night S.D. wanted us to know what was in his will. Stanley made S.D. rip it up."

"Well, this is great. This is our proof. You're in."

"I don't know. I never looked."

"We have to find out. This is our proof," said Evelyn.

The two of them worked with concentration, piecing together the words of a strange language.

"Be—what does 'be' go with?" asked Evelyn.

"'Be'. I have a 'queath.' 'Bequeath.'"

"Here's your name. Maude, that's you. Where's the Mason. Have you got a Mason?"

The task was arduous and absurd. Suddenly Evelyn stopped.

"Listen, this is taking too long. Stanley's going to—he's gonna do something. He'll call the police. We'd better get out of here." Evelyn started to pick up the pieces of the will. "We need more time to fit this all together." She couldn't think where to go. There was no safe place now.

"I'll go back home," said Maude.

The thought of Maude leaving her was impossible. "Can I come with you?"

"Oh no, I don't think so. You have no clothes. And they'll be worried about you."

"That's okay. It'll be better if I come with you."

Evelyn helped Maude pack. Within minutes they were in the cab. Because the train didn't leave for an hour, they drove around in Ron's taxi, not wanting to be seen at the station.

"I know a place, down by the river, where there are trees. We could wait there," said Evelyn. And they drove to the river, where Evelyn had been years ago, wearing Rudy Truman's sweater. Evelyn told Maude the story of running away with the picture. She had never told anyone before.

The table in the bedroom compartment had been pulled out and they headed west, hunched over the tattered scraps of paper, trying to make order. It was one o'clock in the morning.

Evelyn decided she was happier than she had ever been in her life. The sound of the miles clacking beneath her seemed to snip the thin webs that had covered her face and eyes for years.

"You must be tired, dear," said Maude.

"I'm wide awake. What goes with 'volve'?"

"'In,' 'involve.' Can you find an 'in'?"

"There are lots of 'ins.'"

"We should sleep."

"You go to bed. I'll see if I can find some tape to keep this together."

"All right dear."

"Guess what. S.D. hasn't even been buried yet."

"No, that's right."

"Not by a long shot," said Evelyn with satisfaction. "Where will we be tomorrow?"

"In British Columbia. That will be nice."

Evelyn kissed her on the cheek, on the soft powdery skin. "Thank you, Aunt Maude."

She closed the door and walked forward in the same direction as the train was moving. She imagined going footsteps faster than the train. She rocked through the narrow mysterious aisles of the sleeping cars, the dark folds of curtains funnelled on either side of her. She opened the heavy door between the cars, where the terrifying ground of shifting metal plates and screaming wheels scared her. She pushed into the silence of the next sleeping car.

The dark curtains pressed so close that she felt small again, as though

126

in the school cloakroom of heavy winter coats on the day she showed the picture to Helen and ran away. The memory was terrifying and delicious to her, like stolen candy. She sucked in her breath and held it to contain her joy. She wanted to yell, to holler something above the clacking and rocking of the train, something that would zing white light over the dark snow, on the flat land she was leaving. Something sizzling, hot electric and indestructible, clearing a pathway ahead of her. A white pathway through the black notes.

In the observation car with the full sky panoplied above her, she was in a perfect place: moving, yet standing still. She was neither here nor there. The old cloakroom surrounded her, but did not contain her. She was alive over the land. No one could touch her now.

As a child she used to climb over the back seat of the car and lie against the window, watching the sky that covered her, riding through the night. The smell of dusty seat covers seemed like the smell of the sky. It had been perfect then. She possessed everything, and everything welcomed her. The dusty sky welcomed her. There were no black notes.

She was safe again on this train. She was back in the world that had abandoned her. In between, time had been a soft place of waiting for something that might never come. Now she was a conqueror. She had a kingdom.

The steward nodded to her as she walked to her car, against the direction she was going, against the texture of her journey. It felt awkward, the way her hair felt when she forced it the wrong way. She was half afraid that she would be sucked back to Stanley and her mother; she would slide on the ice and fall into their open grasp.

When she reached the door of the room, she opened it quietly. Maude was asleep. The jigsaw puzzle lay on the table. She had forgotten to ask the steward for tape.

Evelyn began to number the pieces that went together. She needed an outlet for the energy which bristled in her hands and all through her body. She channelled it into the puzzle that lay scattered on the table and floor, to make order out of the shapes. Some of the sentences she had made sounded so strange. Lines that read "if any child of mine, then alive," and "at the time of my death." These were S.D.'s words, with capital letters for "I DIRECT," "I WILL": commanding, declaring, pointing. Pointing at Evelyn. The words were S.D.'s voice, telling everyone what to do. Stanley and Muriel had managed not to listen; they hadn't even buried the poor bugger.

Evelyn smoothed out the pieces that declared "My daughter, Maude Mason." That was the important part. There she was, acknowledged as one of them, as an owner, as an inheritor. Instead of numbering those pieces, she put stars on the back. Maude Mason had a special place. She was a daughter to her father, to grumpy old S.D. And Stanley and Muriel couldn't lie any more and try to make it different. The will could be mended, taped back together, connected. As each piece was fit into the puzzle, Evelyn felt restored. Her father's picture had been torn out of some larger puzzle, the rest of which was hidden by her mother. This task softened that fact.

Finally Evelyn turned off the light and raised the thick window shade to see outside. The night was as black as the centre of her mother's eyes. She pulled down the shade.

She climbed the ladder to the top berth, undressed and fell asleep.

Evelyn hated it whenever the train stopped. Someone might come and get them. As she and Maude worked on the puzzle, ate and slept, she was alert and distracted at every station. She had asked the steward how many stops there were between Calgary and Vancouver, and she kept count on the brown puzzle envelope, marking them with match-stick lines. Finally Maude asked her what she was counting.

"Number of times we stop."

"Why is that?"

"To see how many we have left."

Mrs. Mason's ancient passivity waned and enormous impatience entered her voice. "Yes, dear, I understood that that was likely the case. Please answer my question."

Evelyn felt rebuked, as though caught lying. "Every time we stop, I get scared that Stanley is going to come in, or the police. So I'm counting the times."

"They are numberless."

"Pardon?"

"The time you have left to be afraid." And Mrs. Mason went back to shifting the bits of paper.

Evelyn had thought the marks on the envelope would reach a maximum number and then it would be over. Instead, it seemed she was counting her fear as part of an infinite progression of fear.

"Are you afraid?" Evelyn asked.

"Yes, dear," said Maude, picking up a piece of paper, and still not looking at Evelyn. "Does that surprise you?"

"You don't seem scared."

"Oh, I'm not scared, I'm afraid."

"What's the difference?"

"I'm not scared about a particular result, or any special thing. Like the police at the next stop. I'm not scared of that. I'm just afraid."

"But what of?"

"I don't know."

"I don't want to be afraid of everything," said Evelyn.

The idea of being afraid in the way Maude Mason was saying—afraid of everything—was terrible. Things could only be held together through some enormous effort; they'd always be ready to fall apart.

"I want to be certain," said Evelyn, as though putting her stake in the ground and declaring herself.

"Yes, of course you do." Maude Mason was suddenly vague and condescending.

"But don't *you* care about this?" asked Evelyn, pointing to the paper. "About being in the will?"

"Yes, right now I do."

"So if we can get this right, then we're certain. You don't have to be afraid." To Evelyn, Maude's comfort and her own had become the same thing.

"But I've told you, they're not the same, being certain and not being afraid."

"I don't know what you mean."

"No, I suppose you don't."

Evelyn had lost her confidence. She was again standing between the cars of the train, the clack clack sounding horribly in her head as the rushing ground blared at her between the steel plates. She was with Maude Mason who was afraid too and couldn't hold things together.

Evelyn felt homesick for a place she didn't even know existed. She felt lonely for her secure place near the river, waiting. Her mouth tightened and then turned down. She felt her face being marked with the first creases in a mask that would grow old.

"What do you think goes at the end of 'inter'?" asked Maude, carrying on with the task.

Evelyn couldn't hear. Everything yawned and gaped. Maude Mason was thin and insubstantial. "What shall we do?"

"Do?" repeated Maude.

Evelyn could feel tears streaming at the corners of her eyes but when she touched her face it was dry. The tears were behind her face.

"If the police come."

"We're not doing anything wrong. Are we?"

"I don't think so."

"We'll just do what we're doing," Maude said, simply.

"But can't we protect ourselves? Stanley will have Muriel to help him." She thought for a moment. "My teacher. I'll call her at the next stop. She'll help us decide what to do."

"That's an idea."

"What day is it?"

"Sunday."

"They'll be expecting me at school tomorrow."

"Monday. Yes, I suppose so." Maude was still vague and closed off.

"But will I go back?" Evelyn's mouth tasted sour.

"I don't know. Will you?"

"But do you think I should?"

"Well, you've only just gotten away."

"Yes, but do you want me to?" She ached for reassurance and belonging.

"No, we're on our way to Vancouver."

"I'll find a steward and ask when the next stop is." Evelyn left the cabin.

Maude Mason hunched over the scraps of paper—they were scraps to her. Evelyn was trying to make them into a map, a seamed and flawed map. Maude couldn't find her way with this map. Maybe Isabel would be able to.

She had the child now, but not for long. Stanley would do something to take her away. She desperately wanted to keep Evelyn with her. She had never before wanted a child of her own. But she couldn't keep her. Evelyn wasn't hers. She had to remember that. She would try to stay distant, try not to mark the child.

The line had to be drawn; she must not raise false hopes. Whether she was in or out of the will was of no consequence, except that it brought her closer to Evelyn. Isabel was at the end of their journey; she could read maps. She might even care about this map. She would, no matter what, have a lot to say. Evelyn must not depend on her, either. That was dangerous. More dangerous than anything else. Maude had to stay back. Not seem to care. After all, she didn't; she didn't really care; it didn't matter what happened.

Evelyn found a phone booth inside the station and made a collect call to Spin's number.

"Collect call for you from Evelyn," said the operator. "Will you accept the charges?"

"Evelyn?"

"Spin?" said Evelyn, "Oh, my God..."

The operator interrupted. "I'm sorry, do you accept the charges?"

"Yes, yes of course I do." The operator clicked off. "Where are you?"

Evelyn couldn't talk. She felt collapsed: of will, of strength, of all initiative. She was bone-tired.

"Evelyn, are you there? Is everything—are you all right? Talk to me."

"I can't." Evelyn had to concentrate on not telling, on holding back the tears.

"Let me ask you questions. Are you at home?"

Evelyn was able to get out, "No."

"Are you safe?"

"Yes."

"All right, you're safe. Are you alone?"

"No."

"Are you in trouble?"

"Yes."

"Evelyn, please, try to talk. I can't think of all the questions."

"Spin, I'm afraid." She spluttered out the word she had learned from Maude Mason, the word that took up a world.

"All right, start from the beginning."

The words came out between sobs and gasps for breath.

"I've run away with my aunt. I think she's my aunt. I'm going to Vancouver. Maybe the police are coming."

"The police, what for?"

"To take me back. To Stanley and Muriel."

"Where are you now?"

"At a train stop."

"Where?"

"I don't know."

"But why did you leave?"

"Stanley."

"What did he do? Did he hurt you?"

"No. My aunt was there. Everyone ignored her. I wanted her to come over to the house. So then she came but everyone was awful to her, just awful. So then we left, and Stanley came and said he was going to call the police. So we got on the train."

"Oh my. What can I do? Shall I call your mother?"

"No. Don't call her."

"What shall I do?"

Evelyn didn't know. She could only think of the names that had looped

in the circle of a dream years ago. Timothy, Maude, Clarence.
"Clarence. Call Clarence."

"Clarence who?"

"Clarence Rathbone. My uncle. He lives in Elmore. On 6 Raftor
Avenue. Ask him if they sent the police. Don't tell him where I am."

"But I don't know where you are."

"Don't tell him anything. Find out what they're doing. My train is
leaving—I'll phone you from the next stop."

"All right."

"I miss you." Evelyn hurt to say that; she felt tiny paper cuts on her
fingers.

"You may need some legal advice, I suppose, if the police are
involved."

"You mean like lawyers?"

"I'll phone a lawyer I know in Vancouver. Maybe she can help."

Evelyn felt better now, walking back to the train, now that she was
doing something practical. She was able to think. Her fear subsided.

"My teacher is going to help us."

"Oh, yes," said Maude, distant and abstract.

"She's going to phone Clarence and find out what's happening. I'll
call her from the next stop. She's going to phone a lawyer. In Vancouver.
We need to protect ourselves. Do you know any lawyers?"

"No, not really."

"Spin will get us one."

"Spin?"

"My teacher."

"That's an odd name for a teacher."

"Nickname. What do you think?"

"Yes, that's fine, dear."

"Can you pay for a lawyer?"

"A lawyer?" Maude had trouble focussing; Evelyn was too excited.

"One who could meet us at the station."

"Do lawyers meet trains?"

"We need one right away. To protect us."

"Yes, that's fine dear."

At the next stop Evelyn called Spin again.

Evelyn was floating high like the tags ribboning at the end of a kite.
She was anchored to the earth by her teacher. Now she could breathe.
The space around her seemed enormous.

As the operator put through the call, Evelyn sensed that there was
another note sounding, not made by the black or white keys; it was an

over-note, a third sound in the air. There it was. A sound that created itself from nothing. Maybe she didn't have to be quite so certain about everything any more.

Spin came on the line.

"Did you get Clarence?" Evelyn asked.

"You and Mrs. Mason have caused quite a stir, my girl, quite a stir."

"Have they got the police after us?"

"Yes."

"They have? Oh my God." Evelyn was afraid again; there were only the black and white notes, making their contrary sounds.

"I've called them off. Stanley says he's going to charge Mrs. Mason."

"Charge Aunt Maude? With what?"

"I'm not sure. Even Clarence wasn't sure. With some sort of crime."

"That's crazy. What's she done wrong?"

"I think I've convinced Clarence, at least, to hold Stanley off for a bit and let me try to handle it. But I have to give them something in return."

"Like what?"

"Some reason to trust me. Will you phone them, and speak to Stanley?"

"No."

"All right. Will you go back home?"

"No."

"I see. Then will you meet with me?"

"Sure."

"All right, I'll try to make arrangements here with my classes, and fly to Vancouver. I'll make contact with your mother and tell her, tell her that I'll be meeting with you."

"No, don't. Only tell Clarence. He can tell Marty."

"Marty?"

"Marty, my mother. Did you get us a lawyer?"

"I phoned a lawyer. I hope that won't be necessary, though, to have a lawyer."

"Could you both meet the train, you and the lawyer?"

"I suppose. I must say, your family is a bit unusual."

"Yes, like you've always said. Spin, is it going to be all right?"

"Well—I'll try my best. I'll have to convince someone—maybe Clarence. It seems pretty serious now."

And their talk ended.

By the time they arrived in Vancouver, Maude and Evelyn had pieced the will together. Maude said it had been "rehabilitated."

They walked into the crowded hollow of the station. They had been tunnelling across the country to a foreign city; now they were above on firm ground. Strange smells were in the air. Excitement was in the air. The crescendo of voices played on the vaulted ceiling of the station like searchlights. Evelyn sucked on the roof of her mouth.

Spin was waiting for them with Miss Norpin, the lawyer. Miss Norpin was Maude's age, and very efficient, the way a lawyer should be. She arranged for a taxi to take them to her office.

Evelyn got in between Spin and Maude in the back seat of the cab. She loved being in the centre of this new turmoil. She couldn't remember ever being afraid. While winter froze the ground in Saskatchewan, here there was green grass, like a brilliant promise, underneath a thin sheet of ice in front of the station. It seemed unnatural and exciting to Evelyn. The trees were stark but not dead: a pledge of warmth, an expectation of fulfillment. It was a feeling that was associated with the company of her teacher.

The lawyer directed the cab driver to a high rise office building. The attendant, slumped at the desk inside the building, was asleep. Miss Norpin signed a large book without waking him. Then they took the elevator that was marked "Floors 12-39," to a board room at the top of the building at eye level with the mountains.

Miss Norpin opened a black binder and began writing.

"Now I understand from Miss Holgate that she has advised some of the family she would be meeting you here, in Vancouver, to attempt a resolution of this matter. That's fine. I need some background information, so that I understand the picture. Mrs. Mason, your marital status, please?"

"Married."

"Husband's name?"

"Geoffrey."

"His age?"

"Oh, I'm sorry. He's dead."

"You're a widow," said Miss Norpin, dryly, not changing pace, working the facts into her black binder on the table.

"Your father is?"

"Dead."

"Yes. His name?" She looked down as she asked the questions, receiving the information like an officer or a guard at the border of a country.

"We called him S.D."

"Stands for?" Miss Norpin lifted her head and peered above the rim of her glasses, as though wielding a heavy burden.

"Sean De'Ath Rathbone."

"Your date of birth."

"April 21, 1915."

The questions went on in military fashion: the details, the facts of a life. Then she turned her attention to Evelyn and started at the top of the list. She came to the question of father, and Evelyn said, "I don't know."

"Surrogate father?"

Evelyn didn't know what 'surrogate' meant.

"Your mother's husband, Stanley Rathbone"—and she looked up at Spin—"is he acting in the role of her father?" Spin nodded. Miss Norpin went on. "Mother?"

"Muriel Paul. Muriel Rathbone."

"What age were you when your mother re-married?" Miss Norpin's tone softened.

The question wasn't right. She felt hemmed in. All her excitement was being crated up.

"Re-married, to Mr. Rathbone," Miss Norpin said.

"We moved to Elmore in 1948. About then, I guess."

Miss Norpin blinked rapidly a few times as though sand or dust had been tossed at her. "And you've come to Vancouver, from Saskatchewan, of your own free will, with Mrs. Mason?"

Evelyn looked at Spin and then said, "Oh, yes. I wanted to come here."

"All right." Miss Norpin spent a long time over her book, everyone fixed on the tiny indecipherable words she wrote. As she turned each page she made a bold, almost aggressive line down the right side of the paper. Every now and then she wrote something in the free zone inside the right margin she had created. The room was quiet.

"Why did you get on the train?" Miss Norpin teased out the question.

"You see, Maude Mason is named in the will—the one that Stanley destroyed. He's doing all this because of the will, that's what I think. We've pieced it together. Stanley's trying to cut her out." The words tumbled from her mouth.

The lawyer looked at Maude Mason. "The will?"

"Thank you for your help," said Maude. "I must phone Isabel. She'll be wondering where I am." She got up from the table and opened the door. "Just carry on," she said, and closed the door behind her.

"Mrs. Mason," the lawyer called after her. But the door had closed. "I'm not sure I understand. Who is Isabel?" She seemed to flounder.

"Her sister," said Evelyn automatically.

"This is a serious matter. Mrs. Mason should not leave." The lawyer examined her papers as though some secret were contained there.

Evelyn continued, not noticing that the lawyer was displeased. "I'm not sure we put it together right. We did it on the train. Stanley thinks it's gone. He doesn't know about this." Evelyn brought out the tattered patchwork paper. The will was their salvation, and she was almost reluctant to give it to the lawyer. Miss Norpin handled it as though it were unclean.

"You say that Stanley will lay charges because of a dispute over this will?"

"Yes," said Evelyn, and then, afraid of being absolutely certain, added, "That's what I think, anyway."

Miss Norpin studied the paper, and asked more questions about the names of everyone mentioned in the will. Evelyn answered, without mentioning the question of Maude's real father.

"Miss Holgate, would you mind finding Mrs. Mason for me, please?" said Miss Norpin. She resumed studying the will as Spin left the room. "These are very serious allegations, Evelyn," said the lawyer in a confidential tone. "These things—I hope you understand—could split your family apart. Do you understand that?"

"But it's already split." The lawyer stared at her as though she could make Evelyn back down by long looking. "It's the truth."

"There will be different versions of the truth."

"Things shouldn't be hidden any more."

"All right." Miss Norpin put down the paper and sighed. "All right. And you say the issue isn't that you left Saskatchewan with Mrs. Mason, but because your father is trying to challenge your aunt, under the will."

"Yes. My step-father. Stanley."

Spin brought Maude back into the room.

"Mrs. Mason, it appears we have grounds to contest whatever charges are laid. There also may well be grounds to prove the intention behind this will. We'll have to examine that in more detail. May I have your instructions to proceed on both these matters?"

"Proceed?" asked Maude Mason.

"Yes, to establish this as the will and to defend you, if necessary."

"I don't need defending." She paused. "Do I, Evelyn?"

"No, I don't think so. I mean, you haven't done anything wrong, just like you said."

"You go ahead then and do what you have to do. I couldn't get Isabel. She may be out having her hair done."

"I'll call you tomorrow," said the lawyer. "Let me get you a cab."

The three left the office. When they reached the door of the home shared by the two Rathbones, Maude couldn't find her keys. While she was checking her bags, a tall portly woman opened the door. She was dressed in lavender, and the collar of her dress rose high onto her neck, raising her chin up. She looked down on them.

"Oh, Isabel. This is Evelyn, our niece, and this is Evelyn's teacher, Miss Holgate. They've come for a visit."

"Haven't you got your key, Maude?" asked Isabel, nodding to the guests. "You should always make sure about your key. Please, come in, come in."

Isabel didn't know anything about what had happened, yet she started making coffee and tending to her guests as though they had long been expected. She accepted the return of Maude in the company of strangers as though it only meant taking four cups and saucers from the cupboard instead of two. Evelyn hated that.

If Isabel was, in fact, Maude's mother, the secret was sunk into the household, deeply hidden. Evelyn was on the trail of it: her limbs had energy to disgorge all that had been so carefully buried. Yet her face was at odds with itself, like a face pressed inside a nylon stocking.

"Tell me all about it, then. Evelyn, you're Stanley's adopted daughter. And were you at the funeral?"

"Yes." But her voice felt distorted and bagged.

"And Miss Holgate?"

"No, no I wasn't."

"Ah, too bad. Cookie?" She handed the plate to Spin as though making amends for her missing the funeral. "Maudie, there are other sweets just cooling, could you get them?"

Isabel was silent as Maude left the room and returned with a plate of cake. "So, is everything all right?" she asked, turning to Maude, and smiling a doughy fixed smile that seemed to Evelyn to be full of caution. "I mean—well, will our guests be staying long? They are very welcome. For as long as they want."

Isabel gave and took at the same time.

"Oh yes, Miss Holgate is Evelyn's teacher," Maude repeated. "She has a plane to catch some time. But Evelyn is here to help us." The end of Maude's sentence rose to a question.

"Miss Holgate, did you fly here, from Saskatchewan?" Isabel ignored the last part of Maude's statement but Evelyn was sure she had just pocketted it for later.

"No, I didn't. I'm teaching in Winnipeg."

"Yes. More coffee?"

"No, I'm fine, thank you."

"And you're here because of Evelyn?"

"Yes, that's right. I'm really not sure I can be of much help any more. The matter seems to have gone beyond..."

Isabel cut her off. "Well, that's nice. And your plane goes..."

"Tomorrow."

"Good. There's plenty of room here. Maude, is the guest room neat?"

"Well, I don't know. It's never not neat, is it?" said Maude, helpful and uncertain.

"No, I suppose not. I hope you don't mind sharing a room. I have a roast for dinner. Evelyn, you go to school in Winnipeg?"

"Yes, I do."

"I see."

Maude, as though trying to lift the weight of a heavy curtain, said, "We had an interesting time at S.D's funeral. There was—quite a to-do."

"He did get buried, didn't he? It would be so like him not to."

"Well, he didn't actually, at least not on the day of the funeral. The ground was too hard," said Maude.

"Too hard? Good heavens, are they going to wait until spring?"

The curtain was stuck and the light on the conversation was diffused.

"People do get buried in the winter, in Saskatchewan," Isabel continued. "I supposed it's the same in Winnipeg, Miss Holgate?"

"It's very cold there. I do prefer this climate, as much as I've seen of it," said Holgate, folding into the confusion.

Evelyn was crazy with impatience. There was so much to be done, so much to discuss, and instead Isabel herded the conversation into trivia. Evelyn wanted to claw something, to scratch. Underneath her impatience was a fear of the lethargy of deceit which Isabel induced. Evelyn would not wait any more.

"I take it, then, you haven't been to the west coast before?" continued Isabel.

"No, I haven't actually. Although I've been to the east coast. It's quite different."

Evelyn hated Isabel. She hated the way Isabel talked. She hated the way Isabel looked, the solid weight of her body sitting there. Maude was dormant. Even Spin, who preached courage, was trapped into compliance.

"I had supposed you could dig a grave any time," said Isabel.

"Of course you can," said Spin.

"It's just a question of money," added Maude.

"Well, he'll get buried eventually." Isabel turned to Maude. "Did you mind that I wasn't there?" It was the first question of substance. Maude stammered under the attention.

"Everyone—some people—people asked about you," she said. Then she was silent. "Evelyn was a great help." She tried to deflect the focus.

"Oh, yes. Evelyn. That's very nice," and Isabel smiled.

Evelyn felt as though hot wax had been poured on her and cooled quickly. Speaking was like cracking a thin, hard layer of wax. "Yes, but..."

Before Evelyn could finish, Isabel continued, "You people will be wanting dinner, eventually. Maude, stay with our guests. Perhaps they'd like a drink." She left the room.

Maude seemed less assertive now but, in a way, more comfortable. She poured the sherry, carrying a cloth in case she spilled.

The house looked down onto the city and across to a view of the mountains. As the day failed Evelyn began to think of Isabel as one of the mountains in darkness. The conversation, like the lights on the mountains, only more clearly marked the location of her dark and stubborn form. Evelyn was jealous of Isabel. She wanted to be alone with Maude and Holgate.

The talk over dinner was about birds. Maude had given Isabel a bird cage as a present before leaving for Saskatchewan. Isabel wanted to use the cage as a plant stand and asked "her guests" to take sides in the debate. Spin tried to opt out, saying she didn't know anything about plants or birds.

Evelyn was edgy. "I like birds, except in cages," she said.

"Of course," responded Isabel. "That's exactly my point. Much better to have a plant."

"But plants need looking after too," said Maude. "Birds are more alive, even if they're in a cage."

"But I'll have to look after them sometimes, and I'm so terrible at it," said Isabel.

"It's not hard, really," said Maude.

"But with plants, the cages are only ornaments," insisted Isabel. "Never mind, we'll work it out ourselves," and she closed the topic, shielding her life with Maude away from Evelyn. "Coffee? I think we might have a liqueur as well, Maude. Let's go into the other room."

The evening settled in, and after two more hours Evelyn had become inured to the vague numbness that pervaded the room. Finally Maude led them downstairs into the guest room. Evelyn undressed in the bathroom, and put on the flannelette nightie that Maude had given her.

Spin turned off the light and Evelyn got under the sheets, lying compact and immobile at the edge of the bed. The long silence made stretch marks between them.

"Sleepy?" asked Spin, finally.

"No," said Evelyn.

"How are you feeling?"

"Yuk," said Evelyn.

"Why?"

"I don't know what I'm doing."

"What do you think you are doing?"

In the darkness Evelyn felt a huge, encircling rage at the question, which seemed coy and manipulative.

"I just told you, I don't know," she said in a voice full of teeth. She rolled over and her head bumped against her teacher's arm.

Evelyn felt herself thaw and freeze in turns.

"You have a hard job," said Spin. "You need your sleep. I'm sorry I have to go back tomorrow but Miss Norpin will take care of things. There's not much I can do now. If a compromise is possible, she'll..."

"We didn't talk about anything," interjected Evelyn. "Not about the will, not about Stanley. We talked about birds, and bird cages. And you didn't help."

"What did you want me to do? You are so full of blame. I understand how hard this is for you, but you're not alone here. You asked for a lawyer and..."

"Isabel didn't want to hear. She wouldn't let Maude talk."

"Be patient. Isabel will come round."

"It was you who told me to do things, and not just to mope."

Evelyn was mean and scared. Her lips felt dry. As she moved her tongue inside her mouth, she felt again the rough edge of the shore and the arched sky containing the nightmare of childhood. "I feel ugly." Then she was choking with tears, for lack of recognition. "Like a monster with a huge head." Her head felt big and her arms tiny. She was all in sections. "I'm all broken up."

"What is it?"

"There's bad in me, too."

"There's bad in all of us if..."

"Maude Mason. She said she was like a rotten apple."

"You're not bad, Evelyn, don't you know that? You're taking on an

140

rotten empire. That's what's bad, and not you. You need your rest.''

"Don't say that, please.''

Evelyn tossed and turned, trying to keep still but wriggling under discomfort and annoyance. She wanted to get away from the monster inside her face and in her limbs. And she remembered sleeping with her mother, before Stanley came along. Being scolded for moving in the bed. Told to keep still. Told to please keep still. Never able to move.

She was in anguish. She longed to be alone again, as she had been for so many years, and yet she was now addicted to these people. Spin, Maude, even Isabel. Muriel? Even Marty? Where was she? Why didn't Muriel call? Or even Marty, with her shrill accusing tone. She never called. She didn't care, damn her. Not even after all of this.

Evelyn tossed and turned. It was better to be waiting, near the river, knowing that no one would come. Finally, no one. But it had all changed now. Spin had filled her with hope. Spin was her connection.

"Go to sleep, Evelyn. You've got a big day tomorrow,'' said her teacher.

The alarm rang at 7:30 a.m. and Evelyn was angry at the intrusion into her sleep. As she listened to it, Evelyn realized that the ringing sound did not care if she woke up or not. It was just a sound the clock had been programmed to make. It carried no blame or blessing. It was object.

Isabel called Evelyn to the phone. It was the lawyer. Evelyn said she would be there at 10:00.

She wanted Spin to go with her, but Spin had to catch a plane. And Maude had abandoned anything to do with the lawyer. Maude was enfolded by Isabel, and Evelyn was on her own.

Evelyn said good-bye to Spin. Out of ambivalence from both gratitude and annoyance, she treated her teacher in a casual manner.

The receptionist ushered Evelyn into an office that had the words "M. Norpin'' on a wooden plaque beside the door. There were books and papers piled on every elevated surface. Finally Miss Norpin came into the room and closed the door. She was more intimate than the day before but also more urgent. She talked quickly.

"Evelyn, I have spoken to Crown counsel in Saskatchewan. His clients—and I'm not exactly sure who they are—although when pressed they seemed to be Stanley and your mother—are determined to lay charges. I'm sorry, but I couldn't dissuade him. Your aunt doesn't seem cognizant of the seriousness of this matter. You will have to take the lead unless there is anyone else. Miss Holgate has, of course, said I should phone her any time. It's a large responsibility for your years, but so be it. I hope I can impress upon you that the charge is of great consequence. I told their lawyer of our defence—your consent. I should warn you that he has instructions—by that I mean that Stanley and Muriel have told him—that you left Saskatchewan because of your aunt's coercion, and definitely without their consent. He sticks to that. You, apparently, are fifteen years of age. It's all preposterous, of course, and I tried to bully him out of it—but their position is firm. I'm afraid it solidified because of Miss Holgate. I think they will agree not to take any interim measures if we can get an early trial date. Do you understand?''

"Yes," said Evelyn, although she barely understood anything that the lawyer had said.

"What is your birth date?"

"I'll be sixteen next week."

"Yes, I see. There is a section in the Criminal Code—taking a girl under the age of sixteen from her parents, without their consent. Unfortunately, Miss Holgate will be drawn into this, on the negative side. They will try to show that she was part of this, had an effect upon you, something coercive. Do you understand?"

"Where do they get that from?"

"In the law it's called aiding and abetting. I don't quite understand her part in it, although she won't be charged."

"She's my friend."

"When she intervened on your behalf that seemed to enrage your mother. Apparently Miss Holgate called Clarence directly, instead of your mother. Again, I don't understand the significance of that. But in any event, let me tell you, if you haven't already gathered it, that they won't stop this thing. We must be well armed. I want you to tell me what they are going to say in court. What do you think they will say?"

The lawyer had spoken too fast and then came to a halt with her question, which confused Evelyn. "Say to what?" Evelyn asked, feeling suddenly quite simple-minded.

"I'm sorry." The lawyer pulled out her black binder and slashed a line down the right side of the page, making a new margin in the same way she had done the day before. Miss Norpin drew in a deep breath, blinked rapidly and then closed her eyes. "Mrs. Mason—your aunt—is being charged with kidnapping." She opened her eyes.

"Kidnapping? Kidnapping—me?"

"Yes, that's right." The lawyer closed her eyes again and nodded significantly and then leaned forward, opening her eyes. "What *are* they going to say about that?''

"Is that why she's a criminal?'' asked Evelyn. Until now the charges had seemed vague, as though they related to something Maude had done a long time ago. But they didn't. They had to do with Evelyn. They had to do with right now. Her hands tingled.

"That's the charge, kidnapping.''

"But it's not me. Like I said yesterday, it's the will.''

"No, I'm sorry.'' And the lawyer stared hard, not blinking. "It has to do with you.''

Evelyn's fist inadvertently hammered the desk in front of her. Miss Norpin's head jerked back and her eyes widened.

Evelyn was embarrassed. "I'm sorry.'' She withdrew her fist from the desk. "I'm sorry, I didn't mean to do that. Maude Mason has a different father. She has a different father than the others. Stanley told her that. I don't know if it's true. She was raised as a Rathbone.''

"Stanley will say she's illegitimate? And who is her mother?''

"Isabel, I guess.''

The idea had become commonplace to Evelyn, but it struck the lawyer visibly, so that she took notes for a long time without raising her head.

"And you don't know what is true?''

"S.D. treated her like she was his. That's all I know for sure.''

"Who will they say the real father is?''

"I don't know.''

"You should tell me, even if it's a guess.''

"I really don't know. No one told me.''

"But if Isabel is the mother, she must know.''

"I guess so. Stanley thinks he destroyed the will, a long time ago.'' Evelyn kept trying to bring the lawyer back to the fact of the will.

"I'm not understanding. Why would Stanley be doing this because of a will he thinks doesn't exist?''

Evelyn suddenly felt confused, as though she was making a mistake about everything. Something was wrong with her argument. But she did know the answer. She had to begin so that the answer would come. "I think—he wants—they want to keep me away from Aunt Maude because—because we're the same, somehow. But Stanley's afraid of her.''

"Surely not. She's so—so slight.''

"She's a threat. It has to do with the will. I don't know how, but that's the key.''

"Your mother seems to be taking a large part in this as well, from what I understand.''

"She backs Stanley. She doesn't like his family very much."

"But she's definitely behind Stanley, your step-father, no matter what the impact is on you, or your future?"

"Oh yes, right to the end."

"All right. Mrs. Mason will have to come in again. And Isabel. Oh, my." The lawyer shook her head. "The charges can be dropped, perhaps, if you return to Saskatchewan."

"I don't want to. There will be a trial?"

"Yes, if you don't go back."

"In court?"

"Yes. And you will have to return for the trial."

"I won't go back now, if that's what you're asking."

"Yes, that's what I'm asking."

"No, I won't go back until the trial."

When Evelyn return to the house, Isabel was serving lunch, as Maude set the table. They absorbed her presence into their domestic routine. Over tea, looking out to the promised green expanse of the city, Evelyn armoured her intention.

"Isabel, the lawyer says Maude is going to be charged with a criminal offence."

"What offence? What do you mean?" Finally Evelyn had secured Isabel's attention.

"Stanley is doing it. He says Maude kidnapped me. He's trying to fight over me as his way to fight for S.D.'s property. We have to be ready. They're trying to get us. To get me back there. We are being attacked by Stanley."

"Stanley?" said Isabel, scorning his name. "Stanley? He can't attack me."

"I think so."

"No, dear, Stanley can't attack me." Isabel passed the sugar bowl to Maude.

Isabel, the mountain, was unmoved. Her granite ways were unaffected by anything Stanley might do, or Evelyn might say.

"Maude, can't you tell her?" implored Evelyn.

"Tell her what?" asked Maude.

Evelyn felt crazy, broken up into sections again, and misunderstood.

"Look, there's going to be a court case. That's what the lawyer said. Maude has been charged with kidnapping. Stanley wants to get back at her. He must know you're going to challenge S.D.'s will."

Isabel turned to Maude. "All right, what is this about?"

"It happened a long time ago," Maude said in a hurry. "I didn't tell you."

"Tell me what, Maude?"

"Everything S.D. had was to be divided among the children. But Stanley told me I wouldn't get anything. He said that at the funeral."

"Be damned," said Isabel, standing up. "Be damned. That rotten scoundrel. I could snub him out with my little finger." Isabel, in her bulky form, looked capable of crushing.

"The lawyer says they'll drop the charges if I go back," pegged in Evelyn.

"You will not. You will live here." Isabel had lost all her vagueness. "Stanley will not lay one finger on you. Let him just try. You tell the lawyer that. Let him just try. Never mind, I will tell the lawyer."

Isabel walked across the room. A mother lode of bile had been mined in her. She seemed to spread out her great size, like a winged animal.

"Do you want to fight for the will, then?" asked Evelyn.

Isabel turned. "That Maude is equal in our family? Of course I do."

"No matter what?" she pressed.

"What exactly do you mean?"

"Do you know what they will say?" Evelyn took courage.

Isabel stepped towards her and her eyes narrowed to slits. "What will they say?"

"Stanley will say S.D. isn't Maude's father." She'd said it. She said it out loud.

But Isabel only turned away. "What does he know about anything."

After Isabel had telephoned the lawyer and made an appointment for the next day, she returned to the table. Evelyn saw that the veins in Maude's neck stuck out, and Isabel was very angry.

"Maude, what happened a long time ago that you didn't tell me?"

Maude looked defended. "You weren't there," she said, in the same halting voice Evelyn had heard in the hotel room, before they'd gotten away. "You wouldn't go, just like this time."

"Yes, what happened?"

Maude's jaw had set. It seemed like a stand-off.

"Please, tell me if you can," said Isabel gently.

"We don't talk about things like that," said Maude.

"No, we don't. But we should start."

"Why? Why start?"

"You don't want to tell me?" Maude kept silent. "All right, that's fine. Maybe tomorrow." Isabel, kinder now, released Maude from the hot attention of her questions.

Evelyn was impatient. She didn't want Isabel to wait for tomorrow. But she was going to wait.

Isabel started clearing away the dishes.

The next day Maude appeared to have forgotten any promise to resume the conversation. She was dutiful in the routine of the house, very kind and guarded.

When Isabel returned from the lawyer's office she had the patched will in hand and spread it out on the table.

"It's pretty serious, what Stanley is up to, don't you think, Maude?"

Isabel wasn't including Evelyn in these conversation. Evelyn had to keep her peace. She had to make herself watch and wait.

Maude seemed confused and shy.

"Stanley made S.D. rip this up?" continued Isabel.

"Yes, he did."

"That must have been when you went home, about the family history and the cairn. Is that right?"

"Yes."

"That's what you never told me about?"

"I kept it with me. All the time."

"The will?"

"The pieces of paper, from that night."

"Why didn't you..."

"We never do," interrupted Maude. "Stanley was angry that I went back for the funeral. He's claiming everything now."

"I'm not so sure about that."

"You don't exist."

Isabel stopped fingering the paper. "Beg your pardon?"

"You don't exist any more, in that place." Maude was stating a fact.

"I don't understand."

"What I said yesterday isn't true. No one asked about you at the funeral. It's like you never were there. Not even Stanley is worried about you. He's only bothered by me. You always stay apart."

"I see. I understand now what you're saying."

Isabel was staying up late again. Every night she would go into her study overlooking the front balcony to write at her desk; always writing at her desk. During the day she was quiet and thoughtful. She'd stopped pushing Maude around.

Evelyn lay in bed thinking that her stay with Isabel and Maude was short-lived. And she couldn't get grounded with them. For days no one

146

had mentioned the will or the court case, and no one had offered her any comfort. She was off balance, pitched forward into the future. They were, all three of them, leaning over into a strong wind that opposed them and also held them up. But then what? What would happen when it was all over? She wriggled inside the thought. Maybe the judge would tell her she was just a trouble-maker, stirring up discontent. Seeking revenge. He might order her to stay with Muriel and Stanley forever. Never get away. Or send her to jail. And she'd have to run away again.

She tossed and turned in her bed. Whenever she lay still her head filled up and grew big with terror. She had to get up.

At 3 a.m. she went upstairs to get a glass of water. Light from Isabel's room cracked through the hall like a pathway. Evelyn knocked on the door.

"Yes, come in."

"Aunt Isabel?"

"Yes, dear? Can't you sleep?"

As with her mother, Evelyn expected Isabel would be half drunk, with a glass of liquor in front of her. But Isabel was drinking tea.

Evelyn sat down on the edge of the sofa. She was glad Isabel was awake. "What are you writing?"

Isabel looked down at the notebook on her desk. "Well, I'm trying to figure things out."

"May I read it?" Evelyn was immediately afraid Isabel would be angry.

But Isabel said quietly, "No, I don't think so."

Evelyn took courage. "I'd like to read it, if you'd let me."

"I'll think about that. Are you not able to sleep?"

"I keep wondering what the judge will do. If he'll blame me."

"Oh no, I shouldn't think so. Stanley has pushed things too far. He needn't have pressed charges. If he had any sense he'd blame himself."

"My mother never calls." Evelyn surprised herself by saying this.

"Did you expect her to?"

"No, not really."

"It will be over soon. You should go back to bed now."

Evelyn wanted to ask what would happen after it was all over, but Isabel still seemed like a mountain to her. Not a mountain on earth, but a mountain on water. An island.

"Good night, Aunt Isabel." Evelyn leaned over and kissed the soft skin of her cheek. Close up she smelled the same as Maude.

Over the next few days Isabel grew less withdrawn and thoughtful. She started to take control. She directed Miss Norpin to instruct counsel in Saskatchewan. His name was Erwin Draney. She then had Mr. Draney come to Vancouver and meet with her and Miss Norpin. Isabel was on the move, as though freed from some heavy burden. In the evenings she rehearsed with Evelyn and Maude what they were to say in court and how they were to say it, coaching them as a teacher would prepare for a play. They re-enacted the scene in the hotel room, with Isabel scripting the parts and taking the role of Stanley, wearing Geoffrey's old jacket that barely covered her ample chest and arms. She even played the role of prosecutor, cross questioning Maude and Evelyn in an aggressive style.

Maude's trial was set down for April 12, 1958 in Saskatoon, Saskatchewan.

They were all exceedingly anxious. Whenever their energy flagged, Isabel would say, "We're on trial, all of us. Our whole family is on trial. We must do our best. Perk up, please."

Evelyn could hardly remember her initial dislike of Isabel. She served her now, boosting herself on Isabel's energy and intensity. Isabel seemed more like the over-note, the third sound not created from any source, the sound she had heard with Holgate. Evelyn knew that Isabel had always acted behind the scenes, encouraging Maude to return to Saskatchewan, using Maude somehow as her connection. Isabel was on an ark, a self-sufficient, self-contained ark, but Evelyn came to realize that Isabel needed Maude. It was hard to know which one was the more dependent.

Isabel questioned Evelyn closely about her background, and her relationship with Muriel, Stanley, S.D. and Kathryn. As Evelyn talked, Isabel would make notes, saying "Yes, good. Hmm hmm. We can use that. Good, go on." Evelyn wanted to please her.

Through the lawyers, Isabel made it clear that Kathryn was not to know anything about the trial; she was to be kept in ignorance. She called Spin on the telephone—even she referred to the teacher as Spin—checking on facts about Evelyn and her school years.

On reams of paper, she wrote and re-wrote the evidence. In the evening she held up the paper, fisted in her hands, her back ramrod straight, reading with intense interest what she had written. To Evelyn, Isabel's head looked like a pigeon's, making abrupt sharp movements, her eyes beaded with intent. Beneath her anxious face was the immovable solid weight of her body.

And in the carefully crafted story she developed there was always one omission, so palpable it occupied a space larger than Isabel. They continually walked around it, and screened it from view. There was no explanation of who Maude's parents really were. To Evelyn it seemed this was what could expose them; but she didn't refer to the question again.

On the day before they were to leave for Saskatoon, Isabel bought Evelyn a new dress. It was black with a white collar and cuffs, very smart and fashionable. Isabel had insisted that everyone wear black for the occasion. "It shows respect, doesn't attract attention. We'll be in the limelight enough, without wearing colour."

Isabel then announced that she had made plane reservations for two and that she wouldn't be going. She wouldn't hear any further discussion. "You don't need me, now," were her final words. She even refused to take them to the airport.

Evelyn was furious.

And their lawyer was furious. When they arrived at his office in Saskatoon the day before the trial, Mr. Draney was appalled that Isabel was not there. He immediately phoned her in everyone's presence. The only message Mr. Draney conveyed from Isabel was, "She considers that justice can best be done in her absence. She will not attend." The word, echoing Rudy Truman's story of his trial, confused Evelyn. She didn't know whether Isabel was being brave or foolish. Evelyn decided that Isabel was a coward.

At 9 o'clock the next morning, they walked up the court room steps and through the throng of people. The newspaper had reported the story the day before and everyone was out to hear the public unveiling of a family's disintegration.

Stanley, climbing the steps a few minutes later, was horrified at all the people. They were the gossips, gawking at him, encouraging his family's tragedy. They should not be allowed. It was no one else's business.

He walked directly into the court room, bumping into the onlookers, his arm clearing the way in front of him. "Good luck, Stan," said one of them. It was his neighbour from the next farm, Gladys Philmore. His neighbour was there, someone who had been inside his house, had eaten at his table. They were all there to laugh at him.

By the time he got inside the court room, Stanley was furious. He went up to John Culver, the prosecutor. Culver was ordering his papers on the podium below the imposing structure where the judge would sit. He was tall and thin, taller than Stanley. He looked down on him, his glasses resting halfway down his face.

"Get them out of here."

"Mr. Rathbone?" said Culver, not comprehending.

"Get them out of here," he repeated.

"Who?"

"All these people."

Culver took off his glasses and lifted his head, looking over the top of Stanley's thinning hair to the farmers, housewives and reporters filing into the court. "I'm sorry, Mr. Rathbone, the courts in this country are open to the public."

"I want them removed."

"Perhaps, but you have brought your case to the courts, and the courts are open. There's nothing I can do." The prosecutor replaced his glasses and resumed turning the papers in his file. Stanley was left high and dry. Muriel came to his side. "Stanley, what is it?"

Stanley was confused. He only wanted to talk to the judge. To get things straight, once and for all, that Maude couldn't come barging in, take Evelyn and disrupt his plans. These others, they were outsiders. "He's going to let them stay."

"Stay? Who?" asked Muriel.

"Everybody."

"Mr. Culver, is there some place we can go?" Muriel wanted to protect Stanley. He was awkward and upset. She wanted to take him away from there.

"We'll be starting shortly, please sit down." Without looking he pointed to the front row of the gallery.

Muriel took Stanley by the arm. He was trembling under the thick cloth of his dark overcoat. "Don't think about them. They don't exist." She guided him to a seat and placed her hand on his leg. She tried to look straight ahead, but in the periphery of her vision she saw her daughter, Evelyn, across the aisle. She looked older, much older than she should be. She was just a child. Maude and another woman were beside her. That other woman had to be Evelyn's teacher. Muriel pressed her hand on Stanley's leg.

Evelyn, holding Maude's gloved hand, gripped it tighter as she watched her mother go to Stanley and then lead him away from the lawyer. Marty, or Muriel—she had lost the distinction now—seemed almost gentle as she handled Stanley. But she was on the other side. There was no bridge between them.

A gradual hush spread through the room.

"Order in court. All rise," said the clerk.

The judge, an old man wearing black robes, entered and walked up the stairs to his place. He folded his robes around him with invisible hands, bowed, and sat down. The lawyers bowed in return and everyone shuffled to resume their places. Mr. Draney signalled to Maude Mason to come forward. The two of them stood together, while the clerk read.

"Maude Elisabeth Mason, you are charged that on the 18th day of January, 1958 at or near Elmore, Saskatchewan, you did unlawfully abduct and detain Evelyn Rathbone, without the consent of her parents. How do you plead, guilty or not guilty?"

"Not guilty," said Maude without prompting. Evelyn noted that her voice was small but strong. Maude sat down at the counsel table, in the front of the court room.

"Order excluding witnesses," said the prosecutor.

Again Mr. Draney turned, his head and neck moving in one stiff unit. He pointed to Evelyn and Spin, while the prosecutor pointed to Muriel. Both then pointed in unison to the door at the side of the room. Everyone looked at everyone else, not knowing what was intended. A sheriff gathered the three together and escorted them out of the courtroom. "You have to wait out here," he said, indicating the bench where Clarence was already seated.

"This is ridiculous," said Muriel. "Why do we have to wait out here?"

No one spoke. Evelyn sat between Maude and Clarence. She was embarrassed by her mother.

Muriel wouldn't look at her daughter. She paced, shaking her head every now and then, and pausing near the door, trying to listen. "This is ridiculous," she repeated. "No one said it would be like this."

"What did you expect?" said Clarence, almost accusingly. His question went unanswered.

Evelyn was broken off, separated from her mother. She got up and walked to the end of the hall. The walls were pebbled and bumpy, like the halls in the dormitory she had left. Spin came up and put her arm around her, but didn't speak.

Inside the courtroom, the prosecutor said, "Stanley Rathbone to the stand, please, My Lord."

Stanley stood in the witness box above Maude Mason. It seemed to Maude that he was the one on trial. He was the accused.

Stanley was sworn to tell the truth. He kissed the Bible and continued to hold it in his hand.

"Mr. Rathbone, you may put down the Bible and be seated," said the judge.

The prosecutor began. "Mr. Rathbone, what is your relationship, please, to Evelyn Rathbone?"

"She is my daughter, through marriage."

"Your adopted daughter?"

"Yes. After I married her mother, I adopted her."

"How old was Evelyn at the time of the adoption?"

"She was eight years old."

"And did her father consent to the adoption?"

"She didn't have a father. Muriel, her mother, had never married before. Evelyn was raised without a father, until me. I thought that she should have a father."

"And why was that?"

"I wanted to—to make sure she had proper care and education. A proper upbringing. I wanted to make things legal so that she wasn't—illegitimate any more, and—"

"Yes, thank you," interrupted the prosecutor.

"—so that she would be my daughter and under my protection."

"Thank you," repeated the lawyer. "And was she under your protection?"

"Yes, she was. I supported her completely."

"Yes."

"I gave direction as to her education. Her upbringing."

"Please tell me, Mr. Rathbone, of Evelyn's conduct, before the events leading up to the alleged kidnapping?"

Maude put her fist under her chin and looked straight ahead into the wall of the judge's bench. She wished that Isabel were beside her. She felt cold.

"How far back do you want to go?" said Stanley.

"As far back as you need to assist the Court."

"Evelyn was a loner."

"Yes. Go on."

"She never had many friends."

"Yes, please, Mr. Rathbone, tell us what you can." The prosecutor seemed impatient.

"When I married Muriel, her mother, she went through a bad period. I think she resented me." Stanley paused for a long time. "I built a new house for her and her mother. She would hide in her room. She became—unbalanced." He didn't mean to say that. He wanted to take it back.

"Can you give me any examples, Mr. Rathbone, of this state of being unbalanced, as you say?"

"Objection." Mr. Draney rose to his feet. "I can't conceive of the relevancy of this evidence. We're about to deal with events going back many years." The judge listened attentively and then said, "Mr. Prosecutor?"

"If Your Lordship would let me proceed, I am sure the relevance will become apparant."

152

"All right."

"Yes, Mr. Rathbone, continue please," said the prosecutor.

"What about?"

"About Evelyn, your daughter. Being unbalanced."

Unbalanced. That's what he'd said. There were too many people listening. Unbalanced? He was making a fool of himself.

"Mr. Rathbone?" said the prosecutor.

"She killed a bird that had been left in her care, by not feeding it. My brother's bird. She ran away from school and she—"

"My Lord." Mr. Draney stood again.

Stanley looked confused, not knowing where to turn. He had to finish, to get it over with. "We got a doctor to calm her."

"Objection," said Mr. Draney, in a loud voice, but Stanley continued.

"She developed an unbalanced hatred against me."

"Mr. Rathbone," said the judge, "please wait a moment. Defence counsel objects to what you are saying."

"Why?"

"Well, you leave that to me, please, and don't continue until I ask you to. Mr. Prosecutor, I confess I am having difficulty seeing the relevance of this."

"My Lord, let me ask a question to direct the witness."

"All right, but Mr. Rathbone, don't answer the question until I rule on it."

"I want to ask this witness if, as a result of any conduct or concern about his daughter, he made any decision about her schooling."

"My Lord," interjected Mr. Draney, "surely my learned friend should come to the point."

"All right," said the prosecutor. "Mr. Rathbone, at the time of these events, in January, where was Evelyn going to school?"

"Yes, I'll let that go," said Draney.

"You may answer, Mr. Rathbone," directed the judge.

"In Winnipeg." Stanley's response was meagre and confined. Maude felt sorry for him.

"And why was that?"

"She had turned against her mother. And she was having trouble at school; she would be better off in a private school. That's where she developed this connection with Miss Holgate." Stanley was speaking rapidly, trying to cram in his statements before being interrupted. But it was all in a tangle.

"Just a minute, please. You say she was attending school in Winnipeg?"

"Yes. Miss Holgate was one of her teachers."

"And what do you know of their connection?"

"I heard—"

"Objection." Mr. Draney was on his feet. "This is clearly hearsay, My Lord, unless my friend establishes the proper foundation, this witness's basis of knowledge. My friend should control himself and his witness."

"Yes, Mr. Culver, please restrict the witness to what he actually knows," said the judge.

"Mr. Rathbone, have you seen your daughter in the company of Miss Holgate?"

"No, I haven't. They were together in Vancouver, after the kidnapping."

"How do you know that?"

"I was told by—"

"Objection," yelled Mr. Draney, without standing.

"Sustained," said the judge.

"All right." The prosecutor was starting to look harassed. "In any event, your daughter was going to school, in Winnipeg, under your direction?"

"Yes."

"Now, do you have any information as to the events on the night of January 16, 1957, when, as I understand it, Evelyn left Saskatoon with Mrs. Mason?"

"Yes, I do. I went to the hotel where Mrs. Mason was staying."

"Why?"

"Because she had been at our home—it was the day of my father's funeral. I sent a ticket to Evelyn, in Winnipeg, so that she could come back for the funeral. Mrs. Mason was invited to my home. When she arrived, she began bickering about the division of my father's estate. She tried to draw Evelyn in—"

"Objection," said Mr. Draney, this time standing. "My Lord, Mr. Rathbone should tell what he observed, not what he concluded from what he observed. That is for you to decide."

"Yes, all right," said the judge. "Just tell us what happened, Mr. Rathbone."

"Well, she left in a huff and took Evelyn with her."

"By 'she' you mean Mrs. Mason?"

"Yes."

Maude whispered, "That's not true," loud enough for everyone to hear.

The prosecutor stammered, "And is—and is Mrs. Mason—is she related to you in any way?"

"She was raised with me, in my family."

"And do you know where she was living at the time of these events?"

"In Vancouver, where she lives now. Where she took Evelyn."

"Did you agree to let your daughter go with her?"

"No, I didn't. But I didn't want to make a scene. I'd gone out to try to find them, in the car. They were on foot and I was worried, because it was cold. I found them later in that hotel. I told the clerk I knew they were in there. I asked for the room number. He wouldn't give it to me, so I took the register and found out for myself."

"And then what happened?"

"I went to the room. Mrs. Mason opened the door and wouldn't let me in. She said I had no right to be there. She told me to call the police, if I wanted."

"And did you?"

"Yes, I did."

"Did you see your daughter on that occasion?"

"I tried to speak to her."

"And were you able to?"

"I couldn't with Mrs. Mason there. She was in the way. I thought it was better to get the police."

"That's a lie," said Maude. Her thin tiny voice was like a hat pin poking through Stanley's words.

The judge interjected. "Mrs. Mason, you will have your opportunity to speak."

Maude stood up.

"Yes, that's fine, just listen for now, please. You may be seated," said the judge.

"Did you do anything in regards to your daughter?" continued the prosecutor.

"I told Maude—Mrs. Mason to let her go." Stanley looked white and angry.

"And did she?"

"No, she wouldn't. She refused."

"When was the last time you saw your daughter?"

"Not since then—not until today."

"What happened when you got the police?"

"I went back to the hotel with the officer, but they had gone. I thought they'd go to the airport, so that's where we went. But I later found out they'd taken the train."

"Have you tried to make contact with your daughter? Have you requested that Mrs. Mason return the girl?"

"Yes I have but you said we had to have a trial. I asked you to get her back."

There was laughter in the courtroom.

"Do you know if she is attending school?" the lawyer continued, ignoring the laughter.

"No, I don't know."

"At the time of these events, was your daughter under your care and protection?"

"Yes."

"And do you support her?"

"Yes."

"What is your daughter's date of birth?"

"Her birthday?"

"Yes."

"She has a birthday coming up." Stanley hesitated.

"Do you know how old she was when these events happened?"

"Fifteen, sixteen."

"My Lord." The prosecutor turned to the judge. "I'll be calling the mother to establish the date of birth. Those are my questions." He looked back at Stanley. "Please stay there and answer the questions of my learned friend."

At that moment the court room door opened and Isabel entered the back of the room. The judge looked up and soon everyone was craning their necks to see.

"Excuse me, My Lord," said Mr. Draney, bowing. He walked out of the railed-off area and down the aisle to Isabel.

"I'm here to keep him honest," whispered Isabel.

"Perfect timing," said the lawyer, and led her to the front row, to the place vacated by Maude.

Isabel smiled at Maude and then looked at Stanley. He was older, of course, after all these years, but she still saw him as a young boy. His expression didn't change, and he turned away. Did he not recognize her? Of course he did. They would know one another until the end of time.

Mr. Draney stood across the room from Stanley and began his questions. "Tell me, Mr. Rathbone, how was Evelyn doing in school, in Winnipeg?"

"Fine." Stanley looked up at the ceiling.

"Good grades?"

"Yes."

"In fact, she's always done well at school, hasn't she?"

"Not always."

"She skipped a grade, didn't she? She was ahead of herself in school."

"I guess so."

"Don't you know, Mr. Rathbone?" There was no answer. "Mr. Rathbone, I asked you a question. If you would care to look at me and respond."

"Yes, she's smart." said Stanley, staring coldly at the lawyer.

"And over the past two years, how often have you seen her?"

"Often."

"How often?"

"At Christmas, Easter break. Summer."

"It was you who fostered the idea that Evelyn should go away to school, wasn't it, so that she could be independent?"

"Sure," he said flippantly.

"Why did you do that?"

"I thought it would be best for her."

"And she is independent, isn't she?"

"I guess so."

"In fact it was Evelyn who invited Mrs. Mason to the house on the night you have described."

"I don't remember that."

"You didn't invite her, did you?"

"I don't remember."

"Yes, you do, Mr. Rathbone. You remember very well. Because you didn't want Mrs. Mason to be at your house. You were very upset when she arrived."

"She'd come to make trouble."

"Mrs. Mason had come to make trouble?"

"That's correct. And she has. I was right." Stanley felt better now. He could stand up to this lawyer, this mouthpiece for Maude.

"Why did you think she would make trouble, Mr. Rathbone?"

"That's just the way she is."

"I see. And she has caused problems in the past for you, has she?"

"Yes, she has."

"What trouble has she caused you?"

"Interference."

"With what?"

This lawyer was egging him on. Getting on his nerves. "She has tried to interfere with my family."

"In what way, Mr. Rathbone?"

157

"Trying to break us up."

"Trying to destroy your family unity?"

"Yes, that's right."

"Interfering with your father's wishes?"

"Yes, she's done that."

"Coming between you and your father? She's done that, hasn't she?"

"Yes, she has. She has brought the name of our family into disgrace."
So, let the world know, if that's what they wanted. He'd tell them.

"And she's destroyed your good relationship with your daughter,
hasn't she?"

"That's right."

"And tell the Court how she has done all these things, Mr. Rathbone."

"It's her way. It's always been her way. To disrupt."

"To ruin things for you?"

"Yes."

"Your own sister?"

Stanley snapped his head around and glowered at the lawyer. "She
is not my sister."

The courtroom hushed. Mr. Draney let the silence settle into tension.
"And you've never considered her to be your sister, have you?" he said,
almost sweetly.

"No, I have *not*."

"As far as you are concerned, she's an outsider."

"Yes."

"She's never been part of your family."

"Never," said Stanley, closing the subject.

"Tell the judge, then, Mr. Rathbone, why it was that your father, Sean
De'Ath Rathbone, considered Maude Mason as his own daughter, raised
her as such and remembered her as such."

"He never did," Stanley shot back.

"He didn't? I suggest you think again about your answer, Mr.
Rathbone."

"You can't bully me, sir," said Stanley, standing up in the witness box.

"I'm not bullying you, sir. I am asking you a question."

"You are not, you are telling me what to do."

The court room stirred. "Order," called the judge. "Mr. Rathbone,
answer the question. Mr. Draney, don't argue with the witness."

"What's the question?" snapped Stanley.

"Do you, having carefully contemplated your previous answer, still
maintain that your father did not raise Maude Mason, born as Maude
Rathbone, as his daughter, and remember her as such?"

"I do."

"He wrote a will, didn't he, that referred to Mrs. Mason as his daughter?"

The question shocked Stanley. "There is no will."

"Mr. Rathbone, your father remembered Maude Elisabeth Mason in his will."

"There is no will."

"Answer the question, please."

The prosecutor was on his feet. "My friend is going very far afield, Mr. Lord. I object to—"

But Mr. Draney cut him off. "I am not going far afield. I suggest to you, Mr. Rathbone, that you know very well about your father's wishes, and you know very well about the will, made by him in 1946."

"There is no will."

"You swear to that?" said Draney, turning and walking to counsel table. "You swear that your father never made a will in 1946?" He picked up a file folder from the table and tapped it against his hand.

Stanley watched him, absorbed in the slow tapping of the paper. "What do you have there?" he said finally.

"You know what I have."

"The will was destroyed."

"Ripped up, but not destroyed."

"I saw it. It was destroyed."

"No, Mr. Rathbone, not destroyed."

"You can't do this."

"You convinced your father to rip up his will because you said lawyers would try to cheat him. Isn't that correct, Mr. Rathbone?" The lawyer continued to tap the file against his hand.

"They were trying to interfere."

"That's right. Just like your sister, Maude Mason. Everyone was interfering. Evelyn was interfering."

"I'm not on trial here."

"Perhaps you are, sir." And the lawyer started to walk towards the witness stand. "Mr. Rathbone, I put it to you that Evelyn told you, on the night in question, that she would not go with you. And in response you physically pushed her out of your way."

"*I* did?"

"Yes. And your only endeavour, in these whole proceedings, is to try to get rid of Maude Mason, to prevent her from taking her share under her father's will."

"S.D. was not her father."

"Who was her father, then, Mr. Rathbone," snapped the lawyer, as though he had lost all patience with these answers.

"Clarence. My brother."

The audience inhaled like one body. Maude sunk her head into her hands. The lawyer stopped tapping his paper. Then there was a sound, like a high-pitched groan. The sound came from Stanley. He was being hunted by his own confused declaration. He was in a trap. He got up and stumbled from the witness stand. The judge called after him. "Mr. Rathbone, come back. Mr. Rathbone."

Stanley didn't notice the other people in the corridor, didn't see Evelyn, Muriel or his brother as he walked past them into the cold glare of the sun.

The impossible had happened. With his own mouth he had expressed the shame which had surrounded him all his life. He had said it out loud, under oath.

He didn't have his coat but kept walking, not feeling the cold. When a taxi passed, he hailed it.

Scandal. He was finally possessed by the scandal.

He told the cab driver to take him to Elmore. When the driver protested that it was fifty miles away, Stanley said, "My name is Rathbone. Have you heard of that name?" But the words had no tone, no energy.

"No, sir, I haven't."

"Well, it means I can pay," he said, quietly.

"Up to you."

"Yes." Stanley felt smooth inside, granulated and levelled out. The charred ends of the secret that he had carried were burnt to whiteness now. Clean, like powdered bone in the cold sun.

He directed the cab driver to the cemetery.

S.D.'s grave was in the family plot, in the old part of the yard. Stanley told the driver to wait.

He walked along the path through the trees empty of leaves. There was a statue of a young boy, his hand cupped against his thigh. Stanley placed a quarter on top of the snow in the boy's hand.

By the time he reached his father's grave the snow on his shoes had soaked through to his skin.

The ground was mounded higher on S.D.'s grave and brown earth showed through the snow. Next to it was a small grave marked Maude Rathbone, 1901-03. The first Maude was under a small stone. The second one, still alive. And his father, dead for only four months. The family scandal out in the open for everyone to see. He had named Clarence. He was a fool. Fault. Whose fault? Clarence? Evelyn? Maude? Whose fault?

His life had gone on too long. He wished that he was buried under the ground, instead of being on top of it, cold and heartless. His life had emptied out now, like a cup that had fallen. He had no passion left. It had all been spilled.

He could hardly untangle what the dispute was about, what he had been trying to achieve. He had become enmeshed in his own trap. It was because of Maude. He looked down on the small grave of his sister. Small and dead. Maude Rathbone. She didn't die in a fire. No one was killed by a fire. He'd saved her because his mother's twisted face looked at him and begged him. Kathryn loved Maude and he could have let Maude die. He had been frozen back then, wanting her to die.

She was the scandal.

He was trying to protect the family name, trying to get Evelyn away from Maude, trying to get control of—what was it? His father hadn't loved Maude, the second Maude—or he shouldn't have loved her. She was a mistake, an error. He'd gone to court to prove it, to prove he was right and she was wrong. Wasn't she?

He looked at his wide open hand and his empty palm. Nothing. Nothing but his own shame. He could almost see through the white skin into the bones that made the structure of his hand. They seemed so small, his bones, so insignificant. He was a failure. Through his spread fingers he could see his father's tombstone. Sean De'Ath Rathbone.

"Father," he said out loud. "Help me."

Tears broke the cold grimace of his face. He hadn't cried since he was a child, when he had held his breath to lure his father's love.

He was ugly. Like a gargoyle in this winter garden, with part of its ugliness broken off and lying beneath him, where his father lay under the ground. Stanley was repulsed by the man he had become. Part of him was buried there; an essential part that had nourished him was now gone. He had never lived his life, somehow. Never occupied it. Always wanting to be like his father. He had failed. S.D. had kept everyone together in his way, kept the family as a unit. Now there was nothing left of that family because of him. He had hurt the brother that he loved.

Where was he?

He was like the statue of the boy in the graveyard, frozen back in time, his hand cupped against his thigh, still, immobile and dumb, a quarter in his hand. He had grown cold in the shadow of his father's life, suspicious and cold.

He had to find Kathryn.

He went back to the taxi and directed the driver to Talaru Boulevard.

Kathryn was sitting at the front window of the house and waved as he came up the walk.

"I know, Muriel called," said Kathryn as he stood in the doorway. The house was hot and stuffy.

"What did she say?"

"She said there was a mess. She kept saying 'mess.' Something about court. Were you in court, Stanley?"

"Yes, because of Maude."

"Our Maude? What about our Maude?"

"I told the judge. I said Clarence is her father."

"Clarence, her father? But that's crazy, Stanley. Why would you say that?"

"I don't know. I've done it all wrong."

"Maude is our daughter."

"I mean the second Maude, not the first one."

"There's only one Maude, you know that. You shouldn't have lied, dear. Will they send you to jail?" Kathryn seemed as though she too were made of something thick and indiscriminating.

"No. Not yet, anyway. I'm going to tell the lawyer to stop the case. To divide the estate amongst all of us, including Maude."

"The estate?"

"S.D.'s property."

"Yes, that's right. Maude gets her share. And Isabel."

"It's public now—" Before he could finish, the phone rang.

"That will be Muriel, I expect," said Kathryn, predicting past and future.

Stanley answered the phone. He told Muriel to come home, to tell the lawyer it was all over.

The phone rang again. It was a newspaper reporter.

"Could I have a statement, Mr. Rathbone?"

"No."

"I understand you made allegations in court today about incest in your family."

"Well, you heard wrong," Stanley said quietly and hung up the phone. He took it off the hook.

Do simple things. Slowly. If he could stay close to his mother and be simple, like her, he could start all over again. Make some tea for Kathryn. It took him a long time. The world had a gossamer, fragile quality, best understood if he could submit to serving his mother, waiting on her. His skin felt papery thin, the way her skin looked. He sat near her, on the floor, looking up from a small place. She seemed ancient and full of wisdom, as she held her teacup in hands that trembled.

"You normally sit on a chair, don't you?" she asked, looking down at him. "You look so small."

"I haven't sat on the floor like this since I was a boy."

"Yes. You are very young, sitting there."

"I feel young, Mother."

"Yes, I think you do."

Stanley wanted to put his head on her lap, but he couldn't bring himself to do that. Instead, he placed his hand on her knee, and gently touched the smooth silk of her dress. He could almost imagine the world that he had lost contained in the pattern of her dress: an ordered, perfumed world, that repeated itself at regular intervals, to show him that he could know it. A world he could rely on.

"What was I like, as a child? Do you remember?"

"Oh, yes, I remember. I remember each one of you."

"Did you like me?" And the words sounded so pathetic and needy that he regretted them.

"But of course I loved you. How could I not love you? I held you in my arms."

Stanley looked at her skin netted in thousands of tiny lines. He imagined he could hear the blood flowing slowly, so slowly through her veins. He was adrift in that slow pulse.

"What was I like?"

Kathryn mused. "You loved your father. You imitated him, even as a young boy. I remember once, you were what, four years old? You must have heard him say the word b-u-g-g-e-r."

"Bugger?"

"Yes, that word. He must have said it, although he never swore. It's not a very nice word. You didn't know what it meant. We had guests. You were playing on the couch. In the middle of our conversation I heard you say—and I'll say it just this time—'bugger, bugger, bugger' as you turned the pages in your picture book."

"I said bugger?"

"Yes, you did. Over and over again. Your father got all red—the way he used to. I had to hush him. We all listened to you saying 'bugger bugger'. Well, I started to laugh. We all laughed, even S.D. I remember so clearly. You looked up, with this expression in your eyes, and stared at your father. He was laughing and so you started to laugh. But then something happened. I guess you thought we were laughing at you. You began to cry. You screamed and cried. I could barely calm you."

"I don't remember that."

"No, you don't."

"Bugger, bugger, bugger," said Stanley. Kathryn laughed.

"What are you doing?" Muriel demanded from the doorway.

Stanley looked up and kept repeating the word as he laughed.

Muriel was in a rage. "You might laugh and say bugger. But you have created a very large scandal. I was mauled by reporters."

Stanley kept saying "bugger bugger" and smiled at each repetition of the word.

"Bugger is right. I've been trying to call. The phone must be off the hook."

"Is Stanley going to be arrested?" asked Kathryn in a quiet voice.

"Oh, so you know of the mess your son has created?"

"Muriel," said Stanley from his place on the floor, "why don't you sit down?"

"Stanley, for God's sake, get up. Maude and her gang are about to descend."

"How do you know?" He was alarmed at having to face other people. He needed more time.

"Clarence told them to come."

He wouldn't hurry. He'd take his time; he'd hold his breath if he need to and create calm. But Muriel was pacing. "Please, if you could sit down."

"I will not sit down," she yelled.

Stanley had only once before seen her in such a rage. He was afraid of her anger now, and her bigness.

"Maude? Is Maude here then?" asked Kathryn.

"Yes, she is. With reinforcements," replied Muriel.

"Maude doesn't have reinforcements, Muriel," said Stanley. He waved his hand across his eyes, trying to clear his vision. "Couldn't you sit down? Have some tea. Have a drink. You could get yourself a drink, Muriel."

"I see. You won't even pour me a drink, is that it?"

"You could pour yourself one, couldn't you?"

Muriel turned on her heel, and Stanley could hear the clinking of bottles from the other room.

"Here comes a car," said his mother. Stanley couldn't, didn't want to move from his place. He wanted to stay down there, beneath eye level and accountability. "It's Maudie. And Evelyn. For heaven's sakes. Maude and Evelyn."

"They were in court today," said Stanley, trying to be matter-of-fact.

"Well, they aren't here to arrest you anyway. There's someone else— my goodness, it's Isabel. Isabel. Can you imagine? All my children. Where is Clarence? And there's another woman. Stanley, get the door." Kathryn was excited in a sublime way.

"Can't they can let themselves in? It's not locked."

Muriel reappeared with a drink in her hand. "So they've arrived, have they? Stanley, you'd better stand up to the attack."

"I'm fine where I am. Please sit down."

"Stop saying that. I will not sit down. What's happened to you?" Kathryn was waving to them from the window. "Stanley, Clarence has just driven up. This is wonderful."

"Not so wonderful," said Muriel, leaning against the wall and bumping a picture of Blue Boy. "Stanley, what are you doing?"

"Nothing," said Stanley. "I'm doing nothing."

"Well, you'd better do something."

"Why?"

"Because—you fool, you have an explosion on your hands."

"This is wonderful," Kathryn repeated. "We must make more tea. And dinner. Stanley, the family's home. We'll have to get dinner for everyone. Call Edna to come over. She's only down the street. She'll make dinner for us all."

"It's all right. Someone will call her later, Mother."

And the doorbell rang. Kathryn called "come in" in her feeble voice. The door opened.

"Well, well, you've all come home. And Isabel too." Kathryn's eyes started to tear. "Isn't it wonderful. This is cause for celebration. Please, we'll all have a drink. Stanley?"

"Clarence can manage it. Or Muriel," he said from his place on the floor.

"Grandma," Evelyn said, "I'd like to introduce you to my teacher and my friend. This is Miss Holgate, and this is my grandmother, Mrs. Rathbone."

Spin stepped forward and Kathryn took her hand. "You are very welcome in my house on this blessed occasion," said Kathryn. Stanley nodded like the bob of a head on a spring, as though in a wooden way he had convinced himself this time could be blessed.

"Isabel, I thought you would never come back," said Kathryn, her voice unsteady with emotion.

Clarence began serving sherry from a silver tray. When he had finished there was a long silence. Everyone seemed to be waiting for an event that had passed. Stanley continued to sip his tea.

"Clarence," said Kathryn, "come sit by me, bring a chair over here."
Clarence obeyed. "Now, that's nice. I have my two sons here." She
touched them both. "And my daughters, my granddaughter, and her
teacher."

"And your daughter-in-law, Grandma," Evelyn reminded her quietly.

"Yes, of course, and Muriel."

Silence again swarmed through the group.

Evelyn hated the lull that seemed like calm but wasn't calm. The last
four months had cleared away like steam, with nothing answered. Maude
and Isabel had given up; they'd closed rank against her. Evelyn bit the
skin on the inside of her mouth.

Stanley, still sitting quietly on the floor, knew that Muriel was right;
he would have to get up. But he kept seeing the statue of the young boy
in his father's graveyard and the quarter he had placed in the boy's frozen
hand. The brown earth showing through the snow on his father's grave.

He looked into the dining-room. Past events seemed immediate now:
the night that S.D.'s will was torn up, all his useless fears.

"Do you remember," began Stanley, looking up at everyone in turn,
"do you remember the night that Father brought out his will?"

Evelyn swallowed air. No one answered.

"I remember it very well." Stanley got up and walked slowly across
the room, through the hall, and stood, his back to the group, looking
into the dining room. "S.D. sat over there." He pointed to the head
of the table. "I sat on his left side."

"No, you didn't." Maude claimed a speech she hadn't been trained
to deliver. "That place was reserved for Isabel."

"Isabel wasn't here," said Stanley, not turning around.

"There was still a place for her," continued Maude.

"On the left of S.D.?"

"Yes."

"Are you sure?"

Maude went into the dining-room. "Yes, right there. You sat across
from Clarence, on Mother's left."

"Wasn't I next to S.D.?" asked Kathryn.

Soon others were drawn into the room, pointing and talking. Stanley
went and helped Kathryn.

"Sit here, Mother, where you sat that night. Maude, over there.
Clarence?" said Stanley. He could get everyone reassembled, just like
before, to start over. "Isabel, I think Maude's right, there was a place
for you here. Would you mind?" He drew back the chair and she sat

down. "Now, we should have more sherry. As I recall, we had a lot to drink that night. I'll get the sherry."

When he left the room everyone sat more stiffly in their places, like museum pieces.

"Here we are." Stanley refilled the glasses. He seemed jubilant and full of motion.

"Why are you doing this, Stanley?" asked Muriel. "Why are you doing this?"

"I don't know." Stanley paused. Except for getting everyone reassembled, he had devised no plan and was surprised at being without one.

"Mother, do you know what happened in court today?" asked Isabel.

Kathryn looked up, startled. "You mean about Stanley lying?"

The simplicity and apparent correctness of Kathryn's answer unnerved Isabel, who hesitated. Stanley filled the gap.

"Father sat here." Stanley moved to the head of the table and sat down. "Father said everything would be equal. Isn't that what he said, Maude?" She didn't answer. "Everything will be divided equally?"

"Yes, but you took the will from him, and made him rip it up," said Maude in a tight, defended voice.

Muriel intervened. "Stanley, I'm going home. I've had enough of your antics."

"So have I," echoed Isabel. "Don't you care about what you have done? You're up to your old tricks again."

"Old tricks?" he repeated dumbly. Stanley tried not to look at her, but was unavoidably drawn to her face. She was so familiar to him, as familiar as his own name. "I haven't seen you in—not for years."

"And so that means I have no right to speak? Is that what you're saying?" Isabel pushed back her chair and rose to her feet.

He had to keep his voice calm. Be quiet. Count one, two, three. Don't stand up. Keep lower than the rest of them. "No, I'm sorry. That's not what I meant. I just remembered..."

"Stanley, you've gone out of your mind," Muriel interrupted.

"I went wrong, somewhere, on that night. Do you know where I went wrong, Clarence?" asked Stanley, hoping Isabel would sit down.

"We've all gone wrong," Clarence said, slowly.

"Isn't it a bit late for this?" Muriel said wearily.

"It should never have ended in court," Clarence said, focussed on Stanley. "You lied about me."

"Where did I go wrong?" Stanley repeated.

"I don't know," said Clarence, struggling with the question.

Evelyn finally erupted. "Everyone is playing cat and mouse again. I have a question, and I want to know the answer: I want to know who my real father was. I'd like to know that. Do any of you have the nerve to tell me that one, simple fact?"

"Not now," said Muriel. "We've had enough for one day."

"Why don't you tell her?" said Stanley simply.

Kathryn was distressed. "Why is everyone so concerned about fathers today?"

"You could tell her, if you wanted to," urged Stanley. "We have to start over again, and do it right this time."

"I don't understand you, Stanley." And Muriel looked at him as though he were a complete stranger.

"Couldn't you tell her?" he repeated, almost hopefully.

Muriel's anger came to the surface. "All right. All right, you want me to play your foolish game?" She went over and stood, towering above Evelyn, her face red and bloated. "Your father," she said, trying to control herself but her voice full of accusation, "your father was an alcoholic. He died in the gutter."

"That's not true," Evelyn shot back.

Then Muriel lost all composure and sputtered with fury, "It is true. You want the truth? That's the truth."

"Tell her who her father was, Muriel," said Stanley.

Muriel wheeled around and glowered at him. "I've told her, you bastard."

Kathryn interrupted again. "That's enough, thank you. We'll have no more talk like that in my house."

Muriel was on the attack. "This house now belongs to Stanley. You can't kick me or anyone else out."

"That's enough, Muriel. No more of that. This is my mother's house, and you—we all are—guests," Stanley said, firmly and without rancor.

"Stanley, why are you doing this to me? After all I have done for you," she protested.

"Because I'm tired of you, the way you are. And I'm tired of the way I am, the way we all are. Your father," he continued without a pause, looking at Evelyn, "was Timothy Sutton. When your mother got pregnant, he wanted to get married. But your mother didn't want to. They were very young."

Muriel stared at him, not moving or speaking.

Stanley continued, "I think your mother loved him. But she has always had big expectations. She wanted financial security, and he couldn't give it to her."

168

"You're talking as though I'm not here," said Muriel, quieter now.

"Please, I want to know this," interrupted Evelyn. "That picture I found, was that a picture of my father?"

"Yes," said Muriel. Her face was in a pinched mask of defeat and distaste.

Stanley went on; he couldn't help himself. "Your mother"—he turned and looked at Muriel—"you were—you are strong willed. I like that about you. It was never going to be right with Timothy. So you tried to do it alone." He turned back to Evelyn. "She had to put you in a foster home for a while."

Muriel flinched.

"In a foster home? For how long?" asked Evelyn.

"I didn't want to. I tried not to," said Muriel, her voice starting to crack and strain.

"Until you were two or three years old," continued Stanley. "She got you back as soon as she could."

"Are they still alive, my other parents?"

The question hurt Muriel.

"They were old when they had you."

"Are they dead?" persisted Evelyn.

"Yes."

"Is my father still alive?"

"We heard he died last year," said Stanley.

The stone cracked against the glass, and it splintered, shards fracturing. All this time, all this way to find out the truth. And it was too late. All the time that was a lie. "I could have met him. I could have talked to him." Her fists were curled on Spin's knees. "You didn't tell me. I could have known him." She wanted to tear at Stanley and her mother, to scratch them and make them bleed.

"He wasn't any good," said Muriel.

Evelyn dug her fingers into her teacher's leg. "But he was my father. He never knew me."

"He saw you once," Muriel said, feeling sick that she had to go on. "I came for you at school, and took you to the park. You were in grade three. Timothy was allowed to be across the street, to watch."

"How could you? How could you do that?" Eveyln felt unclean.

"I wanted to protect you."

"You wanted to protect me from my own father? Turning him into this peeping tom, this creep." She pounded her fists against Holgate's legs. "I can't believe you did that. You broke him. Like you tried to break me. I hate you."

"I gave you everything, Evelyn. I did it for you. Don't say this to me."

"You left me. Two times. Two times, not just once." Evelyn arched her back, straining to look at her mother.

"Two times? What do you mean?"

It was so much Stanley's habit to interrupt Evelyn on Muriel's behalf that he had to bite the inside of his mouth in order to stay quiet.

"Why didn't you tell me who my father was? Why did you lie?"

"Because—" Muriel yelled, and then she hesitated. She couldn't remember why any more, not exactly. She had been ashamed. She had wanted something better. The past would go away.

The room hung with the passion of mother and child. Evelyn laid her head on Spin's legs, and Spin gently stroked her hair. Evelyn wept.

Muriel had to find a way out. Like a cat with teeth bared, she turned to Holgate. "Well, you can give comfort, can't you?"

"Leave me out of this, please," said Spin quietly.

"Who are you, anyway?" asked Muriel, as though noticing Holgate for the first time. "Have you come to take away my daughter?" The question was strange, as though fossilled, from a different time.

Spin ignored the question and continued stroking Evelyn's hair.

"Do you have any children of your own? You don't, do you? And you come barging in playing—playing wet nurse to my child." Muriel turned away from Holgate. If she'd had wings, she would have enfolded them around herself.

"Evelyn appears to me to be very upset."

"Don't you speak of my child," repeated Muriel, sour and petulant. "Anyway, there's something not right about you," she added, like a fish hook under water.

"There's something not right about this whole family, if you want to know," echoed Stanley from the S.D.'s end of the table. He looked around. "Where is Clarence?" Clarence was nowhere in sight. "Clarence," called Stanley. The house seemed suddenly empty and it echoed. "Don't anyone move."

Stanley went upstairs. The doors in the hall were all closed, his mother's habit to contain the fire. He opened each door and whispered his brother's name, like a secret, into each room.

Clarence was huddled in the corner of the bedroom that had been theirs in the wintertime when they were children.

"Clarence." Stanley leaned over him. "Clarence, are you okay?" Clarence had his arms hugged around his head, and was rocking back and forth, making a small sound, almost a hum. Stanley touched his shoulder, and then squatted on the floor beside him. "Tell me."

170

"Too much noise," Clarence finally said. "Too much talking."

"We have to talk now," said Stanley. "Evelyn had to know."

"He did it."

"Who? Did what?"

"To Isabel."

Stanley watched the repetitive, compulsive movements of his brother, back and forth, back and forth.

"You lied about me," Clarence said. "I was there. Hiding."

"Where were you hiding? I don't understand."

"Came into her room. I wanted to scare her, hiding under the bed. Mother was away. In the city. I heard them. They were on my head. The bed touched me. They touched me with their w-weight. I wanted to scream, but I d-didn't."

"Clarence, I don't understand."

"Maude is our s-sister, Stanley."

"Come down with me." Stanley took his hand and pulled him up. "It will be all right."

As they walked down the stairs, Stanley's horror at these revelations, whatever they meant, was mixed with an odd hint of pride, almost a smugness. He wanted to unearth the truth; he wanted to be smeared with it.

"Will it be okay?" asked Clarence. He was shaking.

"Yes."

"What do I s-say?"

"Whatever you can."

They re-entered the dining-room, arm in arm.

No one had moved. Muriel sat bleary-eyed in her chair. Evelyn was kneeling on the floor, leaning against her teacher. The three framed an image of despondency. For an instant Stanley felt his pride as an overburden of deceit. He wondered if he had already gone too far.

Kathryn, at one end of the table, was pale.

"Mother," Stanley said, "are you feeling okay?"

"Yes, I am. I think I should phone Edna, about dinner. It must be past dinner, isn't it?"

"Yes, I'll phone soon."

"All right, dear, whatever you say. I'm tired."

Stanley continued. "Mother, do you want the truth to be told?"

"About what, dear?" she said wearily. "Is there a lie? Oh, yes, you told a lie today."

"Should we tell the truth?"

"You should always tell the truth."

171

It was a discussion in primary colours only, in red and yellow. Kathryn treated her children as though they were in their infancy.

"Then it's all right with you?"

"Yes, dear. But do phone Edna."

"I will." Stanley walked Clarence to the other end of the table. "Clarence and I have been talking. Maybe he'll stutter. But he has something he wants to tell you." Stanley moved away from him slowly, to make sure he could stand.

Clarence cleared his throat and looked up. His mother was directly in front of him. He had been in a daze, out of time, and the sight of her there started his speech. "Mother, I'm s-stuttering again," he said, and his head dropped.

"That's fine, dear. It's not how you say it, but what you say."

Clarence raised his head again. "Evelyn learned who her father was. She wanted t-to know that. Does M-Maude want to know?"

Maude jerked her head as though in sleep.

"There's no secret to that, Clarence. S.D. is Maude's father," said Kathryn.

Clarence was confused. He looked at Maude, but she only looked away.

"Now that's enough," said Kathryn. "That's enough of all of this. We're going to have some dinner." She turned to Muriel and Evelyn. "You must make amends with your daughter and you, with your mother." Kathryn rose and slowly left the room.

Dear Evelyn,

While you were staying with us, as you know, I started to write some things down. You asked me then if you could read what I was writing.

I haven't been able to show it to Maude. I am sending it to you now.

Should I say more? Understand that I send this to you with relief and dread. I am unearthed and my skin is mushroom-thin and unwholesome. I do not expect, even if I could hope for, protection. I am passing on a legacy to you that it may be broken.

Please write to me.

Love,
Isabel

I am doing what I want to do. Most important. Remember that; even hold on to it if necessary. It avoids self-pity. Now, the issue. Maude. Dear Maudie. And Stanley. And S.D.'s will. How can I think of all of these things.

First, Maude. She didn't want to tell me about the will. She kept it from me because she takes her direction from me. Do I encourage that? I must try not to. I am the only star that revolves in her universe. If I disappeared, what would she do? I only wonder if I cultivate her dependence on me. In a way, she is my only friend.

Such a strange family. Stanley. And Evelyn, another forgotten child, turning up on my doorstep.

I've tried to keep myself neutral, answering Maude's questions and nothing more. I haven't settled her mind, or disturbed it. That's what I've wanted to do, to stay neutral—to stay out of it. She returned to Saskatchewan when S.D. called a summit and then when he died; it was up to her, it was completely her business. But did I encourage her to go? Was she doing what I chose not to do? I find it difficult to untangle all of these things. And now she is keeping things from me.

When she decides she doesn't want to stay and have lunch with me, she calls me before and after lunch to tell me what she is doing, to account to me, as though she has let me down. I'm amused. I don't care if she stays for lunch or not. Did I care whether she returned to Saskatchewan?

She says I am aloof, that I don't exist.

She's told me before she looks at me as though through the wrong end of a telescope. What does that mean? I should get a telescope and look through the wrong end, to see what she sees. It's probably a blur. Or things are tiny rather than enlarged. Did she say she saw me that way, or I saw her that way? I can't remember. I must try to remember. I assume she is talking about how she sees me. And if I cultivate dahlias, doesn't she? Or roses—suddenly she has a passion for roses, seeing them in a vase in our house. If I wear a big hat, so does she. It hurts me. We walk down the street, arm in arm, and although I know she's trying to hold her head up, there's something squashed about her gestures, fledgling and hairless, as she peers out from under the wide brim of her hat with big scared eyes. I want to gather her up then. Sometimes I begin to hum under my breath in a nonchalant way, thinking that might give her courage. Or I disengage our arms, and push her out—that too. It's annoying that she didn't inherit any of her father's traits. But she is tenacious. If I moved to another city, and didn't leave a forwarding address—how unlikely that would be—she would still find me.

Sometimes I think I don't care. At a certain point I disengage and it—

she—has nothing to do with me. Nothing personal. Her failure is not my own, nor is her success. But I do exist. Surely I do exist.

Something serious has happened. I must try to look at it. Otherwise I will be overwhelmed. I have trouble focussing on what has happened—Evelyn, Maude, Stanley—they all shed my attention.

I am in layers. I want to gather Maude up and push her away at the same time. I do nothing. The earth is in strands of different minerals, different colours—that's how I am. The childhood layer is sun-coloured, but soft. It erodes easily. Then there is a harder layer, a black layer, like pitch. Then the ground lightens again in earth tones, but still hard. Easily chipped but not erodable. Rocks are made by such layers.

If I read a letter from my mother, or think of S.D., it's as though the light shines *up* through those layers. And I look through light saturated with the old days. I'm not one whole person, except in layers.

I'm not even sure what it is like to be me. My voice, the shape of my face: annoying to some, pleasant to others. But how am I different, inside? How can anyone distinguish me from anyone else? It's in the layers, I suppose.

I must try and figure this out, finally, once and for all. Just for myself.

Everyone thought of S.D. as being all of one consistency, as though he had bloomed out of rock and that was him—a hard statue of himself, looking down on everyone. But he made mistakes. He was proud, of course, but not as proud as Stanley is.

And there is a buried strand in me crystallized from one short afternoon which makes a difference. How can I look at that now, after so long? If people knew, and the people were earth, they would try to spit me out, erupt me, turn me out like a stomach turning. But my world isn't the earth. Not quite yet. Not unless Stanley has his way.

This is so difficult to write, even to myself. Present time lies between things, like rainbowed light. Or like the spaces between stone thoughts.

Trying to explain. Exegesis. I am writing. Exodus. Genesis is the beginning. Exodus—means leaving. I left, never to return. Leviticus. Numbers. Deuteronomy. To explain, if only to myself. To be at Revelation. To stomach revelation.

"We don't talk about things like that." I have bequeathed to Maude a code of silence, of unknowing. That silence must come to an end somewhere, even if only here. Must it? Oh Lord, must it, after all these years? I have only myself.

Why did he come into my room? I think he was lonely. How can I write this? Even he was lonely on that day.

Mother had gone to town early, before the heat.

By 11 o'clock the air pressed against my skin as though trying to close my pores. I went out into the back garden. Lawrence was in the field; I could see the umbrella of dust following the tractor; but even the dust settled quickly against the pressure of the heat. The sound of the tractor was far away. I leaned against the house, in the shade. The sun followed me wherever I went. At noon it had absorbed all shadows.

He came in from the fields because he had a fever. He was never sick before. Pale beneath sun-worn skin. I must write quickly.

I took his lunch to him. There were cucumbers from the garden, and tomatoes, thick bread and cheese. His face was flushed with fever; and he was gentle, like a child, but not needy and demanding, the way he sometimes was, fretful and assertive. If I write quickly, maybe it will all get out, and then can be put to rest. He told me he didn't want to eat, but could he have a cool towel for his forehead. I especially remember that, his asking for the cool towel. He didn't tell me, but he asked. He was like a son with full-flushed face, hot and feverish, wanting someone to love him enough to get him a cool cloth for his forehead. Certainly I loved him that much. Certainly I loved him more than that.

I did. Damn me for that if you will, but I did.

As I fetched the cloth and ran the water, warm at first and then turning cold, I thought that his mother must have seen him this way, and loved him, right from the beginning and on through, with infinite patience for his distemper and his pushy ways, knowing that he was a child wanting to be loved just enough.

I broke off writing just then. I stared out the window into the realization that I am writing this for you—a reverie, a diary—what do I call it—I am writing for you, Maude. In my old age, when all the separate strands have blended, I too may merge into someone who cares little for you. I may only have left the part now that I fear so much—the part that cares for nothing. I suspect that will be the case. Something like death takes over these memories and makes the only living layer the one on top— and even that is a burden.

Years ago I tried to write this down. Before you came to the coast, before you married Geoffrey. I kept writing "I can't tell the difference." I couldn't tell the difference between the inside of me and the outside. I lived in shame, and the outside condemned me. I was moving through my life the way a leaf floats on water. And I didn't occupy any place from which to look out. There was nothing there. I ran the bath water and slowly took off my clothes, folding them neatly. The water felt warm like my blood. And when I pressed the razor into my wrist, it cut me without hurting. But the blood was so red, dripping into the water. I was shocked at the colour of me, flowing out, different from the water, bright and contained inside me, flowing out.

I wrapped my wrist in a towel and went to the telephone. I called my mother. We talked about the weather, about the crops. The blood kept seeping through, colouring the towel with the stain of me. I was bleeding to death, talking to my mother. And she had no idea. I removed the towel, and while I asked about Maude, S.D. and Clarence, my voice was completely calm, until I fainted. I was only out for a minute or two. She was still talking when I regained consciousness.

When I hung up the phone I bandaged my wrist. I was tired. I decided to compose my own life, create it, as I had created you. What I had done was—I want to say immaculate. Sun-coloured. That's the way I decided it was. I went to sleep. I have survived.

I do exist. How can they say I don't exist?

It hardly matters if I tell you, even if Stanley gets his way. I have shaped you, as I have shaped myself, entirely out of my imagination, out of a dream I had one afternoon. It was a dream.

I took the cool cloth in to him, and put it on his forehead. His eyes were closed, but he said the coolness was "wonderful." It was a long, full word, not one he ever used before. Then he wanted to get up; his room was too stuffy. It was a sick man's room. He said we would go into my room, and we would have a picnic there. He was determined, and carried the tray into my room, where we sat on the bed.

He had his night shirt on and his legs looked shapely and handsome, even the coarse black hairs. He dipped a piece of bread into the oil on the cucumbers. It dripped onto his leg and he massaged the oil into his skin. I laughed, and the room filled with colour; it had colour, like gold, and dimension, in my laughter. Things in the room were separate from one another. He was separate from me. I watched him breathe, and my breathing came in unison with his. We were close. Like one person. But separate. Then he held a cucumber above my leg and let oil drop on me, and he touched my skin with his warm hand, spreading the moisture into my legs. He didn't stop. He spread my legs and touched me—touched my genitals, touched my breasts. I opened. I couldn't help it. He was inside me; it didn't hurt. It was earth meeting sky, the bird

176

between. The desire was long—spread, elongated and hot. I was thick and light. I was something winged and something that has to do with desire. I was sponsored by the air. And then he got up. As he left he said, "This didn't happen. Remember that. It never happened."

Am I damned? Am I wrong, forever blamed? And you, banished now as well? I learned not to regret that afternoon. I learned to forget it. But then I gave you up. I gave you up to Kathryn. That part, I have remembered and regretted. And now Stanley wants to separate us, wants to condemn you. He can't do that. Surely not.

Kathryn made herself forget your origins, forget that you weren't her own. By naming you Maude she began the confusion that took hold in me and displaced all of the ways the truth could have been told. She claimed you thoroughly. She was never told what happened that afternoon. For him, and for me too, the secret didn't exist in real time. Maybe that was the way we treated you as well—not being in time, in everyone else's time. Because you weren't.

When my belly started to swell, it was Stanley who started teasing me, saying I was getting fat like a cow. My legs and arms weren't fat, only my belly. I didn't know what it was. Stanley, being older, seemed to know about things, like a sly man knows secrets, or like a traitor knows the betrayal. I was afraid of him in those days because he always played the conqueror in our games, the part of the invader. He always seemed to know what had happened. He was clever about that sort of thing. I must go on.

Then one night after dinner, when Mother was preparing dessert for the next day, Stanley announced that I couldn't have apple pie any more because I was too fat. Something about the way he said it, predatory and ominous, made me scared—not of Stanley but of what was happening to me and what I had done. He wasn't teasing me any more. He was declaring a scandal. Mother felt it too; the knowledge started in her back. Her hand stopped slicing the apple. And knowing came in a wave of motion. It seemed to ripple through her as she paused, the knife held just above the cutting board. Her back grew rigid. The same knowledge started in me—that I had a baby inside me. And at the same time as I knew this, I knew you were then four months old and you were my father's child.

Kathryn didn't turn around. She resumed cutting the apple. Father was at a cattle auction in Regina and wouldn't be home until the next day. Stanley didn't know what had happened, but he knew, unerringly, that something was wrong and the family had to close rank. I've always thought of Stanley—and these are my unkind thoughts, for there are some kind ones—that he has had a germ theory of the family. He could tell when something was wrong, when there was an outside element abroad which he had to eradicate. He wouldn't, of course, try to eradicate me, because I was part of what he had to accept. But you were different. I fear, in my absence, he treated you like an evil thing to be eliminated. Because I did leave you, and never went back. I left you to all of them.

Kathryn came into my room that night. I woke up as she was stroking my head in the way she sometimes would, as though my hair were thoughts that she was trying to untangle and smooth away. I looked at her and saw that her eyes were kind. She held me and shaped my head with her hands. I asked her to rub my back, which was the old way she had of helping me go to sleep. I remember I had on one of those long nightgowns that used to ride up around my neck. It was winter. Kathryn put her hand underneath the thick flannel of my nightgown and lightly fingered my back, pressing and feathering the skin. I thought then how much I was in the middle. I was between my mother and father the way a bird is between the earth and the sky. I felt completely safe and completely in between. My mother and father were connected in me in a way they didn't ever connect with one another. My mother was the sky, and my father the earth. Without some explanation in me, the bird in between, there was no way to connect them—they were separate thoughts who then thought of me. In me they were innocent. And my innocence was kept by them. It was a fair trade, in a way, wasn't it? What I bridged for them in that brief period in my life was their own shame. I accepted them in a way they couldn't for each other. I believe that. I needed to believe that, you see. Otherwise I would hate everything, you and S.D. included. And I set my face against that hatred. That was the only way I could be any good. And it had never happened. Isn't that funny. It never did happen. All was clamped down, closed down, ignored. It didn't happen. I was immaculate. Until now.

Evelyn has just interrupted me. She asked if she could read what I am writing. She wants to know, more than anyone, what it is that has happened. She needs a golden bough to take her through this underworld. You would never ask. I am sure of that. But Evelyn burns, the way I burn now.

I walked around my study and stared out into the dark sky. All I can see through this window, with the light on inside, is my own reflection. My face looks at me like an accusation. I am saying as much truth as I can manage. I am in agony. But I can go on. I do exist. It did happen.

I don't remember my mother leaving that night. In the morning she told me we were going to Regina. I didn't ask why. The boys were told it was for shopping. She gave them a long list of chores and then wrote a note to S.D. because I saw it in an envelope underneath the honey jar on the table.

And we passed S.D. on the highway, but Mother didn't notice.

She took me to a restaurant on the Crescent, and ordered cocoa for me, and she said she'd be right back. We hadn't spoken very much the entire time. As I drank the rich chocolate, I remember feeling excited at being with my mother in the city and drinking cocoa in a restaurant. I was getting what I wanted. I knew that I wasn't like the others. I had tried to suppress this knowledge but it was always there, as close as the smell of my skin. Now something different was happening to me. I liked everything for that fact alone. I knew only the excitement then.

When Mother returned she ordered a coffee. She was shaking as she raised the cup. We had an appointment with the doctor in half an hour. She then asked me the only question which she ever asked about the pregnancy—if it was Lawrence. I was confused for a moment, but I could answer the question because nothing had anything to do with Lawrence. I said no. I think she then believed it was the hired hand who'd been there during the summer. I don't know. I believe even if she knew the truth, she would still have loved me.

When we went to the office, I was left alone with Dr. Gammon, and he didn't ask many questions either, but he touched me inside; it was cold and humiliating to be touched that way. But that was nothing compared to what came later, of course, because childbirth is a terrifying experience, when you curse having a body. This was the cold, almost external part.

Afterwards I sat in the waiting room while my mother went in to talk to the doctor. Still, I wasn't upset; I only felt lonely then. I wanted her to come back. She did, after a long time, opening the door, holding out her hand for me to take.

Mother and I went back to the restaurant. It occurred to me that she didn't really know any other place to go. She was as much out on a limb as I was—the two of us were out there together, not knowing what to do or where to go. If ever I doubt her courage, I always remember that day when she kept taking on her own fear and overcoming it, time after time—taking the initiative, arranging the appointment with the doctor, sitting in that cafe with her pregnant daughter. Many times, before and after, I have seen her bow to the demands of her husband and her sons; that day, she was supreme.

And so the question of courage comes up for me again. I believe my mother was courageous on that day, and the days that followed. Was

179

it cowardice that she didn't confront S.D.—or me for that matter—with the further question? Was it cowardice that she didn't ever really challenge the gossip that almost overwhelmed our family? And was I a coward not to tell you what I know, or to tell anyone? The questions have followed me like a light; they have never led the way.

And was I wrong to abandon you? That question is bound up with the question of courage, like the root ball of a plant is bound over a rock. This writing might only be a catechism which confirms my guilt. Does it? Ask yourself, now, if you wished *not* to be born. It's an impossible question—to subtract from your existence now, to nothingness. I can't do it for you. I am glad you were born. You are, in fact, my only friend. But if you suffer it's not as though that could have been avoided. Some, but not much.

I know. I am doing my usual trick. Being rational. What else can I do? There are bones in the sun and in the earth. I am full of regret. But I do exist.

Over lunch, Mother said that I was healthy, and she was grateful for that. I would be sent away. She said, "everything is changed for you, now." I wouldn't end up with spiders growing out of my hair. That was the most important thing then—it invigorated me and helped me. For whatever it's worth, I've tried not to let cobwebs grow in my hair, the hair my mother stroked, the thoughts my mother had. Is that enough?

Kathryn took me to a shop not far from the doctor's office—it was a fancy lady's shop. We must have looked like the country bumpkins we were. She bought me a silk scarf, a long blue scarf with the shape of a bird on it in the midst of the blue sky of the scarf. It was perfect. Maybe that's why I came to think of myself as the bird in between.

She put the scarf around my neck, tied it loosely, and kissed me. It cost a lot of money—I don't remember how much. I was, then, on my own. With that gift, I had sprung loose.

That scarf wore thin; it even became stained, although I did everything I could to prevent that. My fingers left marks on it. It never gave me warmth, but it was exotic and I loved it. She crowned me as the bird I imagined I was. Later, I gave it to you.

And then we left. It was dark by the time we arrived back at the farm. I thought she would ask me to put the scarf away before we entered the house, but she didn't.

One month later, I was on the train with Kathryn, going to the home in Winnipeg. She left me there, in that cold city, in that horrid place. And then, believe me, I cried. I felt as though I had come to the end of my life. My fantasy had gone and I was in the world, and in hell.

I hated S.D. and I hated you, you unborn, killing me. I tried to eliminate you. Do you bear any imprint from that time, any memory of the fierce hatred I had? You were a malignancy. There was another girl there, Fiona, who told me what to do. I took hot baths. But none of it worked, of course. I had chosen you as much as I had chosen the colour of my hair. I wanted you, then, as something that I had done, something I represented.

And later there was the brilliant colour of my blood in the bath.

Outside my window now, on the deck, a leaf scuttles across the boards, making a bony sound, a horrid scratch of dead tissue. It's nearly dawn. Nothing has been the same since you. We have a conspiracy. I am grateful to you for being more related to me than anyone else. We are almost the same. We are almost one person. But the leaf reminds me that death touches us both, all the time, and will break us up. It's close now, but still abstract, the idea of our death. Then, in the beginning, death pressed in hard.

I was fifteen years of age, five months pregnant, living in a foreign town, in a home for unwed mothers. I took my school by correspondence. My mother pretended, or believed, that I was in a happy place.

In my—or your—seventh month, a kind of hysteria went through the school. It was March. Even in Manitoba the winter gave hints of breaking. Then, one day, there was a chinook. Overnight there was a sudden burst of warmth, and ice began to melt. I think we got hopeful. Fiona, who was eight months, thought her baby would be born that day and she could go home. It was as though the universe had declared a party, with all our sins absolved.

All the fat girls, so young you'd think that God would not allow us to have babies, sat on the front porch, wearing shawls or light coats. Then Fiona found a baby carriage and said that anyone who wanted to take a ride should come along. Everyone tumbled down the stairs and lined up for the ride. I was first. I got into the carriage with you in my big stomach; it was one of those high-wheeled black carriages. Fiona tucked me in with a crocheted baby blanket and said in a simpering tone, "Now, there, there, is beeby comfie, eh, is she comfie" and she gave me a bottle. She stuck it right in my mouth, and the nipple tasted bitter. "Drink your bah bah," she said. As I drew the liquid forward, I realized it was liquor—brandy I think. "Let's go for a ride, little beeby." Fiona started to push me as I sucked on the bottle, resting it against my huge belly protruding from the carriage. As we started to move down the hill from the house, all the fat girls screamed and cheered. The carriage went faster. Then Fiona started pulling it back rather than pushing it, yelling

181

"whoa, there, whoa." Then she stumbled and let go. You and I were off, ferociously rumbling down the sidewalk hell bent for leather, as S.D. used to say. It was wonderful. I could hear the fading screams of the other girls. I screamed. Fiona screamed. We were out of control. But there was traffic ahead on the road. I thought, in an instant, that I would take whatever might come. If we were hit by a car, then we would die together, so what. As we bumped along the sidewalk with the sweet wind in my hair, I changed my mind. I didn't, in fact, want to die in this way, inside a black baby carriage with an unborn child defining the end of the line, smashed up on a March day. I leaned hard, with all my strength, forcing the carriage off the path and onto the iced slope. We skidded forward even faster. There was a tree in front of us.

And slowly a long sentence went through my mind, in an instant, as though it had had all the time in the world to shape itself and to come through to me: "the un-inevitable is about to happen." Whereupon we smacked into the tree and were thrown onto the ground.

The world bristled and shivered in gold. The tree was plated in gold sequins. The breath had gone out of me and there seemed no hurry to get it back, with the world gone to gold and the voices around me quiet, in whispers, as though secrets were being told. The faces were shielded in gold, too. And then the colour went as my breath returned. I regret that gold going.

An ambulance came. I had cushioned the impact against the tree. But you were safe. You were going to live.

Fiona gave birth to a boy. She gave the baby up for adoption, and cried all night and then left. She came back the night before you were born. Mother had come, and a special cot was set up in a room for her, and another for Fiona.

I think Kathryn was the first person to hold you, after the nurses. I cried louder than you did. It was just as well you went to my mother, because I couldn't have comforted you.

You went away with Kathryn, returning to a place I could not. I went on to the west coast. I never returned. My mother had taken my child.

The agreeable and the disagreeable memories have left me with a sense of loss. Has this writing weakened me? I am in layers, and there is a fault in the earth through which I have looked.

I mark the day. Now, let it rest. I have done what I wanted to do.

They have gone now, Evelyn and Maude. I've sent Maude away, as I always do. I didn't intend to open this notebook again. But now I feel lonely, indescribably empty. I have nothing more to do. I'm at an end. There isn't even an obstruction ahead to mark my finale, like a tree or an unborn child. There is only Stanley, and his version of the truth. That's what they will say: she couldn't face the shame of the trial. I am a coward. My blood, red, brilliant, shocking, will make no difference.

Can I bear what I have done, with my own father? Can I say it out loud? I am as gnarled and misshapen as Maude, and Evelyn. My world is the earth that I corrupt, that tries to spit me out.

I do exist. I do exist. And now, I suffer. I suffer with the rest of them. I must stand up with Evelyn. Please, stand up.